PROHIBITED
PORTRAIT

ABOUT THE AUTHOR

R W Kay was born and schooled on the Isle of Man. After graduating from the University of Nottingham, he was commissioned into the Royal Air Force in 1966. Following subsequent RAF training and gaining an MSc at Lancaster University, he became a Chartered Engineer and was awarded a Fellowship of the British Computer Society.

He retired in 2005. His first novel, *A Nastia Game*, based on his tour of service at the RAF Staff College, Bracknell, was published in 2009.

BOOKS BY R W KAY:

A Nastia Game
Bin Laden's Nemesis
Iraq's Retribution
The World is Empty

PROHIBITED
PORTRAIT

R W KAY

The Book Guild Ltd

First published in Great Britain in 2019 by
The Book Guild Ltd
9 Priory Business Park
Wistow Road, Kibworth
Leicestershire, LE8 0RX
Freephone: 0800 999 2982
www.bookguild.co.uk
Email: info@bookguild.co.uk
Twitter: @bookguild

Typeset in 11pt Bembo Std

Printed and bound in the UK by TJ International, Padstow, Cornwall

ISBN 978 1912881 314

British Library Cataloguing in Publication Data.
A catalogue record for this book is available from the British Library.

To the Super and all devoted police officers everywhere without whom civilisation would cease.

I would like to express my gratitude to friends who have helped with their comments on early drafts, especially Julia Hamilton and Paul Watson.

AUTHOR'S NOTE

Prohibited Portrait is a work of fiction based on unfamiliar history. For example, the line of succession of the Caliphs, Mohammed's representatives on Earth for nearly 1,300 years, is as well documented as the ancestry of the Roman Catholic Popes. The names and timescales of the Caliphs in *Prohibited Portrait* are accurate.

In 1941, Syria's Vichy Government and the Nazis planned a *coup d'état* to replace the pro-British Iraq royal family. The defeat of the Vichy plot by the Allies occurred as described.

The dates of events impacting on the story, such as the formation of the United Arab Republic in 1958 and the Gary Powers U2 incident of 1960 are also authentic.

The story of Abdullah Quilliam, a descendent of Captain John Quilliam RN who was First Lieutenant on HMS Victory at the Battle of Trafalgar, is factual. After visiting Morocco and becoming a Muslim, Abdullah Quilliam opened the first British mosque in Liverpool in 1887. For converting hundreds to Islam, he received the honorary title of *Sheikh al-Islam* from the Ottoman Caliph, Abdul Hamid II in 1893.

The Caliph's Great Seal stems from the widely held acceptance by historians that a badge of authority was passed on by successive Caliphs as their mandate to be Mohammed's representative on Earth.

CHAPTER 1

November 1959 had been a stormy month with westerly gales raging in the North Irish Sea and South-West Scotland. In the early hours of Thursday 19th, the wind veered south-easterly and began to increase. The Isle of Man Steam Packet Company's ship, the *Tynwald*, departed from Liverpool at 10.30 am for its regular four-hour journey to Douglas. An hour after the ship had departed and emerged from the protection of the Mersey basin, the sea began to get progressively rough. There was no indication of what was to come. The *Tynwald*, heading west, passed the Liverpool bound ship, the *King Orry*, that had left Douglas at 9.00 am, steaming east. The two ships customarily blew their ship's whistles to acknowledge each other.

A further hour passed and it was becoming clear to all the passengers that they were in for a wild crossing. In the heavy seas, the *Tynwald* was rolling from side to side and making little progress. As progressively more travellers on board became seasick, theories began to emerge that it was "all in the ears" or that the answer was to find the ship's "pivotal centre of movement". Passengers seeking to find the centre of gravity of the ship discovered it was next to the warm engine room where the smell of fuel oil was worse than the fresh, salty air on deck. Others sought refuge in the theory that the answer was to "settle the stomach" by drinking whisky.

As two o'clock approached and the stricken ship should have had the island in sight, members of the crew came round to say that the *Tynwald* would be unable to dock in Douglas, and the ship's captain had decided to head for Peel on the west side of the island where there would be more protection from the force 10 storm. The expected time of arrival would be approximately 9.00 pm.

By three o'clock, the storm clouds ensured it was dark. By 3.30 pm, it was pitch black. Almost everyone on board had been stricken by *mal de mer.*

In Douglas, the storm's winds were uprooting the palm trees in the gardens along the front of the Loch Promenade. Sand, pebbles and seaweed were being thrown onto the roadway with such force that the windows of parked cars were being broken. The lucky car owners were those who had rescued their cars before the police shut the entire length of the promenade.

None of the passengers who disembarked that evening would ever forget their experience. For twenty-four hours afterwards, most would imagine the ground swaying as it mimicked the ship's motion.

It wasn't until the following morning that the extent of the damage to the Douglas seafront could be seen. The Borough Surveyor, John Quine, left home at seven o' clock to walk the entire length of the promenade from the Victoria Pier to the Derby Castle. Back in his office by nine o'clock, he had made notes of the damage. A meeting had been convened for 9.30 am by the Mayor of the Borough that included not only town council staff, but the Isle of Man Government's Director of Finance. Superintendent Bob Kinley, the Deputy Chief Constable, also attended.

'The damage to the Loch Promenade is largely confined to the gardens between the roadway and seawall,' began the surveyor. 'We should be able to clear the road as far as the Sefton Hotel by lunchtime and Broadway by the end of the day.'

'That will reduce inconvenience to out-of-town workers and shoppers to a minimum,' remarked the senior policeman. 'There will be no parking restrictions today, as long as cars don't cause an obstruction.'

There were cursory nods around the table.

The Borough Surveyor continued, 'However, there is a chasm in the sea wall opposite the Palace Theatre where the promenade runs much closer to the shoreline. The breach that has appeared is approximately a yard wide. I'm afraid the repairs to the wall will take several weeks. It will be necessary to close the road to guarantee safety.'

'What will the repairs cost?' asked the Mayor.

'Four, maybe five thousand pounds.'

'That will be quite a chunk out of the town's contingency budget,' observed the Town Clerk.

'I will arrange for a grant from government funding,' observed the Director of the Manx Treasury.

'So what you are saying,' said the Superintendent, 'is that the promenade beyond Broadway will be closed until just before Christmas?'

'Except to residents, I'm afraid so.'

'When can work start?' asked the Mayor.

'Our council workers have already started to clear the Loch Promenade. When this meeting finishes, I will begin a detailed inspection of the fissure. I will have a report ready by Monday that will include accurate costings.'

The meeting closed. The Mayor called for the next meeting at 1400 hours on Monday, 23rd November.

★

3

By Friday afternoon, the extent of the damage to the seawall on the Central Promenade had become apparent. Workers, released from the initial clearing operation, had been transferred to the cavity opposite the Palace Theatre.

However, while clearing the site of tons of sand and pebbles, it was discovered that the storm had badly cracked a sewer that ran from the pumping station behind the Palace Theatre, under the promenade and out to sea. Effluent had begun to spread around the sewer's cavity.

'There's shit everywhere,' exclaimed the foreman to the Borough Surveyor.

'Unfortunately, it's already dusk and emergency repairs can't begin until daylight,' replied the Surveyor.

'It's time and a half tomorrow,' the chargehand reminded his boss.

'I know, but we can't leave the repairs until Monday, can we? The sewer must be our priority. I'll tell the Town Clerk that the work will last all weekend.'

'Sunday is double time.'

'It's got to be done; otherwise, the health risks are too great.'

'I'll tell the boys there'll be a big bonus in their pay packets for Christmas,' smiled the gaffer.

Exhausted, John Quine went home, hoping nothing else could go wrong.

★

When he arrived on Saturday morning, worse was to follow. Half an hour had passed when the gang's foreman called, 'You'd better come and look at what we've found.'

'What?'

'You'll see.'

He followed the gang's boss, who pointed: 'There.'

In the rubble and excrement was a body. Mostly clothed, it was bloated by its time in the sea. Its face was badly gashed, discoloured and unrecognisable.

'Could it have come down the sewer?' asked the foreman.

The interior diameter of the sewer pipe was three feet.

'Impossible. It would have caused a blockage in the pump,' replied the surveyor. 'If it had been in the sewer, then it would have had to enter downside of the pumping house.'

The foreman nodded agreement. 'Shall I go and get the police?' he asked.

'There's a police box at the bottom of Broadway. Use that.'

★

In the 1950s, the Manx Constabulary had a network of public phone boxes that were directly linked to the permanently manned police stations at Douglas, Castletown, Peel and Ramsey. The boxes had a flap that, when opened, gave callers access to a mouthpiece that directly connected them to the duty officer at the nearest station.

Within ten minutes of the call being made, a sergeant and a constable had arrived from the police HQ. They agreed work had to stop.

The sergeant gave his PC orders. 'I'll drop you off at the station. Ring Superintendent Kinley at home and ask him to come here as quickly as possible. I'll carry on to Noble's Hospital and arrange for the pathologist, or one of his staff, to come.'

By one o'clock, the island's only pathologist, Dr Tim Parton, and one of his small team of lab technicians had arrived. They immediately began scraping away the debris and uncovering the body. The police photographer had arrived and was photographing the details. The Deputy Chief Constable and his Head of CID, Sergeant Turnbull, had also arrived.

'Well, George, this is one for you. You might be busy over Christmas,' joked the Superintendent.

'Thanks for nothing, boss.'

The island's CID was only two strong – a detective sergeant and a detective constable.

The DS asked the doctor, 'What age is the body?'

'Hard to say; maybe he's a man of fifty.'

'How long has he been dead?'

'Judging from the state of adipocere, I would guess he's been in the sea for about two or three months. He was obviously washed ashore in the storm and I guess he drowned. These abrasions and cuts seem to be consistent with him hitting and scraping rocks. The crabs have been at his face too. I'll know more when I carry out the post-mortem.'

'Is there any ID on him?'

'Nothing obvious.'

George sighed. He knew there hadn't been a murder on the island since 1943 when a fight had broken out between pro-Allied Finns and pro-Russian Finns in an internment camp at Ramsey. He also knew that the policeman involved in clearing up the investigation had been Detective Constable Kinley.

Now his boss, and standing next to him, Superintendent Bob Kinley was a local man, born and bred. He'd left school at fourteen to work on his father's smallholding. When eighteen, in 1933, he'd applied to join the local police force as a cadet. Six feet two inches tall, and weighing a healthy fourteen stone, he'd passed the fitness test with flying colours as well as the English language and arithmetic exams. He'd prepared to pass the entrance exams for constable when he became twenty-one by taking a Pitman correspondence course. Within a few years, he'd passed the promotion exam for sergeant. In 1952, he was the first Manx policeman to attend the National Police College at Ryton-on-Dunsmore to prepare him for promotion to inspector. His innate intelligence was demonstrated by him having won the Irish Correspondence Chess Championship in 1958 and having been the island's chess champion for eight consecutive years.

George was hoping the mystery would turn out to be nothing more than a body washed ashore during the storm. If there was evidence of foul play, then he might have to call for assistance from Lancashire Constabulary – a prospect that didn't appeal.

George's record in World War Two had been exemplary. A PC before the war, he had volunteered to join the Manx Regiment soon after war broke out. Excelling in aptitude tests, he was enlisted into the newly formed Army Intelligence Corps in 1940 and trained to become an imagery analyst. He was in the team that identified the V1 rocket sites near the Pas de Calais in 1943 and the V2 sites a year later.

A native of Colby in the south of the island, his intellect was reflected by him being one of the very few who could complete the annual King William's College General Knowledge Paper set for the boys over their Christmas holidays. He knew he would be stretched if an investigation was to last more than a few weeks.

'Well, Tim,' began the Superintendent as the body was about to be removed to the mortuary, 'when will you be able to perform the post-mortem?'

'I'll start tomorrow, Bob, after I've been to church. All I can tell you so far is that there appear to be no man-made wounds. If you want to watch the PM, meet me in the hospital at noon.'

'We'll be there,' replied the Deputy Chief. Then, turning to his detective, he casually remarked, 'I have a funny feeling about this one, George.'

And the Super's hunches are usually right, thought the detective.

CHAPTER 2

The two police officers arrived at Noble's Hospital promptly to watch Dr Parton begin his post-mortem. The path-lab technician had previously thoroughly cleaned the corpse. He had removed his clothing, confirming there were no objects in his pockets or manufacturers' labels on his clothes that could aid identification.

At each stage of the PM, Tim explained what he was doing to the policemen. His commentary was logged on a tape recorder while his technician took photographs as required.

'The body is a man aged about fifty, plus or minus five years. Caucasian, but his swarthy skin suggests southern European – possibly Italian or Spanish. Weighing twelve stone and five pounds, his height is five feet ten inches. He has a muscular build, suggesting he kept himself fit. He has been circumcised. No obvious distinguishing features, except a scar on his left shoulder which I will examine later. The abrasions and cuts to the face, hands and legs are consistent with the body being dragged over rocks. Exposed soft tissues, particularly his nose and lips, have been partially eaten by fish. Some of his teeth have been removed professionally; others have been filled with mercury amalgam. The hands are abraded and some of the skin rubbed away, so there's little chance of getting a meaningful set of fingerprints.'

'Dental records could identify him,' commented the Super to his detective.

George nodded but said nothing, knowing that identification would prove critical to the investigation.

Having overheard the Deputy's remark, the doctor looked up from the cadaver. 'It's not the best of starts, Bob. The amount of adipocere, which causes the bloating, suggests he has been in the sea for about two months, which rather surprises me.'

'Why?' asked Bob.

'Bodies drowned in the sea normally sink to the bottom, and even a storm like last Thursday's wouldn't usually bring them to the surface.'

Tim then partially filled a test tube of fluid taken from the man's lungs with a syringe. He passed it to the technician for analysis.

'The amount of water in his lungs confirms he drowned.'

Minutes passed. The pathologist was examining the shoulder scar with a magnifying glass when he was interrupted by the technician returning from his laboratory.

'Would you come here a minute and check my results?' the lab assistant asked.

The pathologist looked up, 'Why?'

'The water in his lungs is not seawater.'

'Are you sure?' Tim queried.

'Certain. Not only that, it is tainted,' replied the technician.

'What with?'

'I haven't tested it that far, but my guess is there are flukes in the water.'

The doctor stopped the autopsy and left the room. Returning a minute later, 'I'm afraid, gentlemen, you have a problem. This man did not drown in the sea.'

The two policemen looked at each other, their faces registering surprise.

'Then how on earth did he come to be washed up on Douglas beach?' asked the Superintendent.

'That's your province, Bob, not mine,' replied the pathologist. 'But let me explain something. Freshwater is more similar to our own blood than saltwater. When someone drowns in freshwater, the water that's been inhaled into the lungs passes rapidly into the bloodstream through the lungs' walls by osmosis. In less than two minutes, the body's blood becomes so diluted that cells burst, leading to organ failure. Remember the body's temperature is 98°F; that's a lot hotter than a summer's day. The organs begin to decompose immediately, producing gases that will help keep the body afloat. The decomposition will slow down depending on the temperature of the water, but it could take weeks before it stops.

'However, seawater contains far more salt than human blood. When seawater is breathed in, the body transfers water into the lungs from the blood – the opposite process. Consequently, rapid decomposition does not occur and organ breakdown takes longer to begin, perhaps up to thirty minutes. Hardly any gases are produced and the body is more likely to sink. It's not a hard and fast rule of course; much depends on the density of the body, which varies according to its amount of fat. Fat people tend to float more easily than thin people; just as lard floats on water. And this guy was not fat.

'My findings are going to depend on the temperature of the water where this man drowned, as that will determine the amount of decomposition and gases in his organs. I wouldn't mind betting this man drowned in relatively warm freshwater that had somehow been tainted. He has been floating in the sea, probably just below the surface, for several months.'

'So, the body could have come from anywhere?' asked George.

'Yes, although it's most likely local. I can't see it drifting across from the mainland. Can you?'

'To be honest, I'm more interested in how he died,' replied George. 'Was it an accident? Or was he drowned deliberately?

Could he have been held down in a bath? Are there any signs on the body of a struggle?'

'He was alive when he drowned, although he could have been unconscious when he entered the water. He appears to have been a strong, fit man. If he was held under the water, it would have taken two people. There is no evidence of pre-mortal bruising because his body received considerable damage while coming ashore. If there were pre-mortal injuries, they have been hidden. His clothes are the ones he drowned in. Although they are badly torn, they appear to have been expensive – continental in style: tapered trousers with an expensive leather belt, a silk shirt, and low-cut lapels on his jacket. Strangely, there are no manufacturers' labels. There is no evidence to suggest the labels have been cut out either. His shoes are missing, although they may have come off in the sea.'

'Could he have been drugged?'

'We won't know until we've done blood tests. I'm afraid those will have to wait until tomorrow.'

'Could his legs have been tied to a heavy weight?' There was a hint of frustration in the detective sergeant's questions.

'There is nothing suspicious. If he was weighed down and thrown into a pool, then you may be looking for something like a lead belt.'

'A lead belt?'

'Yes, the sort used by divers or frogmen,' replied the pathologist.

Tim had resumed examining the scar on the shoulder blade with his magnifying glass. After some murmuring to himself, he stopped to look at the policemen.

'This man has been shot in the shoulder blade. I would think the scar is about twenty years old.' He asked his assistant to take close-up photos as he held a ruler next to the scar.

'A bullet wound? What calibre is it?'

'It's definitely from a .303 rifle. When I was a doctor in the Army, I saw several examples of men who had shot themselves

11

when cleaning their 303s. I would say he was hit from a distance of about half a mile or more.'

'How do you know?' asked the Super.

'Two things: firstly, the slightly ragged edges of the entry wound suggest the bullet was slowing down. Had he been shot from close range, then the edges would have had a cleaner cut. Secondly, there isn't an exit wound, which suggests the bullet was near the limit of its range. I think he could have been shot when trying to escape.'

'Shot in the back?'

'Yes, and from the evidence of the scar tissue, the bullet was extracted by a professional surgeon.'

'Hang on a minute,' interrupted George. 'He must be German.'

'How do you make that out?' asked the Super.

'Only British and Commonwealth troops used .303 rifles.'

'Are you saying he's a Nazi?' asked Bob.

Like most pathologists, Tim had a quick wit and interrupted. 'The island is hardly Paraguay, Bob. And anyway, we fought more than simply the Germans. There were Italians, Japanese, Yugoslav Communists, even the Vichy French.'

The two policemen saw the joke, but were hoping they had their first breakthrough in identifying the body.

Dr Parton began to examine the corpse's large intestine. After several minutes, he exclaimed loudly, 'Aha.'

'What?' asked George hopefully.

'There is something inside here.' With a small pair of tweezers, and after some fiddling, he removed a minute object. 'A schistosome,' he declared.

'What's that?' asked George.

The pathologist didn't answer — he was now in his element — something had turned up that was different from his usual humdrum investigations.

He began talking to the two observers as he used his scalpel.

'I'll have to cut open the liver and anal passage. Schistosomes breed like rabbits. This one could have reproduced hundreds of eggs that would have been excreted in the usual way, but some eggs could have become lodged. If some worms are in his liver, they can live unnoticed for months – even years. It might give us a clue as to how long he was dead before entering the sea.'

'Where could the schistosomes have come from?' asked the DS.

Dr Parton looked up from the cadaver. The question had interrupted his train of thought.

'Sorry, what did you say?'

'Where could they come from?'

'They're common in southern Europe and North Africa. He probably picked them up abroad; they're very rare in Britain. Our climate is too cold.'

The pathologist turned to look at his assistant. 'I can't remember us getting any human stools for analysis containing schistosomes before. Can you?'

The technician nodded agreement. 'There's been plenty of roundworm and even threadworm cases, but never schistosomes. If I remember correctly, there was a child from a farm in Marown and a school teacher who lived in the Ballaugh Curraghs who both had bad cases of roundworm.'

'I wouldn't mind betting we will find roundworms in his lung water. If the water this chap drowned in was stagnant or he lay on dirty ground afterwards, then the roundworms could have entered his body and begun to reproduce.'

'It sounds nasty,' commented the Super.

'Not really, Bob. Unless there is a bad infestation, roundworms don't do much harm.'

'Where in the island could there be that sort of water?'

'In theory, it could be anywhere. I would rule out most of our rivers – they're especially clean and fast flowing with the exception of the River Dhoo. It's slow as it flows through the Douglas-Peel gap, particularly around Crosby.'

13

'Crosby is in Marown, and the Curraghs are renowned for being swampy,' said George, looking at his boss.

Dr Parton had stopped. 'Look, Bob, what I would like to do is send the sample of schistosomes to the School of Tropical Medicine at Liverpool University. My guess is this chap picked them up in a warm climate. The university may be able to narrow it down a bit. This investigation is going to take some time. I suggest you don't hang around any longer. We'll wrap up now and I'll resume tomorrow. As soon as I've a report for you, I'll let you know.'

★

Next morning, instructions were given to all the island's policemen to look for possible sites where a drowning could have taken place. On Monday afternoon, a constable from Peel had traced the River Dhoo from Crosby to its source – a small, peaty lake in the middle of one of the island's largest plantations at Archallagan. The pond was oval-shaped. Forty yards long by fifteen yards wide, it appeared to be no deeper than three feet and was mostly surrounded by reeds.

However, the constable based in Sulby village didn't need to investigate. He knew the teacher who lived on the edge of the Curraghs and had suffered from roundworms. He directed the government analyst to the schoolmaster's home at Ballaley. 'You'll find plenty of places to take a sample of the water there,' he remarked.

★

By mid-December, the results from Liverpool University had arrived. The School of Tropical Medicine's report suggested the schistosome type was common not only in northern Africa, but south-eastern Europe – Greece and Albania. Analysis by the

Manx Government's Environmental Department had confirmed the existence of roundworms in the damp soil around the Archallagan pond, the Curraghs and a further six sites dotted around the island.

Dr Parton's report established the corpse's anus and intestines were mildly infested with schistosomes that had bred for several generations. As they had passed through the corpse's body, some had lodged as parasitic worms in his organs and venous walls. Dr Parton's conclusion was that they had been in the cadaver's body for as long as a year but were not the cause of death. However, the water in his lungs could have come from any of the sites where samples had been taken by the government analyst. The report's summary was concise:

> *The victim died by drowning in freshwater that was mildly fetid. The decomposition of the organs suggests the temperature of the water was approximately 70° F. His body had subsequently entered the sea shortly after drowning between mid-September and early October. The contents of his stomach show that he had eaten fish about an hour before death. There was no alcohol in his blood, nor any drugs. There is no evidence to suggest that he had been forcibly held under the water. Consequently, my recommendation to the coroner will be to return an open verdict.*

CHAPTER 3

Monday, 4th January 1960

'It's been over six weeks since that body was washed ashore, sir, and I'm no nearer finding out who he was. The dental records have come up with nothing. The clothes we sent away for analysis – nothing either; other than they are continental in style. The trousers are tapered and have no turn-ups, that sort of thing. It's time for a new approach.'

'What do you suggest, George?' asked the Superintendent.

'I thought at first we should put a photograph of him in the local press. However, even with his face cleaned up, I'm unsure if he is recognisable to anyone who knew him.'

'There would probably be a protest from the more squeamish members of society too.'

'Quite. So what I have in mind is to get an artist who specialises in portraits to sketch him as she imagines he may have looked, reconstructing details such as his nose.'

'I've read in the *Police Gazette* that the Met are experimenting with a new technique called photofit. If we sent them a photo, then perhaps they could send us back a drawing suitable for printing in the *Examiner*.'

'That could take weeks. I was thinking of using a local

portrait artist who has an outstanding reputation for her work. She's a niece of my wife, and I'm certain she can be trusted to be discreet as well as build a close likeness.'

'OK, George, let's see what she can come up with.'

'There may be a fee.'

'What does she normally charge?'

'Fifty guineas.'

The Super took a deep breath. 'Not cheap, then?'

'I think she will do it for less; particularly when I tell her she will be breaking new ground as her portrait will be restructuring the face instead of copying it. If she is successful then other police forces may want to use her in future.'

'OK, go ahead.'

★

The following day, George met his wife's niece. She was both intrigued and flattered that she should be asked to help identify the dead body and looked forward to the challenge. Consequently, she agreed to waive her fee. On the Friday of that week, she initially drew a sketch of the man's face from the hospital technician's photographs. Then, while sitting with the cadaver, she took measurements of the nose, mouth and jaw before completing her portrait that would be published in the local papers the following week.

★

Chief Constable Ben Powell, affectionately known behind his back as either Baden or BP, had been one of the youngest colonels in the Military Police during the war. He had been the island's police chief since 1955. Appointed by the Home Office, he had a wide range of contacts from his war years in the intelligence services and gave the local force strength of purpose with a disciplined leadership style that prevented it from becoming parochial.

In front of him sat his deputy, Superintendent Bob Kinley. 'I want to keep you in the picture about what I've agreed with DS Turnbull,' said the Super. 'I'm concerned that the unknown man was either murdered by drowning in a pool of freshwater or, having drowned by accident, was then dumped in the sea. I've seen the artist's sketch that's going into the papers. Hopefully, someone will recognise him this weekend.'

'OK Bob, keep me informed. Are you happy that you and DS Turnbull have the resources to cope if it turns out the cadaver was murdered? After all, this could be the island's first murder since the war, and I want you to take the lead, not some unknown detective from Lancashire CID. Use your deputy to take the load off your shoulders and give this investigation your priority.'

'We'll cope, sir.' Unseen by the Chief, the Super's fingers were crossed.

★

The following weekend, the impression of the man washed ashore appeared in three of the island's weekend newspapers: the *Examiner*, the *Ramsey Courier* and the *Isle of Man Times*. The headline read: *Appeal for witnesses to come forward. Do you know this man?* The article gave few details, but asked the public for help with his identification.

The following morning, a woman rang the Douglas Police HQ in Athol Street. The duty sergeant answered.

'I know who that man is,' she said in a strong Manx accent.

'Can you come to the police station and see the detective in charge of the case?'

'I live in Ballaugh Glen,' she replied. 'I haven't a car.'

The sergeant could tell from her voice that the woman was elderly and knew that to get to Douglas she would have to catch a bus to Ramsey, change, and take another bus to the island's capital – a journey that could take up to two hours.

'Tell me exactly where you live and I'll get Detective Sergeant Turnbull to come and see you. What time would be convenient?'

'After lunch; say, half past one.'

★

Mrs Winnie Craine turned out to be a sixty-five year old widow who lived alone in a small, detached stone cottage situated south of the village centre. It was about 200 yards from the village pub, the Raven, and the humpback bridge, famous as a feature on the motorcycle TT course.

DS Turnbull arrived, accompanied by his DC to take notes of the meeting.

Mrs Craine invited the two policemen into her parlour where a log fire was busily burning away; occasionally, an odd spark flew onto the stone hearth, worryingly close to the woollen rug that fronted the fireplace. The room was warm, with an aroma of pine that reminded George of his upbringing in a similar cottage in Colby.

'Before we begin, I insist on making you a pot of tea,' she remarked. 'It's a long way for you to come on such a raw day.'

The two policemen smiled at each other. They wondered what would come next, as she wore a pair of National Health glasses in a steel frame that looked as if the lenses had not been cleaned for some time.

While she was in the kitchen, the DC whispered, 'I think this could be a wild goose chase. She wouldn't recognise Winston Churchill if he walked into the room.'

'Shh, these old biddies can be cannier than you think.'

Minutes later, Mrs Craine returned with a tray carrying a plate loaded with slices of Manx fruit loaf, as well as cups, saucers, a milk jug, a sugar bowl and the teapot.

'That's very nice of you, Mrs Craine,' said George appreciatively, 'but what makes you think you know the man in the *Ramsey Courier*?'

'It's like him,' she replied, as she began pouring the tea. 'His nose is a bit bigger, but otherwise it could be Mr Lemont.'

'Mr Lemont? Is that two words or one?' asked the young DC with his notebook at the ready.

Both George and Mrs Craine looked vacantly at the DC to explain.

'When the Huguenots came to Britain from France, there were a lot of people with the name of *Le Mont*. Some anglicised the name to Lemont, some didn't.'

'He spelled his name as one word. He could have been French. He had a tan and spoke excellent English. Now I think about it, there may have been a trace of a continental accent; not that I've met many foreigners. I cook for him when he's here, and I clean his house and do his laundry.'

'You said, "When he's here." When did you last see him?' asked the DS.

'Oh, it must have been four months ago,' she replied.

'Last October?'

'He left soon after the September races – the Manx Grand Prix – had finished. He was keen on motorbikes. There are several in his garage.'

Puzzled, George asked, 'I don't quite follow. Perhaps I think you'd better tell us everything you know. Start at the beginning. When did you first get to know him?'

'Mr Lemont came to live in Ravenswood about eight or nine years ago. Time goes so quickly, I can't remember exactly.'

'Ravenswood?'

'It's the name of his house. It stands in about an acre – half a mile up the glen.'

The DS nodded for her to proceed.

'Soon after he arrived, he advertised in the window of the village shop for a part-time housekeeper and cook. I applied as I had recently been widowed, and got the job. It entailed the usual cleaning as well as preparing meals – casseroles, and so on. He was hardly ever seen by the locals. When I was in his house, he was either in his library writing or in the garage fiddling with his motorbikes. On one occasion, he told me he was writing a book. When I asked him, "What's it about?", he said something about World War Two in the Middle East.

'He was a quiet man who liked his own company. He agreed to allow some of the adjacent farm's sheep to graze the land that surrounds his house. Mr Lemont was fond of the sheep and I often saw him talking to them. He gave some of them names, and they would come to him when he called them. I remember him on one occasion saying he preferred sheep to people.'

'I thought sheep were stupid,' muttered the DC.

She smiled. 'No, they're cleverer than you think – a bit like old biddies.'

Both policemen blushed. They realised they had been overheard.

Embarrassed, George coughed. 'So, you go to his house. What, twice a week?'

'He pays me well. If he's at home, I go and prepare his meals every day – sometimes twice a day.'

'But you haven't seen him for quite a while? Why didn't you report him missing?'

'Why should I? He often went away; sometimes up to six months or more.'

'He still pays you?'

'Oh, yes. He's very generous. I always get a bonus at Christmas. He insists I keep the house warm, dust the furniture, clean the windows, and so on.'

'So how does he pay you – when he's away?'

'When I got the job, he opened an account for me at Lloyds Bank in Ramsey. I receive a monthly allowance.' Her reply hinted a degree of indignation; she was upset that the DS thought she should not have a bank account. With her hackles rising, she asked, 'And anyway, you've not told me why you're here.'

Realising he had trodden on her toes, George attempted to smooth the waters. 'Last November, a body was washed ashore at Douglas,' he began. 'We have been unable to identify him by the usual methods and resorted to the reconstruction portrait that appeared in the local papers. You have been most helpful.'

'So you think the body is Mr Lemont. How did he die?'

'We're unsure. I can rely on your discretion to keep that to yourself.'

'Of course.'

'Do you know if he has any relatives?' asked George.

'Not that I know of. He's never mentioned anyone, and there are no photographs of anyone in the house.'

'There is one more thing I would like to do. Presumably, you have a key to his house?'

'Yes.'

'Would you be good enough to take us to the house so we can have a preliminary look around? I'm going to have to undertake a more thorough examination, but that will require a search warrant. We will come back with it next week.'

They finished their tea. The young DC finished up the bonnag. He paid her a compliment: 'It's delicious.'

★

They arrived at the entrance to the house, which stood about fifty yards back from the road. They drove up the single-track tarmacadam drive. The imposing double-fronted house stood in the middle of a field, about the size of half a soccer pitch. To the south side, standing at right angles to the front of the house, was a triple garage with ample space in front for parking further cars. In the field there were, perhaps, fifty or more sheep. George, with a country-trained eye, recognised two rare breeds – Lincoln Longwools and Manx Loughtans.

Mrs Craine unlocked the front door and they entered a grand hall. The double-width staircase rose to a mezzanine balcony facing them.

'Would you like to look in the library?' she asked.

They nodded and entered the first door on their right. In front of them, at the far end of the room, was a large bay window that looked onto the grazing sheep and the hills beyond. In the recess was a large desk made of light oak that matched the rest of the furniture.

'I think our search could take some time,' remarked George. 'However, we'll just have a quick look in the desk.'

'You'll find the drawers are locked.'

'Where does he keep the key?'

'In the wall safe.'

'Where's that?'

She moved to one side where there appeared to be nothing but shelves. She knelt on the carpeted floor and felt under the lowest shelf. A hidden spring released a section of the shelf. Mrs Craine pulled and revealed a built-in safe.

George saw it was a Chubb model – one of the best. It measured four feet high and two and a half feet wide with a large numerical dial in the centre of the dark grey door with a brass handle underneath.

'Do you know the combination?' George asked.

'No.'

'We'll not be able to open it today,' remarked the DS. 'On Tuesday, we'll come back with our expert on safes. I think that's all we can do for now. If you let me keep the front door key, then we won't have to disturb you next week.'

After dropping Mrs Craine off, George told his DC to drive to Ramsey. 'While we're up here, we might as well pop in and see the manager of her bank.'

'Will he tell us anything?'

'I'm not after her details, although I would love to know how much she is getting paid. I want to know where Lemont is getting his money from. Are his accounts on the island, or are they abroad?'

★

'George, I can't give you that information without a court order.'

'We've known each other since our schooldays. This is a murder inquiry. All I want to know is where does Mrs Craine's monthly allowance originate? I'll come back next week with a letter of authority if I have to.'

The manager sighed. He pressed a button on his desk, and his senior clerk entered moments later. 'Bring in Mrs Craine's file, will you?'

'We have three Mrs Craines. Which one?'

'The one who lives in Ballaugh Glen.'

A few minutes passed while the clerk was fetching the file. It allowed the two former school friends to catch up with each other's news.

The manager inspected the file briefly. 'She receives £50 monthly from the Westminster Bank in Douglas.'

'That's £600 per year – almost as much as I get,' commented the detective sergeant.

'If you want to know where Lemont's money comes from, then you will need a court order,' the manager warned. 'Old man Barlow, the manager of the Westminster, is a stickler for correct procedures.'

CHAPTER 4

On Monday morning, DS Turnbull acquired warrants from the Deemsters' office to search Ravenswood and an authorisation for the Deputy Chief Constable to inspect Lemont's accounts at the Westminster Bank.

In 1960, all banks closed promptly at three o'clock. However, the DCC immediately arranged an appointment to see the manager at 4.15 pm that afternoon. 'No time like the present,' the Super commented as George handed his boss the warrant.

Sergeant Turnbull briefed three constables to assist the search at Ballaugh. 'In essence, we are searching for anything that might confirm the identity of Mr Lemont. We want to know where he has been since last autumn and a lot more about his background. At present, we know very little other than what Mrs Craine has told us, which is practically nothing. The Chubb safe will be opened, hopefully, by Jim Ridgeway. I think you all know him. Be ready to leave Douglas at 0800 hours.'

Jim Ridgeway owned a jeweller's shop in the main shopping street in Douglas. He was the island's leading horologist, being qualified to service Rolex watches, as well as the only Manx retailer of Chubb safes. He was also a part-time special constable.

★

At 4.10 pm, the Superintendent left police HQ to stroll around the corner to the Westminster Bank at the bottom of Prospect Hill.

Mr Barlow, a man in his mid-fifties, was dressed immaculately in a dark three-piece suit. Wearing a stiff, separate collar shirt with his tie kept in place by a diamond pin, he inspected carefully the authorisation that had been signed by one of the island's Deemsters. Somewhat reluctantly, he handed over Lemont's personal file containing his accounts.

The Super began making notes of relevant details. Initially, a sum of £1,000 had been deposited to open the account in October 1951. A month later, a further £3,500 had been paid in. A few days later, £3,000 was transferred to Qualtrough and Quine, Advocates, Ramsey.

Presumably to buy his house, thought the DCC.

There was a standing order for £50 paid monthly to Mrs Craine's account at Lloyds Bank, Ramsey. There was a copy of Mr Lemont's birth certificate, purporting to show he had been born on 15th February 1915 in Harrow.

That makes him almost forty-five, the same age as me, about right.

The account showed a monthly sum of approximately £400 was paid in from a coded source: CHZur000CD3286917. The amount was never quite the same and tended to have gradually increased over the years.

'Lemont's initial deposits and monthly income, where do they come from?' asked the Superintendent.

'Zurich, Switzerland.'

'What bank?'

'No way of knowing. The Swiss banks use a centralised clearing house system. They could be from one of a dozen banks.'

'There must be some way of getting around Swiss secrecy?'

'Not without knowing which Zurich bank, the eleven-digit account number and its password. It's what makes their banks so

26

secure and wealthy. Why do you think Switzerland has most of the world's gold? It's because hundreds of accounts were opened by senior Nazis who raided the European Banks from Norway to Greece and everywhere in between. They're now dead and they were the only ones who knew their account details.'

'These entries marked *Cash*...'

'What about them?'

'They appear at irregular intervals for similar sums. What are they?'

'It's where he has withdrawn cash from various Westminster branches.'

'But why are some different from others?'

'The bank has a system known as arrangements. If Mr Lemont knows he will need cash when he is in London, say, then he will make an arrangement between our branch and a particular branch in London. When he needs the money, he will go to that branch and can take out what he requires up to a limit. In his case, it is £200 per week. However, if he goes to a branch where there is no arrangement, the branch will ring here for clearance and the cost of the phone call would be deducted from the cash – leaving him with, say, £49 16s if he wanted £50.'

'Suppose he was abroad?'

'Ah, altogether different. There are currency restrictions as I'm sure you are aware. To take cash abroad over £25, he would either have to apply for exemption from the Treasury or have a bank account in the country he was visiting. The chances are, however, that he simply draws money direct from his Swiss account. Foreign banks will be happy to accommodate him and turn a blind eye in order to get their hands on Swiss francs.'

'I don't follow.'

'Suppose he was in Spain. He'd withdraw 1,000 Spanish pesetas and the bank would receive that amount from Switzerland in Swiss francs.'

The Super nodded. 'Thank you for your help. One thing, though, why is his monthly income different each month?'

'The original standing order would have been made out in Swiss francs. Sterling has been dropping against Switzerland's currency ever since the war.'

★

On Tuesday, the search team arrived at Ballaugh in two cars. The DS allocated their work areas: one constable took the garage; one – upstairs, while a third combed downstairs and the library. Meanwhile, Jim Ridgeway knelt in front of the safe and explained to DS Turnbull what he was doing.

'This is a top-of-the-range model,' he explained as soon as he had seen the safe. 'Six numbers are required between 0 and 99 to open it. I've never sold this type to anyone on the island. Therefore, I can only assume the owner had someone from across install it. Unless I'm lucky, this could take a while. I will describe to you what I'm doing in case you need to do it in future.'

He then took a stethoscope from his holdall, put the earpieces to his ears and placed the bell-shaped diaphragm directly under the numeric dial.

'To start, the dial has always to be set to 10. So I begin by turning the dial clockwise to the number 10. Many users choose their six numbers based on a word. So, for example, if their word began with the letters D and A, then their first number would be 41.'

'Why 41? Why not 4 and then 1?'

'The numbers must at all times be more than eleven spaces apart. Both 4 and 1 are too close to each other as well as to the number 10. Furthermore, each number has to be selected by alternating the direction of selection. So I am going to turn the dial anticlockwise to 22 and begin there.'

He listened and, seemingly satisfied, he continued clicking the dial anticlockwise, one numeral at a time: 23, 24, and so on. Always he stopped to listen carefully before proceeding to the next digit. Intrigued, George watched, holding his breath.

When he reached 41, Jim smiled. 'Ironically, the first number is 41,' he said.

He then moved the dial clockwise to 29. Then slowly, unit by unit, he continued in the clockwise direction until he stopped at 13. 'That's the second number.'

'The thirteenth letter in the alphabet is M; the word could begin DAM,' remarked George.

Jim nodded, saying nothing, but moved the dial anticlockwise to 25.

He continued moving the dial one number at a time. Jim had moved the dial almost through a full circle before stopping at the number 1. 'The third number,' he nodded.

'The letter A? The only word I can think of is damask,' said the DS.

Jim looked up at the detective, shrugged his shoulders and said nothing. Then moving the dial clockwise, digit by digit, from 88, the next number turned out to be 62. Continuing, Jim found the last two numbers: 47 and 16.

'The last thing I have to do is go to zero and twist the handle. Hey presto!' announced Jim with a grin. The safe door opened.

'So the combination is 10, 41, 13, 1, 62, 47, 16, 0' said George as he wrote down the numbers, thinking there was no word that could match Jim's theory.

They began removing the contents when PC Trevor Rimmer, who had been searching the garage, appeared. 'I think you had better come and look. I think I've found another hidden safe.'

The two men put down the safe's contents and accompanied the PC.

As they walked to the garage, the PC explained: 'There are the usual items in the garage, such as tins of paint, boxes of assorted nails, screws, tools, and so on. There are also three motorbikes covered with sheets. However, two things struck me as odd. The first motorbike I uncovered was a DOT scrambler.'

'What's unusual about that?' asked George.

'I wasn't expecting it to have a Manx Motorcycle Club, MMC, sticker on the mudguard. It means the club could have some details about Mr Lemont.'

'True. What was the other peculiarity?'

'The Morris Traveller was parked over an inspection pit. I reversed the car out of the garage and took a closer look.'

They had arrived at the garage, and the detective could see what was unusual. The four-feet-deep rectangular pit had on one side a small, grey metal door, measuring about three feet by two. In the middle of the door was a keyhole with a brass surround showing the manufacturer's name – Dotteling AG.

'That's a Rolls Royce-quality safe,' Jim remarked, 'the best there is.'

'I couldn't find a key and it's definitely locked,' added the PC.

'What are your thoughts, Jim?' asked George.

'It's made by a German company that has specialised making bespoke five-bolt safes since before World War One. Without the key it is unbreakable as its walls and door are made from five-inch-thick, top quality steel.'

'You can't pick the lock?'

'Sorry, George. No one can.'

'Dynamite?'

'No use; the heat would melt the lock's mechanisms that are partially made of brass and fuse the lock forever. This is the first time I've ever seen a Dotteling; in the trade they're legendary.'

After a cursory look around the garage, they walked back to the library.

'How have you got on?' the DS asked the PC in the library.

'There's a whole section devoted to chess books – at least fifty; some are in Russian and others in German. He also has a section on BMW motorbikes.'

'He has two in the garage, an R26 and an R50S. What other books are there?'

'There are collections of Jules Verne, Alexandre Dumas and Victor Hugo novels written in French that are leather bound. There are also several books that could be in Arabic.'

'How do you know?'

'I don't – I'm guessing.'

'So it looks as if Lemont was something of a linguist,' commented George to no one in particular.

'While you were in the garage I looked through the things in the safe. The keys appear to be for the desk, and spares for his car and the house. The most interesting things are these two passports – one is British and one is French. The other unusual item is this envelope sealed with wax and marked *To Whom It May Concern.*'

The PC handed the passports and envelope to the DS.

'The photo is the same in both passports. Our artist's portrait is quite like him, don't you think?' asked George, as he showed the passports around.

'The British one is in the name of Peter Lemont, and the French one – *Pierre Le Mont,*' continued George. 'They're clearly fakes as the British one says he was born in Harrow, Middlesex, while the French one has him born in Marseilles. They have the same date of birth, however – 15th February 1915. I think we are going to have a lot of enquiries to make.'

George then broke the wax seal of the envelope and read aloud:

To whom it may concern,
    You have presumably opened the library safe to investigate my disappearance. I have deposited my will, its codicil and my

instructions with Qualtrough and Quine, Advocates in Ramsey.
There you will find information to help you with your inquiries.

However, only Superintendent Kinley, who is one of the few
men I can trust, will be able to gain access to the documents. He
will have to answer some questions on a chess game we played
some years ago when I was in the Ramsey team that played
Douglas in the Manx League. Anyone trying to impersonate
him couldn't possibly know the correct replies.

The key to the safe in my garage will also become available
and instructions on how to proceed.

'It is signed – Peter Lemont. I don't know what the Super is
going to make of this,' said the DS. 'The Super never recognised
Lemont at the post-mortem, yet it appears he played chess against
him.'

At this point PC Rimmer returned from the hall. 'I've just
made a phone call to the secretary of the MMC.'

'And?' asked George

'They have no member called Lemont. However, the owner
of the DOT is registered as Michael Fellowes at this address.'

'Anything else?'

'Fellowes used to take part frequently in the club's scrambles
at Bride, but hasn't been seen for about a year. Apparently,
Fellowes is a life member of their club.'

'If Lemont uses aliases, maybe that isn't his real name either?'
asked Jim.

'Look, Trevor, you and the others carry on with the search.
Jim and I will go back to Douglas. I'll brief the Super about
what we have found and get several copies made of the passports.
Then pick up one of the copies when you get back and take it
out to show the MMC secretary. It'll be interesting to see if he
recognises Lemont from the passport. I expect the Super will
want a meeting tomorrow morning to brief the Chief. Make sure
you lock the place securely before you come back to Douglas.'

CHAPTER 5

Intrigued, the Superintendent listened to his senior detective. 'I don't remember playing anyone called Lemont or Fellowes at Ramsey. You said it could be seven or eight years ago?'

'Yes, sir. He has a large collection of chess books in his library – some in Russian.'

'That's not unusual – I have several Russian chess books myself. It doesn't make me a communist.'

George looked blankly at his boss, who was smiling at his own joke.

The Super continued, 'The two surnames ring no bells. I keep a record of all my games and when I get home this evening I'll look to see if I can find the game against him. I have to admit that neither the sketch of the dead man nor the passport photos jogged my memory. I think the best bet is for you and me to meet here tomorrow morning at ten o'clock and plan our next move. If we have to contact the French Embassy in London, we may need someone fluent in French. We'll also have to get hold of the Liverpool Passport Office to see if the British passport is genuine. On the basis of what we know, I'll make an appointment to see the Head of Chambers at Qualtrough and Quine tomorrow afternoon, after our meeting.'

★

'Last night, I checked out all my games played in Ramsey,' began the Super the following morning. 'I played someone about my own age called Michael Fellowes in October 1953. I've never seen him since. He played a wild opening and pieces were soon flying all over the board. The game was eventually drawn. I was lucky to escape with half a point.

'After finding the game, I decided to ring the secretary of the Ramsey Chess Club and asked him about Fellowes. He remembered him, but hadn't seen him for several years. He told me Fellowes spent a lot of time off the island. I asked him if he had seen the picture of the missing man in last week's *Courier*. He hadn't, so I waited while he went and fetched his copy of the paper.

'When he returned, he asked, "Are you suggesting this artist's impression is supposed to be Fellowes?"

'I replied I was.

'He answered, "It could be; there's some resemblance."'

'So he wasn't convinced?' asked George.

'No, he wouldn't commit himself.'

'Will you go to Qualtrough and Quine's this afternoon?'

'No, I can't. Old man Qualtrough is in court all afternoon. I've an appointment with him at ten o'clock tomorrow. I think our priority is to sort out the name of the dead man. Is it Lemont, *Le Mont*, or Fellowes? One of them must be his real name, surely?'

'Although the Morris estate car is registered in the name of Fellowes, the same as the DOT motorbike, the land registry has the house owned by someone called Peter Lemont. It would seem the clever money is on that being his real name,' replied George.

'George, I want you to fly to Liverpool tomorrow with Lemont's British passport. I'll ring Liverpool's passport office and tell them why you're coming. Get the early flight so that afterwards you can catch the train to London. I've told the Chief Constable what we're doing and he will get the island's French Chargé d'affaires to contact the French Embassy so that they can check the French passport and will be expecting you. If you can't catch the evening's return flight, you may have to spend the night in London. If you like, I'll get you booked into the Union Jack Club near Waterloo Station. It's very comfortable – I've stayed there several times when I've been on courses with the Met. We'll meet when you get back.'

★

The next morning, Superintendent Kinley was driven to Ramsey sitting in the back seat of the force's black Austin Westminster saloon driven by class A1 driver, PC Hector Duff. On their way over the mountain road, the Super remembered how his early career had begun in Ramsey as a police cadet before the war. In 1939, he had volunteered to join the Royal Navy, but the Chief Constable had stopped his application. The CC had been allowed to retain only five of his junior constables for the duration. Those not retained were allowed to join the Armed Forces and were replaced by former retired policemen and volunteer "special constables" who were too old to enter the Army. Consequently, the Super had moved up several steps on the seniority ladder by the time his former colleagues had returned from the war. PC Duff was one such example, who had returned having won the Military Medal when a sergeant at El Alamein.

Ironic, he thought. *Had I entered the Navy, and Duff stayed in the police, I may have been driving him this morning.*

Nonetheless, the Super had always resented being kept back from joining the armed forces. His three younger brothers had entered the Army; one had served in Burma with Wingate's Chindits. No one in his family would admit it, but the war had driven a wedge between himself and his brothers.

35

Qualtrough and Quine's office was in Parliament Street, the main shopping thoroughfare in the northern seaside town. It was close to the police station, where PC Duff parked the car. The senior partner, Harley Qualtrough, was the very model of a solicitor with his dark grey pinstripe suit, white shirt, black tie and half-moon spectacles. He greeted the DCC, whom he had known for many years. Formerly, they had clashed professionally in court, as the police in the Isle of Man prosecuted all but the most major criminal cases.

'I apologise for all this hush-hush business, Bob. It does seem unnecessary as I know who you are. However, Lemont's instructions are clear. If we were approached by anyone, then before handing over this package, I have to ask you three questions about a chess game played by Mr Lemont.'

'So, that's his real name?'

'Is there some doubt?'

'To be honest, we're unsure. He seems to have used several aliases. Is this a likeness?'

The Super handed over a copy of Lemont's passport photograph.

The solicitor nodded. 'Yes, I'm pretty sure that's him; if it isn't, then it's a damn good likeness. However, my memory isn't what it used to be. After all, it was almost nine years ago when we handled the purchase of his house in Ballaugh. He used the name Lemont then, and his cheques from the Westminster Bank were in that name too. When he handed this package to us for safe-keeping, I was on holiday, so I never saw him. That was last April.'

'We have seen the Westminster Bank's file, and are trying to establish his true identity. He called himself Michael Fellowes when I played chess against him in 1953.'

The advocate peered over the top of his glasses as if to query whether the bank had gone through the correct procedures, but he made no comment.

Instead, he asked, 'The first question is what opening was played in the game?'

'It was the Blackmar–Diemer Gambit.'

'What was unusual about how the game finished?'

'He sacrificed a rook to get perpetual check and, hence, a draw.'

'Finally, what was the date and where was it played?'

'It was Wednesday, 15th October 1953 at the Mitre Hotel.'

'Good. Here is the sealed envelope. It has Mr Lemont's signature over the seal as well as my company's stamp.'

The Super looked at the seal. 'Your stamp is dated 1st April 1959.'

'Yes, it was a Wednesday; it was my sister's 60th birthday and I'd gone to Scotland to stay with her.'

★

The meeting had lasted less than fifteen minutes. As the Superintendent walked back to the police station, he realised how little the shops had changed since he was based there. Memories flooded back to the war years. A regular task on night duty was to check the shops' doors were secure. On a quiet, hot August night in 1941, in the early hours of the morning, he and a retired PC, conscripted for the duration, had gone for a dip in the sea to cool off. *God knows what would have happened had there been an emergency.* The thought made him smile as he wondered what he would do if he caught one of his PCs in a similar situation.

The duty sergeant offered him a cup of tea. The inspector of the Northern Division, Tommy Lowey, had been expecting him and had ensured the station was in shipshape condition in case the Super undertook an informal inspection.

'Any problems I should know about, Tommy?'

'No, sir. All is quiet. I'm in court tomorrow prosecuting a dangerous driving case. It's fairly cut and dried.'

'Who's defending?'

'Old man Qualtrough, whom you've just been to see.'

'Will he pull any tricks?'

'He doesn't usually; although he might plead guilty to the lesser charge of undue care and attention.'

'Your inclination?'

'Accept, as there wasn't anyone else involved.'

'Fair enough. Now, I must get back to Douglas, but first of all there is something I want to see in Ballaugh.'

★

'Hector, I'd like to return via Ballaugh and see the house where Lemont lived.'

'Very good, sir.'

During their ten-minute journey, the Super opened the envelope to find a bundle of papers and a sophisticated key with a blade that had many grooves, suggesting it fitted some type of tumbler lock. He had little time to examine the papers before they arrived.

PC Rimmer was checking the property before locking up. He saluted his boss. 'We've now completed a thorough search, sir, and I was just leaving. We'll have our reports ready tomorrow. Last evening, I went to see the MMC secretary and showed him a copy of the passport photo.'

'What did he say?'

'He thought the likeness was quite good.'

'But not definitive?'

'No.'

'OK, but before you go, Trevor, open up the garage and let me see the maintenance pit, will you?'

The PC opened the garage and backed out the Morris Minor to reveal the inspection pit.

The Super jumped into the pit with the key that had been inside the sealed envelope. It fitted perfectly, and the officer turned the key twice. He pulled and the door opened to reveal a metal strongbox, approximately two feet long, one and a half feet wide by eight inches deep. PC Duff gave him a hand to help him climb out of the pit and the Super showed the grey box to his two PCs.

'I think this could be the key to opening the metal box, sir,' said Constable Rimmer, as he handed his boss the bunch found in the library safe the previous day. 'We've tried this key everywhere in the house and it didn't fit anything – until now.'

'Thanks, Trevor; I'll take that key and the box back to Douglas and open it later.'

His reluctance to open the box in front of his PCs had been triggered by him having had sufficient time to read the first words of Lemont's letter while on the journey to Ballaugh. He had been intrigued, like the Ramsey lawyer, by Lemont's hush-hush approach and had previously been asking himself several questions: *Why would Lemont only allow me to read the envelope's contents? Why am I the only one he can trust?*

It had all seemed over the top until he had read…

If you intend to proceed with the investigation, you should contact Agent Tom O'Boyle of the Irish G2 when you have finished reading my file. He may put you in the direction of Colonel Paul Paillole of France's DGSE (their Military Intelligence). You will then have to decide what to do…

He'd had no time to read further, but he'd immediately understood the political implications of possibly having to liaise with the Irish and French Secret Services. Only he and the Chief Constable were positively vetted in the Manx force. PV clearance allowed them to handle TOP SECRET material, which had involved them signing the UK's Official Secrets Act. The Manx force didn't have a Special Branch – there was no need for one. He was unsure if George's security clearance in World War Two as an intelligence analyst could have lapsed. He made a mental note to check.

★

As soon as he returned to his office, the Super went to see the Chief Constable.

He explained the dilemma. 'If Sergeant Turnbull is going to get involved with the Irish and French Secret Services, then we need to check if his wartime vetting is still valid, and damned quick; otherwise, we can't go any further.'

'I can do that easily. He was an NCO in the Intelligence Corps, if I remember rightly. I suspect his clearance is even higher than ours! I'll do that before close of play.'

'My other worry is Lemont may not be the cadaver's real name. Firstly, there's the fact that he was circumcised; he could be Jewish or Muslim. Then there's the colour of his skin: is he Middle Eastern? There appear to be some Arabic books in his library; he would hardly have them if he couldn't read Arabic. Finally, Mrs Craine said Lemont was writing a book about World War Two in the Middle East. Is that where he was shot during the war?

'If George is not PV cleared, then we may have to call in help from the Lancashire Force after all.'

'We don't want them tramping over our patch, Bob. I still have my contacts in the right places. If he's not cleared, renewal will be a formality. Take that as read. He'll be cleared within days. You carry on while I ring an old pal of mine in MI5 to check Turnbull's records.'

★

The DCC returned to his office and opened the metal case. He didn't know what to expect, but the contents surprised him. Wrapped inside a waterproof canvas bag was a rectangular, beautifully coloured block. It was apparently solid and fitted snugly inside the metal box. The patterns on the two faces were different.

On what appeared to be the top face, mother-of-pearl shapes had been arranged to resemble Arabic writing.

Is it a phrase that means something?

The writing was framed by a border of flowers made from red, white and blue coloured glass.

What an exquisite object.

He turned it over. The reverse face was made of alternate black and white one-inch squares that resembled a chess board. He counted them – thirteen by ten, 130 in total. He noticed that, when he touched some of the squares, they could be pushed down as if they were sprung.

Is the block hollow? Is there something inside?

He shook it gently near his ear; there was no sound.

CHAPTER 6

The Super received a phone call towards the end of the afternoon from George. 'I'm about to leave the French Embassy, sir. Firstly, Lemont's UK passport is a clever forgery. The Liverpool office wants to send it to London for further investigation. I have agreed. I hope that's OK?'

'I don't suppose we've much option, George, as strictly speaking all passports are the property of the Government. When it's counterfeit, that may be open to discussion. What's the second point?'

'I'm in the cultural liaison department at the French Embassy. Everyone here has been helpful, and they also want to keep the French passport. They think it's fake, and want to send it to Paris for tests. Are you happy with that as well?'

'Can you hand me over to the officer who has been dealing with you?'

'Yes, sir.'

A new voice came on the phone, speaking with only a hint of a French accent. 'Hello Superintendent. How can I help?'

'*Bonjour.* I'm George's boss. Has DS Turnbull told you we believe Pierre Le Mont may have been murdered?'

'Yes, he has. We have examined the passport and although the document appears genuine, the serial number and date of issue don't tally with our records. We would like to send it to Paris where our central files are kept.'

'I've no objection. Our police photographer has taken copies. However, can you help me to locate a Colonel Paul Paillole of the Military Intelligence Bureau?'

'Can I ask why?'

'His name has cropped up in our enquiries with Le Mont.'

'Obviously, I've no idea who the colonel is. All I can do is make enquiries with the *SDECE*, our *Service de Documentation Exterieure,* and get them to contact him. That department will handle the irregularity of the passport and liaises regularly with military intelligence.'

'Thank you; you've been most helpful. Can you put George back on the phone?'

'If I hurry, sir, I should be able to catch the late flight back.'

'OK, George; see you tomorrow.'

★

The Super's mind reverted to the enigma of the tablet and the instruction to contact the Irish Secret Service. He decided to finish reading Lemont's letter, despite knowing his driver would be waiting to drive him home.

When World War One ended, the League of Nations was founded at the 1919 Versailles Peace Conference. At San Remo, in June 1920, the League approved the splitting up of the Middle East along the lines of the secret 1916 Sykes-Picot Agreement between Britain and France. Essentially, the arrangement gave mandates for France to control Syria and Lebanon, while Britain would govern Palestine, Transjordan and Iraq. The mandates would last for twenty-five years during which time France and Britain agreed to steer the five countries towards self-government.

The Ottoman Empire was dissolved. Greece and Italy were allocated areas of the Ottoman's territory as well as France and Britain. The territory that remained was to become the core of modern Turkey. However, its leader, Mustafa Kemal Atatürk, who had defeated the Allies at Gallipoli, immediately set about redrawing the country's boundaries. 'Turkish soil for Turkish people' was his cry. Aided by the recently formed Soviet Government, the Turkish War of Independence would last for three years as Greece, Italy and France lost considerable areas that had been allocated to them. The French, however, remained in control of modern-day Syria and Lebanon.

The boundaries of the new, secular Turkey were agreed at the Treaty of Lausanne in July 1923. The previous year, Atatürk had abolished the Caliphate. It had resided with the Sultan of the Ottomans for over 400 years. During this period, the Sultan had been accepted as the leader of over 300 million Sunni Muslims across the Middle East, India and East Asia. The last Caliph, Mehmed VI, had gone into exile in northern Italy in 1922, where he remained until he died in 1926.

Although the British gave up their Iraq mandate in 1932, allowing the Kingdom of Iraq to join the League of Nations, France remained firmly in control of Syria and Lebanon. After the fall of Paris to the Nazis in 1940, the Vichy French Government took over the running of Syria, along with most of the other overseas French territories. Mehmed's son, Ertrugel Effendi, a highly successful wine merchant based in Paris, who specialised in exporting champagne to Germany, saw an opportunity to court the Nazis and thereby re-establish the Sultanate with himself as Caliph. Ertrugel was hoping the Turkish Government would come into the war supporting the Allies and be defeated by the Nazis. In 1940, it looked as if the Germans would quickly win the war. Ertrugel would then be proclaimed by Hitler as the new Sultan and Caliph of Turkey.

Fluent in English, Italian, French, German, Turkish and Arabic, Ertrugel began negotiations with the Germans. His plan was to encourage the Nazis to strengthen the Vichy Forces in Syria in order to capture the nearby Suez Canal.

Instead, the Germans, although sympathetic to his plans, persuaded him to prove himself. They appointed him the High Commissioner of the Syrian Vichy Government. It was stressed that, as the Axis powers were already being squeezed for oil, his priority was to capture the northern oil fields of Iraq. The Suez Canal could wait. Unknown to Ertrugel, the Germans had already begun negotiating with an Iraqi republican, Rashid Ali, to overthrow the pro-British Iraqi Royal Family. The plan for a coup d'état was well advanced when Ertrugel arrived in Vichy Damascus.

Ertrugel suffered from hubris. His problem was whether the Vichy French forces, supported by the Nazis, should concentrate their attack solely on the northern oil fields around Kirkuk or whether to split and take Baghdad as well. The Germans would thereby have a route to the Persian Gulf and he would become a hero of the Third Reich. Self-opinionated and with no military training, he underestimated the strength of the Commonwealth forces defending Iraq and decided to attack on two fronts on 1st April 1941.

When his forces met determined resistance from Australian and Indian troops as well as the Jordanian Arab Legion, the outcome was never in doubt. The Nazi-planned Rashid Ali coup failed miserably. Four months later, the successful counter-attack by the Australian, Indian and Free French forces led to the fall of Damascus. Syria and Lebanon came under the control of the Free French, although the British and Commonwealth forces in Syria outnumbered the Free French soldiers by twenty to one.

At that point the script finished. The next page was blank, except for a scribbled note: *Remember, when a stranger offers you his shirt, ask yourself why.*

The Super pondered: *are O'Boyle and Paillole to be trusted? And what is the significance of the decorated block? Why did it have to be hidden in such a secure place?*

CHAPTER 7

Friday, 22nd January 1960

The Superintendent and the Chief Constable shared a secretary/ shorthand typist, Dolly Kelly, whose office was midway between the two offices of the senior policemen.

'Dolly, I want you to get me the phone number of the Deputy Chief Constable of the Garda in Dublin,' requested the DCC.

'Do you know his name?'

'I've no idea. You will have to do a bit of delving to find his name and number.'

Dolly smiled. She'd held her position for almost ten years. She thought highly of the Super, known behind his back by his first names' initials – "RJ". She knew he was the power behind the Force. The Chief Constable, appointed by the UK Home Office, was primarily a figurehead.

She understood not to ask RJ why he wanted to contact Dublin.

She promised to get the number as quickly as possible, even though she was unsure how to go about the task. However, liaison with the Liverpool City Police was a regular occurrence. She dialled "0" and asked for Liverpool Central 1010. She was soon talking to her opposite number.

'Jill, it's Dolly from Douglas. Have you a telephone directory for the Eire police?'

'What is it you want to know?'

'The name, rank and phone number for the Garda's Deputy Chief Constable. Our Deputy needs to ring him. I've no idea why as I've never known us contact the Irish police before.'

'We have the Garda's internal directory with all their numbers somewhere. Wait a minute while I get it... there are three Deputy Chief Constables. Which one do you want? There's Strategy, Operations, and Administration.'

'I expect Administration might be a good place to start. What's his name?'

'He's Commissioner G D Brady. His number is Dublin 565565.'

'Thanks Jill; I owe you one.'

It took several minutes before the Douglas exchange had the Irish number ringing.

'Commissioner Brady's secretary speaking, how can I help?'

'Good morning; my name is Dolly Kelly and I'm speaking from the Chief Constable's office in Douglas, Isle of Man. Our Deputy Chief Constable, Superintendent Kinley, would like to speak to Commissioner Brady.'

'Can I tell him what it's about?'

'I'm afraid the Super didn't tell me, but it seems important. I had to get your number from the police in Liverpool.'

'I'll patch you through.'

The line went silent for a few seconds during which time Dolly told the Super to pick up his phone.

'Commissioner Brady.'

'Good morning, it's Superintendent Bob Kinley, Deputy Chief Constable of the Isle of Man Police in Douglas.

'Gerry Brady here. How can I help?'

'It's a long story, but we're investigating a complex murder on the island and a name has cropped up. I am hoping you can assist us in making contact with him.'

'If I can. What's the name?'

'Tom O'Boyle, in your G2 department.'

'Bob, that's an unusual request. You'll appreciate I can't give you his number straightaway.'

'I fully understand, but I wouldn't ask unless it was critical to our investigation.'

'I'll ring you back on Monday. Will that do?'

'That would be fine. When you contact him, tell him it's about someone who we believe may be called Peter Lemont.'

★

First thing on Monday, the Super received his return phone call from Dublin.

'Bob, I have spoken to Tom O'Boyle who is no longer in G2. He is now Head of G1, our internal security service. I could have told you last Friday, but as you appreciate, even I have to go through a rigmarole to contact him. When I mentioned the name Peter Lemont, the silence suggested I'd struck a nerve. In essence, he will only meet you face-to-face. Can you come to Dublin? I'll set up the meeting.'

'I'd like my detective sergeant to accompany me, if that's OK? We could catch an Aer Lingus flight later this week?'

'That would be fine. I'll ring back this afternoon when I've checked what day is best for O'Boyle. I'll arrange things at this end and ensure a car meets you at the airport. I'll book you two rooms in a hotel we use in the town centre. I'll meet you that evening for dinner and introduce you to Tom O'Boyle the next morning.'

★

On Thursday afternoon, after an uneventful flight, the Fokker Friendship aircraft landed five minutes early. A uniformed constable drove the two Manxmen to the Gresham Hotel. A plush four-star Georgian establishment in O'Connell Street, close to Nelson's Pillar, it was situated less than three hundred yards from the River Liffey. After both men had unpacked and taken a shower, they took a stroll towards the river.

'I'm glad this is on expenses,' joked George over a pint of Guinness in Gibney's bar fronting the quay.

'George, it's not often we get away from the island on business, so let's make the most of it. Did BP mention your Army's PV clearance has been checked out and it's still valid?'

'No, he never said a word.'

'Well, you know what he's like. I was expecting him to tell you, but it's all OK.'

They wandered back to their hotel to find Gerry Brady had arrived. Over a drink in the toddy-bar, the usual pleasantries about a good flight and their rooms being suitable were made. At the Irishman's suggestion, they decided to eat in the brasserie rather than the more formal silver service restaurant.

Gerry appeared to be known by the waiter, who led the three men to a quiet table.

'Perhaps you can tell me what all this is about,' began the Commissioner.

The two Manxmen began with the mystery of the body being washed ashore, the man having been drowned, but not in saltwater and the difficulty of determining his identity. They described how they had discovered someone known as Peter Lemont with two fake passports, his isolated home and the precautions he had taken to protect his personal documents. The Super explained how he had found a reference to Tom O'Boyle in one of Lemont's papers.

'On Monday, I mentioned Tom O'Boyle is Head of G1. Do you know what G1 does?' Gerry asked.

'Not really,' replied Bob.

'G1 is our department like your MI5. Tom O'Boyle was transferred from G2 and promoted just over a year ago. He

50

has responsibility, among other things, to liaise with the Royal Ulster Constabulary over IRA attacks. He handles the problem of Noraid funds flooding in from America that are being used to purchase IRA arms. Although O'Boyle wouldn't tell me much over the phone when I spoke to him, I formed the impression that he knew who Peter Lemont was. I'll take you to his HQ in the morning. It's north of Dublin Airport at Malahide. I'll pick you up at half past nine.'

★

Despite a motorcycle outrider leading the police car through the morning traffic, progress was slow. The journey to the swanky residential area that boasted several yacht clubs, as well as the headquarters of Ireland's cricket governing body, took over an hour. They arrived in front of a detached, three-storey Victorian house in the Queen Anne style, set in manicured gardens overlooking a marina. A sweep of steps led to a portico colonnaded door. As he got out of the car, George could smell the sea air in the light onshore breeze. Across the road, the blue water sparkled in the sunshine.

'What a beautiful setting,' he said to Gerry.

'Yes, the security services know how to look after themselves,' replied the Garda commissioner with a cynical smile.

As they walked up the path towards the entrance, a wiry man with a haggard face and gingery hair, dressed in a tweed suit, came down the steps to meet them. The Super guessed he was of a similar age to himself. Commissioner Brady shook his hand, turned to the Manxmen and introduced Tom O'Boyle. The four men stood on the garden path for a few minutes as Gerry explained he would organise their return to Dublin for three o'clock.

'Will that give you sufficient time?' Gerry asked.

'That'll be fine,' Tom replied. He then gestured for the Manx policemen to follow him while Gerry returned to Dublin in the police car.

Tom's office, located on the top floor, overlooked the Irish Sea. As the two visitors looked enviously through its large window, Tom joked, 'I'm afraid you can't see the Isle of Man from here.'

'It's a wonderful view nonetheless; there can't be many offices that allow you to watch herons catching fish,' replied the Super.

'It can be different in the winter when there's a howling, easterly wind.'

'Like Douglas! It's ironic, but it's the winter storms that have brought us here.'

They sat around a small table and coffee arrived.

'Commissioner Brady only gave me the vaguest idea as to why you wanted to see me. It may be easiest if you start at the beginning.'

For the second time in twenty-four hours, the two policemen began their story. When the Super showed Tom the copies of the passport photos, Tom nodded. 'That's the man I know as Peter Lemont, although I only met him briefly in 1949.'

The Super proceeded to describe the lengths Lemont had taken to keep his personal effects secure. The DCC explained how only he could get access to further files by describing a chess game played years earlier.

'Can you think of any reason why Lemont would want me to investigate his death and no one else?' asked the Super.

'I can only guess Lemont saw you as an honest cop and felt he couldn't trust anyone else. From what little I know of Lemont's background, it can best be described as murky.'

The Super said nothing, but thought, *that doesn't add up. He's casting aspersions on Lemont, but claims he hardly knew him.*

The Super passed over the comment and began to explain how they had found a decorated block inside one of the most secure safes manufactured anywhere. 'It is a German Dotteling safe and has been built into the wall of the inspection pit in Lemont's garage. You can see from these photos that the tablet is about two feet by eighteen inches by eight. The top is covered with patterns of mother-of-pearl, and underneath, some of the chequered squares appear to be sprung. The fascinating thing is that it seems to be a solid block, but why should Lemont want to go to such extremes to hide it?'

O'Boyle carefully studied the assorted photos that had been taken with a ruler in their background.

'Where is it now?' he asked.

'In Douglas Police Station.'

O'Boyle asked, 'Do you know the significance of the sprung squares?'

'I was rather hoping you might tell us.'

A shrug of O'Boyle's shoulders indicated he didn't know.

Out of the corner of his eye, for a fraction of a second, the Super noticed George eyeballing O'Boyle.

George thinks he's lying too!

As if O'Boyle suddenly felt uncomfortable with the discussion, he suggested, 'Look, it's almost a quarter to twelve. Now that you've explained your reason for coming to see me, this might be a good time to adjourn. There's a cosy pub around the corner, but it fills up rapidly. If we go now, we'll get a decent seat. I can recommend their fresh lobster thermidor. It goes down a treat with a pint of Guinness. The lunch break will give me time to consider what I can tell you when we return. I assume you are both security cleared?'

The two Manxmen nodded.

'Excellent. In that case, I'll tell you all I know about Lemont.'

CHAPTER 8

After an hour's break, and fortified with several pints of stout, the three men returned to the G1 HQ. George noted, as he walked up the front path, that there was no indication of the house's role. It could have been just another well-kept Victorian mansion in its own gardens.

Settled back in his office, O'Boyle began. 'Let me say straight away I can see the problem of having a body washed ashore and the need to identify it. However, I'm afraid you're going to open a can of worms if you pursue this inquiry too far. Let me explain.

'As you may imagine, Ireland's secret services are neither as large nor extensive as the UK's. When I worked in G2, I was posted in 1949 to the post of intelligence officer in our Syrian Embassy for five years. It was a difficult time as the state of Israel had been formed the previous year. The first, so-called, independent Syrian Government was inaugurated in 1946, when the country joined the UN. It fought in the 1948 Arab-Israeli war, and although Syria signed the armistice, their government continued to aid the Palestinians fight a guerrilla war against the Israelis. There were two military *coups d'état* in Syria after I arrived. I found myself wondering what I had come to. As Ireland had been neutral in the war, the street rioters left our embassy unscathed, but the French and British Embassies had to batten down their hatches and use armed soldiers to protect their property.

'The country was awash with World War Two arms and in a bloody mess. Syrian governments were supplying arms to the Palestinians, while on the other hand, believe it or not, the Israeli Government was supplying arms to the Syrian opposition groups to help them topple the Syrian Government. The Israelis wanted their northern neighbour to remain weak and politically indecisive.

'My patch only included Syria and Lebanon. However, although the British had given up their Iraq mandate in 1932, de Gaulle, the arch colonialist, and his Free French didn't really give up control of Syria until about 1950. After 1945, the British had supported the Arab nationalists to make trouble for the French in Syria. They thereby hoped the French would rapidly relinquish their mandate. Consequently, the French retaliated by supporting the Zionist terrorists attacking the British police in Palestine. It explains de Gaulle's attitude towards Britain and the tension between the two European allies that remains to this day.

'Going back to the war. In April 1941, with Nazi support, the Vichy Syrians attempted an unsuccessful *coup* in Iraq. The attempt to capture Iraq's oil fields backfired – thanks largely to Australian and Indian troops. Three months later, Syria fell to the Allies and came under control of de Gaulle's Free French. Despite being outnumbered twenty to one by the Imperial troops, it didn't stop de Gaulle thinking his men had inflicted the first defeat on the Nazis in the war.

'Most of the French civil servants, who had administered Vichy Syria, transferred their allegiance back to de Gaulle. When I arrived, my opposite number in the French embassy, who I got to know quite well, was Paul Paillole of their counter-espionage service, the DGSE. Paillole had arrived soon after the Vichy Government fell, so he knew Syria's problems far better than me. The French Embassy's security officer was Pierre Le Mont, who left a few weeks after my arrival. Consequently, I hardly knew him.

'As I began to know Paillole better, he told me he believed Lemont had been behind the supply of arms to the Zionists fighting the British police. Paillole also claimed some of the arms were finding their way to the IRA. I found this hard to believe as the IRA had been dormant in Ireland for the duration of the war. Most of their hardliners had joined an international Nazi brigade and died on the Eastern Front.

'Paillole's theory was that Lemont, whom he clearly didn't like, hated the British because they had encouraged Arab uprisings in Syria during the 1930s. In one of the Arab raids, they attacked a remote garrison where his father, a lieutenant colonel, happened to be making a routine inspection. Fifteen French troops were killed and Lemont's father was seriously wounded, forcing his retirement. Paillole believed Lemont saw the IRA as a way of stabbing the British in the back. Frankly, I was glad to leave in 1954. That year there was yet another *coup*. It was unimaginable chaos – no one could trust anyone.'

O'Boyle paused.

It gave the Super an opportunity to ask, 'Do you still think the IRA is a threat?'

'During the war, after the fall of France, up to 400 members of the IRA left Ireland to join the Waffen-SS Nordland Regiment, which was largely made up of Fascist Scandinavians. They fought on the Eastern Front. They believed that, if the Nazis won the war, the Germans would unite Ireland and give it full independence.

'Only about thirty returned. They form the nucleus of the present IRA and believe the only way the six counties will ever become part of a united Ireland is through violence. They have been steadily recruiting and now have as many as 1,000 members – not all necessarily military. They have accountants, logisticians, fundraisers, even PR personnel. My department has a few undercover agents in one or two of their brigades. Unless

MI5 wake up, trouble will soon start in Northern Ireland and spread to England. You mark my words.'

'So,' said the Super, 'should I take this investigation any further? As I said, Lemont's papers instructed me to contact Paul Paillole. Do you think he will be able to add anything? I asked the French Embassy in London to get him to contact me last week, but he hasn't come back yet.'

'Colonel Paillole, if he's still around, should be able to bring you more up to date. He might know what happened to Lemont when he returned to Paris and what he's done since. As I said, I hardly knew Lemont in Damascus and that was eleven years ago. If he has been involved with the IRA since then, he hasn't come up on my radar. That doesn't mean he hasn't been active. You could check with MI5; they may know something.'

They stopped for afternoon tea and conversation became social. Tom admitted he had never been to the Isle of Man, but when the Super revealed he had friends in Cork through playing postal chess and had stayed with them two years previously, Tom wanted to know details of the holiday that included kissing the Blarney Stone and visiting Killarney. At three o'clock, the Garda police car arrived promptly. During their farewells, Tom asked a favour. 'If you do meet Paillole, give him my regards.'

★

That evening, the pair walked down O'Connell Street towards the river and found a quiet pub with a restaurant. They discussed their feelings.

'Several things worry me,' began George. 'How did O'Boyle know Paillole was a colonel? O'Boyle asked us to give the Frenchman his regards if we meet him, which suggests he has lost contact, but I have a gut feeling they keep in touch.'

'There could be a simple explanation.'

'I can't think of one.'

'Unless, of course, he is deliberately trying to bamboozle us. You know what these security people are like – no one trusts them; they don't even trust themselves. What else worries you?' asked the Super.

'He told us he'd only briefly met Lemont eleven years ago, and yet he was positive about the passport photo. Up to now, others have hesitated about the likeness. How is he so sure, or is this another attempt to mislead us? Furthermore, I'd swear he knew something about the coloured tablet.'

The Super smiled. 'When I mentioned it to O'Boyle, I saw the look on your face. I could tell you didn't believe him.'

'O'Boyle never asked any questions about it. Doesn't that strike you as being odd? The block must lie at the heart of Lemont's death; otherwise, why did he go to such lengths to hide it? Funnily enough, O'Boyle also referred to Lemont in the present tense, which suggests he thinks he's alive.'

CHAPTER 9

On Monday, Superintendent Kinley, on arriving at his office, was greeted by Dolly.

'While you were away, I was given a Paris phone number from someone in the French Embassy in London – I didn't catch their name. Shall I try and get the number for you?'

'Yes, please, Dolly.'

Thinking it would be faster, Dolly decided to use Scotland Yard's international police exchange in London. A call from Douglas 1212 was patched through by the Douglas exchange to Whitehall 1212, from where it reached Paris 123123, extension 432, in little over a minute. Expecting it would take longer, Dolly panicked when she heard the greeting, '*Bonjour, comment puis-j'aider?*'

She yelled through the open door to the Deputy's office, 'Sir, pick up your phone. Quick!'

The Super's French was rudimentary at best. However, he managed to introduce himself. '*Bonjour, j'ai Police Superintendent Robert Kinley en Isle de Man, Angleterre.*'

There was polite laughter at the other end. In lightly accented English came the reply, 'Ah, Robert, I gather you have been trying to reach me.'

Much relieved, and realising he was talking to Paul Paillole, the Deputy replied, 'Please call me Bob. How much do you know about why I am ringing you?'

'Enough to know that we cannot talk on this line. The passport has reached me from our London Embassy. It is on my desk as we speak. All I can say is the photo is a good likeness. If you want to know more, then we will have to meet face-to-face.'

'I'm about to have a case conference in a few minutes. Can I get back to you later?'

'That will be fine; I shall be in my office all afternoon, but do remember we are an hour ahead of British time.'

★

The Super and his DS sat waiting in the small conference room to brief the Chief Constable on their visit to Dublin. Ten minutes passed before he entered the room looking flustered.

'Bob, I've just had the Head of the Met's Special Branch on the line wanting to know why we have just contacted the French Secret Service in Paris and not gone through the proper channels.'

'I wasn't aware there are proper channels.'

'Nor was I,' admitted the CC, 'but I am now. Apparently, to contact overseas security services, all UK police forces are supposed to go through the Home Office who then decide if MI5 or MI6 should become involved. I fobbed him off by telling him we are conducting a murder inquiry and the Isle of Man is not in the UK, which seemed to throw him. He didn't seem too happy. What did your visit to Dublin reveal?'

'Before we begin, sir, you may remember PC Duff won the Military Medal when he was in Egypt during the war.'

The CC nodded. 'An excellent man; we're lucky to have him.'

'After El-Alamein, Duff remained stationed in Cairo HQ for several years and picked up some Arabic. As I was unsure if the pattern on the front of the slab could have been Arabic, I showed him the tablet and asked him if he had seen anything like it. He told me that, although he could "get by" speaking Arabic, he could only read odd words. However, he recognised two words on the tablet – Mohammed and Allah.'

'What the hell have Mohammed and Allah got to do with a decorated block of wood?' asked the Chief.

'I don't know, but I'm thinking the block may have something inside it.'

'It would explain the function of the sprung squares,' remarked the Chief.

'O'Boyle and Paillole both confirmed the photos in the passports are of Lemont. Assuming they are not collaborating to mislead us, I think we can take it as read that the cadaver is Peter Lemont. O'Boyle claimed he hardly met Lemont while he worked in Syria in 1949. However, he painted a picture of Lemont as a gun-runner and all-round bad egg. George and I weren't convinced he was giving us the full story.'

The Super paused and nodded for George to continue.

'There were some inconsistencies in what O'Boyle told us. He inferred he hadn't been in touch with Paillole since Syria, but knew he was now a colonel. O'Boyle told us he hardly knew Lemont in Damascus, yet after a brief glance at his passport photo, he was positive it was Lemont. Everyone else who has seen the photos has not been so sure. Then there is the coloured tablet. O'Boyle's body language initially showed interest; then he rapidly tried to pass it off as an irrelevancy. I wasn't convinced by his sudden feigned lack of interest. It has to be a vital key to all this, and maybe it does have a religious significance. Finally, he inadvertently referred to Lemont in the present tense. I think he knows Lemont is alive and is lying to keep us in the dark.'

'In other words, you think O'Boyle and Lemont could be backscratching each other. Any ideas, Bob?' asked the Chief.

'When I spoke with Paillole a few minutes ago, the Met must have been listening. Paillole is only prepared to give us further information face-to-face. I think we should meet halfway. Are you happy with that? Or do you think we should close the case now, even though there may still be some doubts about Lemont's identity?'

'George?'

'The cadaver drowned in freshwater, but ended up in the sea. If he wasn't murdered, then after he had had an accident, someone moved his body. We have a legal obligation to get to the bottom of the mystery. There are other questions. Why are there two safes at Lemont's house? Why did he specifically ask for the Super to investigate his disappearance? Where does he go for months at a time? Why did he choose to come and live in the Isle of Man? Why was O'Boyle lying to us?'

There was a pause before the Super took up the discussion. 'I wonder if the sprung squares are a means of unlocking what appears to be a solid slab. I would like to get the hospital to X-ray the block and see if there is anything inside. If you're happy, I'll ask Dr Parton to have it X-rayed.'

'That's fine by me. I believe George is right. The case cannot be closed with so many questions unanswered,' replied the Chief Constable.

'You're clearly not happy with our conversations being monitored by the Met either,' remarked his Deputy.

'Damn right I'm not.'

'Then shall I arrange to meet Paillole at a neutral venue?'

'Ring him and tell him that we will in future write to him. Ask him to agree to somewhere suitable. After this morning, I think the less said on the blower, the better.'

The Chief Constable stood. The meeting closed.

★

For the second time that day, Douglas 1212 reached the Paris number, but through the civilian channels. The Manx Deputy explained that their previous conversation had been overheard by the Special Branch of the Metropolitan Police.

'Can we meet halfway? Say somewhere on the south coast: Folkestone, Newhaven or Southampton?' asked the Super.

'I prefer to fly. There are direct flights from Paris to Manchester and Edinburgh as well as London. Manchester would suit me fine, as I could be back here within the day. You choose where we meet, preferably in a hotel near Ringway Airport. Arrange to deliver your answer to our embassy next week. Our telegraphic communications are encrypted and I will be able to give you a suitable date within minutes. I will give our meeting top priority.'

CHAPTER 10

'I'm sorry we couldn't do this earlier, Bob, but this is a bad time of the year for unexpected deaths with the elderly. There's a virulent strain of flu going around. I had five deaths last week,' explained Dr Parton as he accompanied the Super to the X-ray department. 'I've spoken to our radiographer, but he is unsure if our equipment will be sufficiently sensitive to meet your requirements. X-raying bones is one thing, but spotting irregularities inside what is probably a slab of hard wood is another. Nevertheless, we will try.'

'What exactly is it you want me to look for?' asked the radiographer.

'I believe these sprung squares on the underside may be the key to opening the slab. Can the X-rays see if anything is inside?'

'I'll give it a stab.'

The Super smiled, thanked the radiographer and thought, *Perhaps not the right thing to say to a policeman.*

While Bob and Tim went to the canteen, the technician took X-ray photographs of the tablet from various angles before going to the developing room.

Over half an hour had passed before the radiographer appeared with the results. 'Beneath the decorative exterior of coloured glass and mother-of-pearl, the box is made from a single slab of hard wood. I'm afraid there's very little to be seen. Nevertheless, the fuzzy pictures from the underside of the box show what appears to be a pair of metal hinges on one side. There seems to be a complex metallic mechanism inside the container. The squares on one side have metal rods connected to what could be a shaft. Those squares could be the key to opening the box. The other squares don't appear to be joined to anything.'

'Can you tell if there is anything else inside the box?'

'It's possible there is a separate piece of wood inside, but it would take much more powerful equipment to delimitate the two materials.'

'Is there any way of knowing the sequence the squares should be depressed to open the contraption?'

'I'm afraid not. Even the type of equipment used by crystallographers at universities may not be able to discern what order the keys have to be depressed. Whoever made this container was a genius with a lot of patience. I'm guessing, but I'll bet it's hundreds of years old.'

★

The following morning, the three police officers met. The Super explained the problem of the hospital's X-ray machine being insufficiently sensitive to help with opening the block, other than to confirm the tablet was not a solid object.

'Dr Parton suggested we contact Manchester University's chemistry department. He believes they undertake research into crystalline structures at very low temperatures. Their machine will be capable of seeing what's inside, and he gave me the phone number of a Professor Dan Eley.'

'If you give me his telephone number, I'll ring him as soon as we've finished here,' said the Chief. 'I think the next step is for you, George, to visit the French Embassy tomorrow and find out when Colonel Paillole can meet yourself and the Super in Manchester. When we have a date, I'll hopefully be able to persuade Manchester University to examine the tablet the day before. We can then book the necessary hotel for the meeting and your overnight stay. Any questions?'

There being none, the meeting adjourned.

★

On Wednesday, George caught the early morning flight from Ronaldsway. Paillole agreed to fly into Manchester on Tuesday 1st March. By 7.30 pm, the DS was back on Manx soil. Professor Eley agreed to meet the two police officers with the tablet on Monday 29th.

★

On Sunday, 28th February, the Super and DS Turnbull caught the 3.00 pm sailing to Liverpool with the tablet, arriving at 6.45 pm. By seven o'clock, they had collected their hire car and arrived in Manchester an hour later.

★

The Professor met them the following morning. 'We use X-ray diffraction to determine the lattice structures of compounds,' he explained. 'Liquid nitrogen ensures a clearer picture by lowering the temperature of the compounds.'

'How does that help?' asked George.

'The technique was first discovered by an old boy of King William's College. William Bragg is the youngest ever Nobel Prize winner for physics,' replied Professor Eley. 'Put crudely, it slows down the molecules' vibrations and each material inside the box will have contracted by a different amount. By photographing

66

the box at the correct angle, we should see the different materials inside. With luck, we'll find out how the opening mechanism works.'

The university labs were practically deserted. The block was encased in a thermos–like cupboard and its temperature lowered slowly to a point where, finally, the temperature inside the cabinet was approaching -120 °C. After removing the tablet from the cupboard, it was placed in a glass container to be X-rayed.

The results after developing the plates were revealing.

The X-ray photos showed the top of the box had a tight-fitting lid whose edges had been imperceptible to the naked eye. The X-rays also disclosed a rectangular object inside the box wrapped in a piece of cloth.

'The rectangle inside is a flat piece of wood, but of a different type to the container. It is about half an inch thick. The cloth is finely woven, maybe silk. You can also see there is a gap of about two inches at one end of the case. It's that end that is the most interesting,' said the Professor.

'If you look carefully, you can see these top ten squares have tiny metal rods, made of brass, that are connected to a crankshaft. Push the squares in the right order and the rods will line up to open the hinges. Some of the other squares are sprung, but don't do anything. It's these ten squares that are the key to opening the box.'

The two Manxmen stared – amazed at the complexity of the gadgetry.

'When do you think this could have been made?' asked the Super.

'Thirteenth century? Who knows? It was around then that the Turks began to make automatons and mechanical clocks.'

'That could tie in with the Arab script.'

'I'll mark the ten squares with a felt pen, if you like,' said the Professor.

'Yes, a good idea,' agreed the Superintendent.

'The other things you can see are these small glass phials close to the crankshaft. Their crystals tell me that at room temperature they contain concentrated sulphuric acid.'

'What are they there for?' asked George.

'The glass will crack and destroy the contents if someone tries to prise open the box.'

'So, what you're saying is that to open the tablet, without damaging the contents, we will have to know the correct sequence to press the ten squares?' asked the Super.

'The order, however, will always be the same.'

'Is there any way of knowing the order?'

'No, although you won't need to depress any square twice. Those rods, once engaged in the crankshaft, will remain secure until the box is opened.'

'What happens if the squares are pressed in the wrong order?' asked George.

'The release shaft will jam. If you look closely, you'll see each rod has a bob-weight attached. By turning the block upside down, the weights are just sufficiently heavy to reset the rods. Shall we try?'

The Super pressed the ten squares from left to right and nothing happened. Professor Eley returned to the lab and took an X-ray photograph. After turning the block upside down, he took a second picture. After developing the two photos, he returned and showed the results: the rods were engaged in the first, but had released themselves from the shaft in the second.

'If you ever find how to open the slab, that's the way to close and secure it,' he said.

'We close the lid and turn it upside down?'

'Yes.'

'Well, at least we know how it works,' remarked George.

'How many possible permutations could there be?' asked the Super.

'Ten factorial, whatever that is,' answered the Professor. 'That's ten, times nine, times eight, and so on. Somewhere between three and four million.'

They thanked Professor Eley and returned to their hotel near Manchester Airport to await the arrival of Colonel Paillole the next day.

CHAPTER 11

Tuesday, 1st March 1960

The Air France Caravelle arrived at the airport from Paris promptly at 1000 hours. The two policemen greeted Colonel Paillole, who spoke fluent English.

'When I conduct business with my Dutch or German colleagues, it is always in English,' he sighed. 'It's a shame the Americans have such a hold on the world. In the eighteenth century, the *lingua franca* was French.' He made the remark with a broad smile.

Worried that Special Branch or MI5 may have been watching, they drove a circuitous route from the airport back to their hotel. Satisfied they had not been followed, they settled into a quiet corner of the hotel's lounge, having previously ordered coffee and croissants for their return.

When the tray arrived, the Colonel smiled, clearly appreciating the gesture of the fresh smell of the pastries and the strong aroma of the coffee.

'I understand that you believe Pierre Le Mont was washed ashore and there is sufficient evidence to suggest he may have been murdered?' began the Frenchman.

The Super took the lead, explaining step by step the events

that had occurred prior to their meeting, but excluding the information discovered at the university.

The Colonel listened intently, nodding from time to time, but said nothing.

When the Super had finished, he looked at the Frenchman and asked, 'Can you explain what is going on?'

'I can't imagine why or how Le Mont chose to live in the Isle of Man,' he began. 'Nor can I explain why he should leave such an elaborate set of instructions to you personally. I can only guess he felt you could be trusted after he had met you through playing chess. I knew he had been a good player because he told me on one occasion that at Montpellier University he played for their team.'

They must have been reasonably close for him to know that, thought George, *and yet O'Boyle was sure they didn't get on.*

'In 1932, the British relinquished its mandate and the Kingdom of Iraq joined the League of Nations. Iraq's success as an independent state put the French Government under pressure to surrender their Syrian and Lebanese mandates. By playing around the edges, France deceived the League into thinking that Syrian independence had also begun. They set up various ministries: Education, Transport and Agriculture, for example. However, the reality was that Albert Lebrun, the last President of the Third Republic, and his Socialist Popular Front kept control through a powerful administration of French civil servants and police. One of them was the chief of Syria's security service – Pierre Le Mont, who'd been in Syria since 1936. After the fall of France in 1940, Syria became a Vichy colony. Among the turncoats was Le Mont, who I suspect had always been pro-Axis. When the Allies defeated the Vichy forces in July 1941, the country was expected to accelerate towards full independence. However, with the Allies busy elsewhere, especially in Egypt, the reins of power reverted to the original French civil servants who swore allegiance to de Gaulle's Free French. Syria became theoretically independent after the war and joined the UN, but it didn't really shrug off French influence until about 1950, by which time Israel had become an independent state and Le Mont had left.

'I arrived at our Syrian Embassy as its intelligence officer in October 1941, some months after the defeat of the Vichyites. Appointed by de Gaulle, my function was, amongst other things, to carefully watch the Syrian politicians and our embassy staff. You might think that would be an easy job, but it wasn't. It took patience and a lot of wheeling and dealing in what were essentially corrupt regimes. The political chicanery got worse after World War Two. Government cabinets were changing all the time as ministers were caught feathering their own nests. You hardly ever knew the name of the Syrian Prime Minister from one month to the next. Infighting within the Syrian Army was just as bad. In 1948, they had three Chiefs of General Staff while they were at war with Israel. Can you imagine the bedlam?

'Soon after arriving, I began to build a small Jewish network of informants. Their motive for working undercover was their belief that Britain would neither honour the Balfour Declaration nor set up an independent Israel after the war. Several of their reports suggested someone in our embassy was selling arms to the Arab terrorists attacking Jewish settlements. I realised it could only be Le Mont and put him under close scrutiny.

'Soviet-manufactured weapons were being smuggled into Syria from Turkey via Armenia. Le Mont was the mastermind. Not only was he dealing with the Arab terrorists, but also supplying the Syrian Army. By 1947, a quarter of the Syrian Army's rifles were being supplied by this route. Le Mont was making a killing, in more ways than one. I tried to persuade the French President, Vincent Auriol, that it was in France's interest for Le Mont to be arrested for treason. However, Robert Schuman, who was Prime Minister and a Gaullist, had the ear of Auriol.'

That doesn't add up, thought the Super. *One minute, Paillole's telling us he's a Gaullist, having been appointed specially by him; and now he's criticising a Gaullist prime minister for defending Lemont.*

'Le Mont was eventually persuaded to retire and given immunity from the French courts. Vincent Auriol signed a guarantee that he would not be prosecuted. He left Syria in 1949.

'I came back to Paris in 1952 and have worked within our DGSE ever since.'

'After Le Mont left Syria, did you ever see him again?' asked the Super.

'No. He disappeared off the radar until you contacted me.'

He's lying again. He knows Lemont is alive and we're barking up the wrong tree. Being in military intelligence, he could easily find out Lemont's whereabouts.

'Are you saying that there can be no explanation as to how an international rogue comes to be living on an island in the Irish Sea with a house that has safes as secure as Fort Knox?'

'It does seem strange.'

'More than strange – downright peculiar. Then there's this.'

The Super, suspicious of Paillole's story – it was too similar to O'Boyle's – showed him the tablet.

The Colonel took hold of it and examined it carefully. He turned it over and felt the movement of the black and white squares. He stared at the calligraphy on the front. 'The writing is in Arabic, but I can't translate it.'

'I thought you would understand Arabic,' remarked the Super.

The Colonel ignored the remark apart from shrugging his shoulders.

The senior policeman thought, *that proves Paillole is not being honest. He worked in Syria for over ten years; I can't believe he never learnt to read Arabic.*

'I recognise the name of Mohammed, but that's about all. Images of the Prophet are forbidden, so in mosques, only words can be shown to represent his name.'

How does he know the slab is hollow and there may be a portrait inside?

'This style of sophisticated calligraphy is very common in mosques,' he explained. 'You see the name of Mohammed and Allah everywhere.'

It was lunchtime. The Colonel looked at his watch and suddenly made an excuse to leave.

He's realised he's made a faux pas, thought the Super.

They offered to host him to lunch, but Paillole declined, saying that he had to make contact with France's Chargé d'affaires in Manchester. He called for a taxi and left in an unseemly hurry.

★

It was not a convincing withdrawal. When he had gone, the two policemen ordered sandwiches. Over a beer, or two, they discussed the Frenchman's hasty retreat, agreeing that he'd not been open with them, either about Lemont or the tablet. Both were now beginning to think the cadaver may not be Lemont, who could be still alive. They felt Paillole's attitude towards them had been condescending.

'I suspect Paillole knows the tablet contains a picture of Mohammed,' remarked the Super.

'I agree, sir; in which case we have something both very dangerous and very valuable,' agreed George.

'And it would explain why Lemont took such extreme precautions to keep it safe. But, if he is alive, where the hell is he?'

'I believe O'Boyle and Paillole are in cahoots,' said George. 'Paillole told us he knew Lemont played chess, but didn't know much about him. Then he built a case to have Lemont charged with treason. You can hardly do that if you know precious little about someone. He knows Lemont is alive all right and probably knows where he is. So, what do we do now?'

'Apart from go home? I think we've got to find out more about Lemont. Where he came from? Why did he come to the island? How did he get the tablet? Who is he working for exactly? He's getting paid twice as much as you and I put together. He's either a crook or a very special undercover agent. If we can answer those questions then we'll uncover the mystery. A month ago, I was convinced Lemont and O'Boyle were rowing the same boat, but I'm now wondering if all three of them are in collusion.'

CHAPTER 12

On Wednesday morning, Bob and George met in the conference room with the Chief Constable. 'What have we learned from Paillole?' asked the CC.

'The mystery of Lemont has become murkier rather than clearer. Paillole turned out to be as assertive in maligning Lemont as O'Boyle. We are now thinking Lemont is not the cadaver and could be alive. Both O'Boyle and Paillole overplayed their hands. Consequently, we know little about Lemont that is reliable. Neither George nor I are convinced by the stories we have been given. I feel we are being treated as country plods who can have the wool pulled over our eyes. We both believe O'Boyle and Paillole have a mutual motive to get their hands on the tablet.

'However, we discovered much more about the mechanics of the tablet at Manchester University, where Professor Eley was most helpful. A "thank you" letter would not go amiss.'

'I'll see to it later this morning,' replied the CC.

'The box contains something, although we don't know what. We learned, for example, that it has glass ampules of sulphuric acid that would break and destroy the contents if the lid was forced open. The fact that someone built such a complicated mechanism to protect whatever is inside must mean it contains something very special. Paillole implied it could be a portrait of Mohammed, but he stopped short when he realised he may have let the cat out of the bag. Unfortunately, we still have no idea how it came into Lemont's possession.'

'You really think there could be a religious connection?' asked the Chief Constable.

'Apparently, the script is highly stylised but is undoubtedly Arabic. Constable Duff and Paillole both recognised the word *Mohammed*. It may be time to delve further into the tablet's background.'

'What have you in mind?' asked the Chief.

'I mentioned this to Professor Eley and he told me the centre of excellence in Arabic Studies is at the School of Oriental and African Studies at London University, known as SOAS. His exact words were, "If they don't know something about the tablet, no one will."'

The CC looked at his Deputy. 'I think it would be a good idea for you to go, Bob. The more we know about the tablet, the more likely we will be able to find out why Lemont came to the Isle of Man and what he does. It could go a long way to finding Lemont's relationship with the cadaver. If the tablet contains a portrait of Mohammed, then it would be priceless, which makes it dangerous. It's secure downstairs at the moment, but maybe we should seriously consider transferring it to a vault in the Isle of Man Bank.'

The Super nodded, but continued, 'Apart from my going to SOAS, sir, I believe we should return to Lemont's house and undertake another search. If necessary, pull the place apart brick by brick. I believe we've missed a trick. Mrs Craine told us Lemont was writing a book about World War Two in the Middle East. We never found a draft script and yet she said he used to spend many hours at his desk. Find the script and we may have a clue to unlocking the rest of the mystery.'

'How soon can you leave for SOAS, Bob?' asked the CC.

'I'll ring them in a few minutes and ask for their Director. If it's OK, I could go tomorrow.'

★

Half an hour later, the Deputy found himself talking to reception at SOAS. Having asked to speak with the Director, he was told that Professor Phillips was abroad and was asked what he wanted. After explaining he wished to see a specialist in Arabic History, he was patched through to Professor Mickleman, the Head of the Arabic Department.

'Mickleman here.'

'Oh, good morning; it's Superintendent Bob Kinley here. I'm Deputy Chief Constable of the Isle of Man Police.'

'Really? How can I be of help?'

The Super outlined his problem and explained how a body washed ashore had led them to finding a beautifully decorated tablet that had a message on one face that included the word Mohammed. Furthermore, X-rays had shown the block contained something inside.

The Professor's reaction was enthusiastic. 'Can I see it?' he asked. 'I think I know what it is.'

'Can I come tomorrow? Say, eleven o'clock, assuming the plane is punctual.'

★

After arriving at Heathrow Airport, the Super headed to Bloomsbury where SOAS was located. Professor Mickleman turned out to be the opposite of what RJ had expected from a professor of art. Rather than a crusty, wrinkled-faced man, wearing a bedraggled Harris Tweed jacket, cavalry twills and Hush Puppies, he was the epitome of an art dealer: the suave type who runs a shop in Piccadilly charging exorbitant prices that few can afford. He was in his mid–fifties, polished, fashionably long hair, immaculately dressed in a light beige suit, a white cutaway collar shirt and a royal–blue tie with a large Windsor knot. He spoke with a cut–glass accent.

However, Bob soon realised Mickleman knew his subject. After only cursory glances at the tablet, he announced, 'It's the Great Seal of the Caliphs. The writing translates as *Mohammed is the Prophet of Allah*. The tablet contains the only surviving portrait of Mohammed. The picture was painted shortly before Mohammed died and was carried by his daughter, Fatima, to his funeral. How did you get it? It disappeared when the last Ottoman Caliph went into exile in 1922 and no one has heard of it since.'

'I'm afraid it's part of an ongoing murder inquiry. We believe the tablet has something to do with why the crime was committed.'

'Can I ask who the victim was?'

'A man called Lemont.'

The Professor instinctively shook his head. 'Never heard of him. Presumably he possessed the Great Seal?'

'We think so. What else can you tell me about it?'

'The last Caliph was Mehmed VI who, as I've just said, went into exile in 1922. It's known he took the Seal with him when he went to live in San Remo, but after that things get hazy. Many believe his son, Ertugrul, inherited it when Mehmed died in 1926, but I'm not so sure.'

'Oh, why?'

'Have you ever heard of Abdullah Quilliam?'

'No I haven't. Why?'

'Ironically, he's an old boy of King William's College and is of Manx extraction. He founded the country's first mosque in Liverpool. He converted to the Islamic faith in Morocco where he'd gone for health reasons after leaving school. He subsequently opened the Liverpool Muslim Institute when he was thirty-three in 1889.

'What many people don't know, however, is that the title, *Sheikh of Islam of Great Britain*, was bestowed on Quilliam for his work in converting hundreds of Englishmen to the Muslim faith.

'Later, Quilliam founded a paper, *The Crescent*, but his views that Muslims should never fight other Muslims on behalf of Britain effectively denounced our Government's policy over the Sudan. His familiarity with the Ottomans, who sided with the Germans when World War One broke out, meant that he was seen by many as a traitor. He was committing treason by declaring that Indian Muslims, fighting for us, should not take up arms against Turkish Muslims. He fled back to Morocco, changed his name and returned to Britain through Ireland, as Henry Leon. He then lived out much of his life as the Imam in Britain's first purpose-built mosque in Woking and holidaying at Onchan on the Isle of Man—'

'Onchan?' interrupted the Super.

'I believe he found a quiet, private hotel that suited his lifestyle. There is an unsubstantiated theory that Quilliam was entertained in San Remo a few years before Mehmed died. I suspect Mehmed may have bequeathed the Great Seal to Quilliam as Mehmed's son was immature for his age.

'If I'm right, then it's possible Quilliam hid the Seal when he was on the Isle of Man and your man Lemont somehow found it. It would go some way to explaining your quandary.'

'You've been a big help. Thank you very much. I won't keep you any longer.'

'A word of warning, before you go; if I may?'

The Super looked at the professor, wondering what was coming.

'The Seal, if genuine, is priceless, but at the same time – worthless.'

'I don't follow.'

'If it is proved to be Fatima's picture of her father, then the King of Saudi Arabia would give billions of dollars for it, as he

80

sees himself as the leader of the Sunni sect of Islam. He claims a direct line from Mohammed. On the other hand, there are the Iranian Shias. They have always claimed the Great Seal belongs to them as at one point Fatima's husband, Ali Talib, owned it. Finally, there are countless extremists who would give their lives to destroy it, including the Israelis. Tread carefully. All associated with it are potentially in grave danger, as Lemont has presumably found out.'

Bob left SOAS, the link between Lemont's house and the Great Seal dominating his thoughts.

CHAPTER 13

On Friday, the Super, driven by PC Duff, went to Ballaugh where they met George, who had gone earlier with PC Rimmer. It was agreed that carpets were to be upturned, floorboards checked if they were loose, chimneys swept, wall panels removed, the attic thoroughly searched – nothing left to chance.

Three hours later, they adjourned for lunch at the Raven with each summarising their progress. Nothing of significance had turned up.

That afternoon, they continued their search.

While continuing to examine Lemont's chess books, the Super spotted a German book dedicated to the Blackmar-Diemer Gambit: *Vom ersten Zug an auf Matt!*

If there's to be a clue anywhere, surely it will be in this book, he thought as he remembered his game with Lemont six and a half years previously. Carefully, he examined each page. On page 191 under the heading *NACHWORT* was a paragraph that showed the results from the tournaments that the author, Emil Diemer, had played. Various numbers had a red dot underneath. In order, down the page, ten numbers were highlighted: -1, -0, +9, =2, +7, -4, +3, +5, +8, =6.

Got it, he thought, *the combination to the tablet!* The symbols in front of the numbers appeared to indicate the amount of games that Diemer had won, drawn or lost in each tournament.

As the Super began to make a note of the numbers, his driver called him.

'Sir, come and look.' Hector had removed a loose panel from behind one of the bookshelves. He was waving a file. 'I think I may have found the draft manuscript.'

The constable gave the script to his boss. Examination showed a double-spaced, typewritten volume of some 500 foolscap pages. Included in the file were articles from newspapers and assorted photos. At the front of the bundle was a sealed envelope.

Written by hand, on the front of the envelope: *Private and Confidential – for Superintendent Kinley's eyes only*

Intrigued, the Super opened the envelope.

Dear Superintendent,

You probably have three questions on your mind

1. *Why did I choose to come and live in the Isle of Man?*
2. *Why did I insist with the Ramsey solicitors that only you could be trusted with the investigation into my death?*
3. *Why the secrecy and the leads I gave you about O'Boyle and Paillole?*

Let me explain.

Your father was William James Kinley, born 1885 on your grandfather's farm in Orrisdale, just outside Kirk Michael. Your father's older brother was John Crellin Kinley, born ten years earlier.

The DCC stopped. *I never knew I had an Uncle John. My father never mentioned he had an elder brother.*

When John was twenty-three in 1898, his girlfriend, Ann Cregeen, who was only seventeen and lived in Glen Dhoo, became pregnant. In those days, the disgrace of illegitimacy was considerable and both families disowned their children. The pair left the island never to return…

He stopped reading the letter.

How does Lemont know this?

PC Duff asked, 'Are you all right, Boss?'

The Super looked up from his temporary trance and asked, 'Hector, where's Glen Dhoo? I've never heard of it.'

'It's an abandoned village about two or three miles up the glen from here. The last people to live there left around the beginning of the century. All the dozen, or so, cottages have been in ruins for as long as I can remember.'

'Can you drive me there?'

'The track from the glen road is impassable except on foot. It would take us about half an hour to walk to Glen Dhoo after we've parked the car.'

'I'd like to go.'

'Now?'

'Yes.'

The Super called the others to stop their searches. He explained that the draft script had been found, and "a good deal besides". He expounded no further.

'It will take some time for me to examine the file. Meanwhile, I'm going to visit an abandoned village up the glen. George, will you lock everything up? Oh, and George…'

'Yes, Boss?'

'Next week, find out if Aer Lingus keep passenger lists. I would be intrigued to know whether O'Boyle ever flew to the island. You may have to go back a year or two.'

★

Ten minutes later, PC Duff found himself walking with his boss up a badly rutted track after parking the police car.

'How come you knew where this place is?' asked the senior officer.

'My mother was the last person to be born in Glen Dhoo.'

'When was that?'

'She was born in 1900 and left the village in 1902.'

'What was her name?'

'Phyllis Cregeen; she was the youngest of eight children.'

'Did she have a sister, Ann?'

'Not that I know of. Why?'

They stopped in the lane and the Super took out the letter. He read its contents up to where he had finished previously.

'My uncle got your mother's sister pregnant. It means you may have a cousin, if she is still alive, who would also be my cousin.'

Hector looked at his boss with a wry smile. 'The disparity of dates tallies, even though Ann must have been born nineteen years before my mother. I know my grandfather's first wife, Hattie, died and he remarried in 1896. That would make Ann a half-aunt. But how does Lemont know this?'

'I don't know, but things are getting complicated, Hector. There is now a personal interest for both of us in finding out more about Lemont.'

They carried on walking up the rough track in silence, thinking through the consequences of having a common cousin. At the deserted village, where only the walls of three cottages remained standing, they wondered how people in the 19th century managed to survive on a running stream to provide water, with no electricity or obvious source of heat and light.

'I've lived all my life on the island and I never knew this place existed,' admitted the Super.

'Not many people do,' replied Hector, as they stood gazing at the valley that ran roughly north–south. The remains of hedges

85

on the eastern hillside still defined the borders of fields where cattle and sheep must have grazed. The opposite hillside was predominantly terraced for growing crops.

'This is the cottage where my mother was born.'

'How did they keep warm in the winter?'

'They would cut peat from the hillside.'

'It must have been a hell of an existence.'

'The only lighting was by using homemade candles.'

They continued to discuss the lifestyle led by the crofters as they returned to the car and drove back to Douglas. As Hector dropped the Super off at his home, he promised to ask one of his sisters if they knew anything about Ann.

★

While waiting for his wife to prepare their evening meal, the Super returned to reading the letter addressed to him that he had found at Ballaugh.

John and Ann settled in Wigan where John, who had maintained the machinery on his father's farm, found work as a mechanic in a cotton mill repairing the spinning jennies. Their daughter, Isobel, was born prematurely in 1899, but Ann died some months later of tuberculosis. Distraught, John gave Isobel away to the factory owner and his wife, who were childless, in exchange for £100. With the money, he travelled to France and joined the Foreign Legion. Shortly afterwards, he changed his name from Kinley to the nickname given to him by his colleagues: Le Mont – "the mount". He was six feet five inches tall and weighed eighteen stone. His skills as a mechanic and his rapidly acquired fluency in French eventually helped him to get technician training and he became an armourer "ingénieur". He served in Morocco where he learned to speak Arabic. He married my mother, the daughter of a Foreign Legion Warrant Officer, in

86

1905. I was born a year later and so Isobel is my half-sister —
seven years older than me, but whom I have never met.

That makes Lemont fifty-four, nine years older than me, and not forty-
five as in his passports.

The Super continued reading.

During World War One, my father, your uncle, served with the
French forces at Gallipoli. However, after the withdrawal from
Turkey in January 1916, he was commissioned and transferred
to the 33rd Regiment on the western front as the senior armourer-
engineer with the rank of captain. One of his fellow officers was
Major Charles de Gaulle. They became friends as they shared,
apart from their height, the firm belief that the war should be
dynamic, not static as it had become. At the Battle of Verdun,
however, they both suffered from the effects of a poisonous gas
attack and were captured at Douaumont. They spent the rest of
the war in a German prisoner of war camp. In captivity, they
got to know each other well as they evaluated their theories
about a fast-moving, mechanised army by gaming battles using
wooden models made by their colleagues. The results inspired de
Gaulle to write a book analysing the issues. Three weeks after
the armistice, they were returned to the allies and my father was
sent back to Tangiers where my mother and I had spent the war.
I was twelve years old and hadn't seen my father for almost five
years.

In 1925, Lieutenant Colonel de Gaulle was given the
command of a light infantry battalion serving in Syria. By then,
my father, Jean Le Mont, had also been promoted to Lt Col and
was the senior engineering officer of all the French forces serving
in the Levant. My mother and I had been living with Dad in
Damascus since 1922. When de Gaulle arrived, I was almost
twenty, fluent in Arabic, French and English and had started to
study the History of Art at Montpellier University. De Gaulle

was unaccompanied in Syria and often came to dinner at our house; he was particularly fond of my mother's cooking, especially her spicy Moroccan couscous dishes. He returned to France in 1930 on promotion. Subsequently, we had two holidays with the de Gaulles in Colombey. The first was in 1931 when I was twenty-five and working in the Deuxième Bureau in Paris. De Gaulle's reference had helped me get the job.

In 1936, I was promoted to the grade of Senior Executive Officer and posted to Damascus in charge of the embassy's security. De Gaulle had warned us that war with the Germans was coming.

'It's not if, but when,' he had said to my father and me after dinner at Colombey one evening. 'Unless we rearm rapidly with modern equipment to fight a mobile war, we will be defeated in days. The Maginot line won't stop dive bombers supporting panzer divisions using rapid blitzkrieg tactics.'

The danger, he warned, was that France would have to seek an armistice with the Germans. It would split the country "down the middle".

CHAPTER 14

On Saturday morning, eager to find if the numbers found in the chess book would open the tablet, the Super went to work in his office. He immediately removed the tablet from the station's most secure safe in one of the dungeons. Returning, he laid it on his desk. He carefully pressed the ten keys on the tablet in the order given: 1, 0, 9, 2, 7, 4, 3, 5, 8 and 6.

The lid clicked and lifted from the frame. Cautiously, he opened the tablet and saw something folded in a black silk cloth. On top lay several foolscap sheets of typewritten paper. He removed the papers and lifted the covered object from the container, gingerly unwrapping it. An image of a man's face, painted on a slab of wood, stared at him. The main feature, which struck him immediately, was the man's dark, mesmeric eyes, set well apart. His stare was aggressive – giving the impression of a leader, not a follower – a man with a strong character. Bizarrely, a memory of a print of *The Laughing Cavalier* by Frans Hals sprung to his mind. It had hung on the back wall of his classroom when he was at school. His teacher had made the class walk past the painting while looking at the Cavalier's eyes. Instinctively, the Super repeated the exercise. Sure enough, the eyes followed him wherever he stood in the room.

On examining the portrait further, he noticed the man's short, dark beard adorning his strong jaw. His large forehead was topped with a crop of thick, tousled hair. He had a broad aquiline nose above a large mouth. The face was of a man with whom you did not argue.

Excited, the Deputy decided to take the tablet and show the portrait to the Chief Constable at his home in Ballanard Road, on the edge of Douglas. Arriving, he knocked on the door and, when opened by BP, the Super exclaimed, 'I've come to show you what's inside the tablet. Professor Mickleman was right. We have a portrait of Mohammed.'

The Deputy then described the find at Ballaugh – how he had found the combination to the tablet and the draft book on the history of World War Two in the Middle East, with its notes and photos.

'There's plenty of reading to do,' RJ explained, 'but at last we are making progress.'

'That's wonderful, Bob. Believe it or not, I had the Met Special Branch on the phone again last night. They rang me here – at home. Seven o'clock on a Friday night – damn cheek! We've now got more people on our backs.'

'What do you mean?'

'It seems both the French and the Irish Secret Services are claiming we are acting outside our jurisdiction by investigating Lemont's possible death.'

'That's rubbish. The body was washed up here. That makes it our problem. When we're satisfied there are no living relatives, it will be our responsibility to give the body a proper burial. What did you tell them?'

'I told them we only answer directly to the Home Office through the island's Lieutenant Governor and asked for the names of those who complained.'

'And what did they say?'

'They wouldn't tell me.'

'Something fishy is going on between O'Boyle and Paillole. To misquote Shakespeare's *Hamlet*, *methinks they doth protest too much*.

'Lemont's letter explained why he came to live in the Isle of Man. His father was my father's older brother. Lemont is my cousin. I believe he chose us to investigate his possible murder and the history of the portrait because the two are linked. Blood is thicker than water and he didn't trust anyone. I don't believe the cadaver is Lemont anymore, but we've got to get to the bottom of this. I've asked George to investigate whether O'Boyle ever came to the island. If he did, it will prove he's been lying.

'My worry is we haven't the resources to carry through the investigation. Whoever the cadaver is was murdered on our patch, but trying to find the rightful owner of the portrait will mean travelling abroad, possibly to the Middle East. That's well outside our jurisdiction, and I can't see MI6 being overly helpful, even though you have your contacts.

'I'd like to thoroughly study these letters and the draft script of Lemont's book. Hopefully, there will be something in them about the portrait. If you don't mind, I'll work from home on Monday, so that I won't be disturbed.'

'Fine; while you're away, I'll see if I can get hold of an old army friend who is now the Director of Training in MI6. If I can persuade him to help us, then we may have a chance of keeping the investigation in-house. This triangle with Lemont, O'Boyle and Paillole at each corner and us stuck in the middle is becoming a bloody nightmare. Anyway, have a good weekend; I'll see you on Tuesday.'

★

Over the weekend and on Monday, the Superintendent studied the Lemont papers, including those on top of the portrait inside the Seal.

Now that you have discovered the combination to opening the Caliph's Great Seal, I shall explain what it contains.

When Mohammed died in 632 AD, the powerful elders of the new Islamic faith agreed their leader should be Mohammed's father-in-law, Abu Bakr. He, therefore, became the first Caliph and established Damascus as his capital.

Fearful that Mohammed's lessons may be lost over time, Abu Bakr formed a committee to have the verses and teachings written down. The writings became the Koran.

Abu Bakr also decreed that the portrait of Mohammed, painted before his death for Mohammed's daughter, Fatima, should be deemed to be the only true picture of the "Most Praiseworthy". Although the portrait remained with Ali Talib, Fatima's husband, other likenesses were treated as idolatrous and were gradually destroyed.

Therefore, the picture you have found of Mohammed is unique and over 1,300 years old.

To be certain of its authenticity, I had the portrait and Fatima's hijab, in which it was wrapped, carbon-dated at three universities: the Sorbonne in Paris, Cambridge University and Massachusetts Institute of Technology. Copies of their certified reports and my correspondence with them are attached.

Twenty-four years after Mohammed's death, Ali Talib, Fatima's husband, became the fourth Caliph but was murdered in 661 while at prayers. His son should have succeeded him. However, Muawiya, the powerful governor of the Levant with an army of 60,000 trained troops, declared himself the fifth Caliph. Ali's son, in an impossible situation, handed his mother's portrait of Mohammed to Muawiya.

Ali's son spelled out that possession of the depiction of the Almighty's Messenger, wrapped in the hijab worn by his mother at her father's funeral, gave the holder the authority of Mohammed.

From then on, only subsequent Caliphs saw the picture. It became, in effect, the Caliph's Badge of Authority and gained a mythical status.

However, the Caliph's vast territory was difficult to administer. Over the years it had expanded as far west as Spain and Persia in the east. It began to splinter into different factions with corruption becoming rife. The Army, mostly Syrian Arab soldiers, grew tired of far-flung postings year after year as uprisings spread. The major uprising was the rebellion of the powerful Abbasid family in the north of Persia.

Originally from the Red Sea area, the Abbasids believed they had a direct hereditary line from Mohammed. In 747, led by Abu Saffah with a 10,000-strong army, they overthrew the Caliph's governor of the province of Khorasan. Abu Saffah's Army then advanced west towards Damascus and, after successive victories, controlled considerable parts of eastern Syria and northern Mesopotamia. Total victory came at the Battle of the River Zab, near Mosul, on 25th January 750 when, despite their army being outnumbered by three to one, the Abbasids routed the opposition.

Mohammed's portrait was captured unharmed and, having been briefed of its significance, the Abbasid general ceremonially handed it to Abu Saffah, who became the first Abbasid Caliph. The Abbasids made Baghdad their capital in 762 and it would become the most important city in the world for almost 500 years.

After establishing good relations with China, where paper had been invented, the world's first paper mill was built in Baghdad and the "Golden Age" began. Great advances in science, mathematics, engineering, literature and philosophy came about as universities were built throughout the Caliphate. The library in Baghdad would eventually hold half a million texts. An interest in automatons flourished as imported machines were brought back from China. Water clocks fascinated the educated elite. By the year 1200, Ismail al-Jazari had invented the crankshaft to make reciprocating pumps. He constructed silver trees with birds that sang and flapped their wings to adorn the Caliph's palace and amuse the harem.

In 1201, the Caliph, al-Nasir, who had ruled for twenty-one years, demanded al-Jaziri's presence at his palace.

Al-Nasir offered al-Jazari a job but warned him that if he disclosed the task to anyone then he would forfeit his life.

Intrigued, al-Jazari accepted the challenge.

Al-Nasir explained that beginning with Ali Talib, successive Caliphs had possessed the only portrait of Mohammed. It was the original portrait carried by Fatima at her father's funeral and had become their badge of office that gave the Caliphs their unique authority.

Al-Nasir had decided it was high time the portrait and the hijab should be protected. He wanted a container made with a lock that only successive Caliphs could open.

Al-Nasir handed al-Jazari the wrapped wooden portrait. Al-Jaziri measured the dimensions carefully and sketched a drawing of a flat case. He told the Caliph he would make the box and lid with Bethlehem olive wood as it was exceptionally hard and resistant to disease and warping.

They discussed details such as the most suitable metal for the hinges and the internal mechanism.

On all points, the Caliph agreed, including the decoration of the box.

Al-Jaziri explained he would cover the underside with inlaid nacre squares and that under certain squares he would attach rods. When pressed in the right order, the rods would engage to open the lid. Ten squares would keep the tablet secure by offering over three million possible combinations.

However, al-Nasir insisted on an extra refinement: an attempt to break open the cabinet by force must destroy the contents. After some discussion, they agreed that to prevent an infidel seeing the Prophet's face, several, strategically placed, small glass phials of concentrated acid would be positioned that would break as soon as someone tried to prise open the tablet.

The container took almost three years to make. The ten-digit code mechanism – a rotating crank that had to be aligned correctly by positioning the levers beneath the nacre squares – had proved difficult to get right. Only the ten squares opposite the hinges would work. Once the mechanism was perfected, the sequence of depression was chosen. Finally, al-Nasir decided the pieces of nacre and coloured glass on the top of the tablet should read "Mohammed is the Messenger of Allah". Al-Nasir had been Caliph for forty-five years when he died in 1225.

Around 1206, the Mongols, led by Genghis Khan, began expanding their empire. His warriors swept across Asia destroying everything in their path. The fierce tribal chief had begun to take over the world. Although Genghis died in 1227, he left his son, Ogodei, a territory that extended from North-East China to the Caspian Sea. In total, the area measured eleven million square miles. Genghis Khan had conquered more than twice as much territory as any man in history – before or since.

In 1258, one of Genghis' grandsons, Hulagu Khan, invaded Mesopotamia. His huge army marched on Baghdad. The Caliph in residence immediately saw the impossibility of defending the city. He entrusted his equerry, al-Mustansir, with the Seal and its secret. With the Mongol army of over 250,000 men encamped on the east bank of the River Tigris, the Caliph arranged for his lieutenant to escape. In the middle of the night, al-Mustansir slipped away in a small boat with the Seal and sailed down the River Tigris to safety.

Hulagu's Army ransacked Baghdad. The Grand Library, containing countless precious historical documents and books on subjects ranging from medicine to astronomy, was destroyed. The Tigris ran black with the ink from the enormous quantities of books flung into the river and red from the blood of the scientists and philosophers killed. From being the most influential city in the world, Baghdad became a depopulated, ruined city and never recovered its former glory. However, Mohammed's portrait had survived.

Al-Mustansir had sailed south to the Persian Gulf. Coastal trading ships had taken him to Oman and Yemen, before entering the Red Sea. From there, the safety of Egypt was in his grasp as Egypt was ruled by the Mamluk family – still very much a part of the Sunni Abbasid Caliphate.

As Hulagu's Army was preparing to advance through Palestine, prior to invading Egypt, his brother died and Hulagu returned to Mongolia to claim the succession. He left behind an army of only 20,000 men to control Mesopotamia and Syria. The Head of the Egyptian Mamluks saw his chance. Quickly raising an army and declaring al-Mustansir as the new Caliph before departing Cairo, he defeated the Mongols in a battle near the Sea of Galilee on 3rd September 1260. It was the first major loss suffered by the Mongols who never again ventured south-west towards Palestine and Egypt. The Caliph's Seal, however, had survived and remained in Cairo with successive Caliphs for the next 250 years.

By 1300, the Ottoman Empire was beginning to expand in Anatolia, modern day eastern Turkey. By 1453, the Ottoman Sultan's Army ended the rule of the Byzantines after capturing Constantinople, which then became the Ottoman's capital. As the Empire further expanded, the Sultan began accumulating titles from the empire's subjected peoples. It wasn't until the Ottomans conquered Egypt in 1516 that the last of the Abbasid caliphs surrendered the caliphate to the Ottoman Sultan. With Mohammed's portrait secure, the Seal moved to Constantinople where it remained for more than 400 years.

The Ottomans joined the German alliance soon after World War One began. When the armistice was signed, the Sultan was allowed to retain his title despite vast areas of his empire being allocated to France, Italy and Greece. However, led by Atatürk, the consequent Turkish War of Independence regained most of the territories, and in November 1922 the modern state of Turkey was created. Atatürk abolished the sultanate and the last Caliph, Mehmed VI, left Turkey. As far as history was concerned, the Caliph's Great Seal seemingly disappeared for ever.

You're asking, how did I get hold of the Seal?

You'll remember I had joined the Deuxième Bureau after university. When we stayed with the de Gaulles for the last time in 1936, my father had retired through ill health. I had become the senior security officer in Damascus. Dad and General de Gaulle spent long hours discussing the state of the Army.

I remember de Gaulle telling me, 'The Germans will crush us within weeks, and a puppet government will be set up under the heel of Hitler. Our provinces will be lost. Syria and Algeria will become especially important to the Germans because of their oil fields. Your position in Syria will allow you to play a vital role to those of us who do not succumb to the Nazis'

I replied, 'How will I be able to help?'

'When war is about to start, you will receive a miniature transmitter. Other loyal staff in important embassies such as Algeria and Indo-China will also get them. Later, you will be sent an encryption method using Dumas's Count of Monte Christo.'

In early January 1939, three months after the Munich Agreement, I received a parcel at my private apartment in Damascus. It had been delivered by hand. I never found out how it had arrived. Through the post a few days later, a copy of The Count of Monte Christo arrived, followed a week later with instructions on how to use the book to create codes.

I had become de Gaulle's mole in Syria.

You will see that I have begun to write a history of World War Two in Syria. In it I describe in more detail how I came to befriend Ertrugel Effendi, Mehmed's son, who was the Governor General of Vichy Syria between July 1940 and July 1941. After Ertrugel's arrest, following the defeat of the Vichyites, I visited him regularly in Acre, where he was imprisoned. My reason was to prepare the case for his execution after the war. In order to gain his trust, I had to feint being pro-Nazi. We often talked about his father, Mehmed VI, and on one occasion he mentioned that the Caliph's Seal of Office was a portrait of Mohammed, painted just before he died in 632. He told me that his father had given it to an Englishman called Henry Leon for safe keeping. I forgot about the story until last year when, by chance, I met someone who knew who Leon was. It was a short cut to finding where Leon had hidden the Seal.

CHAPTER 15

By Monday, the Super had started reading Lemont's draft on the history of World War Two in Syria. Lemont had begun drafting chapters with headings, but there were many loose notes bundled together with paper clips and elastic bands, as well as cuttings from newspapers and grainy photos. However, the prologue appeared complete.

Prologue

After Germany invaded France, Marshal Pétain, the French ambassador to Spain and a hero of the Third Republic for his achievements in World War One, joined the government of Paul Reynaud on 18th May 1940. With the invading Germans pushing back the Allies, the British Expeditionary Force began their retreat from Dunkirk. With the military situation seemingly hopeless, Reynaud and Pétain began to realise they must seek an armistice.

Churchill had different ideas and flew to Paris with Clement Attlee for a meeting to discuss the deteriorating situation. The French griped that 80 percent of the British troops were being evacuated from Dunkirk, but only 20 percent of the French. Churchill promised that thereafter they would leave together.

He spoke passionately about the need for the two countries to continue the fight, but it was clear Reynaud was seriously considering the possibility of surrender. Churchill pointed out that in such an event he would have to implement a blockade by bombing the French ports.

Churchill made two further attempts to persuade the French to continue fighting. On 11th June, with Anthony Eden, Britain's Foreign Secretary, he met Reynaud, Pétain and Brigadier Charles de Gaulle at Briare. De Gaulle's account of the military situation reinforced Churchill's pessimism.

Two days later, Churchill flew to Tours in central France with Lord Beaverbrook. It was a business meeting to explain the consequences of Britain going alone. Reynaud acknowledged that France would continue the struggle from North Africa, but only if America was prepared to join the fray. After the meeting, Beaverbrook told Churchill that he was certain de Gaulle was staunch and would come to Britain to lead the French.

On 14th June, Reynaud's Government retreated further south to Bordeaux as Paris fell to the Germans.

Over 100,000 French troops had been evacuated from Dunkirk between 26th May and 4th June. However, the majority, believing the war to be lost, returned to France from ports in the west of England.

Having flown to London from Bordeaux to set up the Free French Army, de Gaulle made his famous appeal on 18th June. Transmitted in French by the BBC, it was repeated four days later. His headquarters were set up at 4 Carlton Gardens in London, but by mid-July he had fewer than 2,000 men at his disposal.

Marshal Pétain became the President of France's Third Republic, and on 22nd June he signed an armistice with Germany. He subsequently established an authoritarian regime when the National Assembly granted him full powers. At that point, the Third Republic was dissolved and Pétain's

French Government established itself at Vichy. It immediately introduced many dictatorial policies. Money was tightly controlled – the banks were nationalised. Unions came under government control. Newspapers became little more than propaganda sheets. Anti-Semitism was encouraged. The gendarmerie and Police Nationale were ordered to arrest Jews and gypsies.

In general, the French public supported the government despite its subservience to the Germans. The Nazis allowed Vichy to keep control of the French Navy and its colonies, including Syria. By avoiding a total occupation, a degree of French independence was achieved. Pétain and Hitler agreed the occupation was to be provisional pending the conclusion of the war – which in June 1940 seemed imminent.

On 11th July, the embassy in Damascus was informed by telegraph that a new Governor General, Ertugrul Effendi, had been appointed by Pétain. The Governor would be arriving the following day, accompanied by the German senior officer appointed to command the Damascus Garrison, Major General von Zürich.

All the staff were to be seated in the embassy's theatre by 10.00 am to await the arrival of the new leaders. Outside, the temperature was over 40°C in the shade.

Having worked in the embassy for four years, I knew most of us were in favour of continuing the struggle against the Germans, but there was little we could do other than accept the status quo.

When our tall ambassador for the last three years, Jacques de Villefranche, walked onto the stage followed by two diminutive, rotund figures, there was a muffled guffaw. Von Zürich, in his military uniform, looked not unlike a bemedalled Humpty Dumpty. Effendi wore a lightweight beige suit. With sweat patches showing under his arms, it appeared as if he had slept in it.

After being introduced by de Villefranche, Effendi spoke first.

'Ladies and Gentlemen,' he began. 'You may be wondering why Marshal Pétain has appointed me to be your Governor General. Apart from being fluent in French, English, German, Italian, Arabic, and Turkish, I have extensive administrative experience. In Italy, I worked for Mussolini, helping him to set up the Government of Ethiopia. Afterwards, I drafted the Italian-German treaty of mutual interest. I look forward to meeting you all in the coming weeks, but this afternoon I wish to hold a preliminary meeting with all my senior staff. Your retiring ambassador has already informed those of you who are to attend.'

Von Zürich was even briefer: 'My task is to ensure the protection of Syria and its people by building a fortress to keep us safe from the British Empire's satellites in Iraq, Palestine and Jordan. To that end I have much to do, but you can remain confident that the Third Reich will not let you down.'

At the afternoon meeting, I formed the opinion that von Zürich was a time-served officer at the end of his career. Presumably, the Nazi hierarchy underestimated the task he was to perform – namely, invade and capture the northern Iraq oil fields around Kirkuk.

The appointment of Ertugrul as Governor General of Syria was an even odder choice. As the only son of the last Ottoman Caliph, Mehmed VI, Ertrugel was the rightful religious leader of over 300 million Sunni Muslims. However, being an Ottoman Turk, he would never be popular with the indigenous Syrian Arabs as they had suffered badly under the Ottomans' rule for over 400 years.

Not only was there no love lost between the Arabs and the Turks, but thanks to the duplicity of Britain and France through the implementation of the 1916 Sykes-Picot Agreement, none was lost between the Arabs and the Allies.

I grew to know Ertrugel well. I was his Principal Security Officer in the embassy and, therefore, attended all his cabinet meetings. There was little happening in Syria or Lebanon that I didn't know about.

It was ironic that I was trusted to be pro-Vichy without any background checks being made by the Nazis. They would surely have discovered my family's close relationship with de Gaulle. Fortunately, the Germans accepted my sworn allegiance to the new regime.

My main worry was making contact with the Free French without being discovered. It needed careful timing as the Germans had a fleet of detector vans in Damascus sweeping the airwaves for illegal radio transmissions. Knowing their modus operandi helped to avoid discovery. My transmitter was safe under the floorboards of my private apartment, but I never felt at ease being a double agent. Nonetheless, during the winter of 1940-41, I was able to give the Free French considerable details of the proposed invasion of Iraq. By February, I was able to transmit the date of invasion – 1st April – and stress it was essential to deny the Nazis access to Vichy air bases in Syria, from where they planned to attack the Suez Canal.

Arab speakers were thin on the ground in the Vichy-Nazi brigades and several embassy staff were co-opted as interpreters. As an honorary major, I was attached to a Vichy squadron and received a flesh wound at Palmyra. I was briefly held as a POW before being released.

De Gaulle left London for Egypt in the first week of March 1941. He was accompanied by General Georges Catroux, the former French Governor of Indo-China. They were received by General Archibald Wavell, the Commander-in-Chief of the Middle East. Perceived as being pro-British, Catroux had been relieved of his post by the Vichy regime, who controlled the French overseas' colonies. De Gaulle had travelled to Cairo to persuade Wavell to airlift a detachment of Free French troops to help capture Damascus after the Iraq Coup had been defeated.

De Gaulle's argument was that the Vichy troops in Syria would change sides if they witnessed the Free French being successful. Although Wavell's troops were desperately overstretched with the Germans in North Africa, Wavell agreed. However, Anthony Eden, Britain's Foreign Secretary, objected. He feared a conflict between the two French armies would be disastrous. However, de Gaulle won the day, but it was the beginning of friction between de Gaulle and Churchill's Government.

The prologue seemed to be complete, but how Lemont had found the Seal remained a mystery. He sifted through newspaper cuttings to find the next chapters – many appeared unfinished. The construction of Lemont's book was clearly a long way from completion. The Super could see there was much more material to be incorporated, but believing further reading would add little to solving the mystery of either Lemont's identity or the role played by the tablet, the Super skimmed over the draft chapters…

The Coup d'état...

The Nazis had realised they could not win the war without adequate supplies of oil. Since 1939, Rashid-Ali, an Iraqi republican politician, and the Nazis had been planning a coup d'état to overthrow the pro-British regime of King Ghazi. The coup began by engineering a car accident in which Ghazi died on 4th April 1939. His son, who was to succeed him as King Faisal II, was only four years of age. The infant's Uncle Abdullah became Crown Prince and assumed control of the country.

The oil fields at Kirkuk were particularly important to the Nazis as they were only 120 miles from the Syrian border. When the invasion of Iraq began, the Syrian forces were a mix of French Vichy troops and Iraqi freedom fighters, reinforced by two battalions of German Wehrmacht and a Luftwaffe squadron.

German intelligence had completely underestimated the size of the Indian and Australian forces disembarking in Basra over the winter. The Indian 20th Infantry Brigade, having steamed up the Tigris, was preparing defensive positions around Baghdad while 25,000 Australian troops were dug in further up the river to defend Mosul...

...the rout of Rashid Ali's guerrillas and the Vichy forces was complete by mid-May. Prince Abdullah and his pro-British Government had survived the attempted coup and ensured the Iraqi oil fields were safe for the rest of the war.

The Plans to Invade Syria...

Overall command of the liberation of Syria and Lebanon fell to Lieutenant General Archibald Wavell, who planned the campaign. It was to be swift, only lasting three months. The campaign remains little known. Churchill and Eden censored the reports, believing that the publicity of fighting against French forces could have a negative effect on public opinion in Britain.

The retaliatory Allied invasion had two aims: to prevent the Luftwaffe from using Vichy Syria and Lebanon as a springboard to attack British troops in Egypt, and to prevent attacks on the Suez Canal. During April and May, massive RAF attacks on Syria's runways began and continued non-stop until 8th June – the date of the ground invasion.

Wavell's strategic plan called for four coordinated strikes. Firstly, a move on the western side of the Golan Heights towards Beirut would initially be largely diversionary. Secondly, the main thrust for Damascus by the Free French, supported by Indian troops, would use the route to the eastern side of the Golan Heights. Thirdly, Indian and Australian troops, commanded by General Edward Quinan, would advance into eastern Syria from northern Iraq. And fourthly, an advance on Palmyra, in central Syria, would be made by the Jordanian Arab Legion...

The Invasion...

In the early hours of 8th June, the 21st Australian Brigade crossed the border into southern Lebanon. The Australians were to ensure the 5th Indian Brigade could advance on the main eastern road towards Damascus without being attacked on their western flank... Despite heavy fighting, the Indians had taken Deraa and then Quneitra by 13th June... After Quneitra had been captured, the Indians and Free French forces advanced on Kissoué, a strong defensive position, south of Damascus. At 0400 hours on 15th June, Indian troops made a frontal attack, while on the Indian left, the Free French forces advanced towards Damascus, bypassing the town, using the high ground to their advantage...

On 21st June, the Free French entered Damascus first – a decision taken at the highest level to placate de Gaulle. The Free French went into the city in style. In an open car carrying de Gaulle and General Catroux, de Gaulle made a ceremonial entrance to the liberated city escorted by mounted troops of the French cavalry...

The End of Vichy Syria...

After the fall of Damascus, the Vichy Governor, Ertugrul, along with his Nazi General von Zürich, sought an armistice. The loss of Damascus, the rapid advance of Allied troops in the east and the losses in Lebanon made the Vichy position untenable. Beirut fell on 12th July and marked the end of hostilities with a total ceasefire... An armistice was signed on 14th July and Syria came under the control of General de Gaulle and his Free French administration. Syria would remain an important Allied base for Mediterranean naval operations for the rest of the war.

The Vichy forces lost approximately 5,000 men. When given the choice of repatriation to Vichy France or joining the Free French, three quarters chose to join de Gaulle's forces.

All the captured German soldiers were held in POW camps on the Palestinian / Lebanon border. Ertugrul and twenty-nine of his most senior civilian officials were detained in Acre until 1945.

The Beginning of the End of Nazi Control...

With the successful Allied invasion of Syria in 1941, Vichy France began to lose one colony after another to the Free French. The success of Wavell's plan was largely owing to the bravery of both Australian and Indian soldiers. Although the success against the Germans in Syria was total, Churchill rewarded Wavell by putting him out to grass: as Commander-in-Chief of India. He later became Viceroy in 1943. He was replaced in Cairo by Claude Auchinleck. Despite Churchill's rebuff, hundreds, if not thousands, of boys were christened with the name Wavell over the following year as British fathers remembered the Allies' first victory on the ground.

Public opinion in France began turning against the Vichy Government after its defeat in Syria. Germany was no longer invincible.

CHAPTER 16

Monday, 7th March 1960

George's phone rang.

'Constable Rimmer here, Sergeant; can I have a word?'

'Yes, Trevor. What is it?'

'My wife and I went out for a meal last night to the Aragon Hotel at Santon. It was our wedding anniversary. It was very quiet, practically empty. A few salesmen staying there; that's all. The place has gone downhill since we had our wedding reception there twenty-two years ago.'

'It's a great shame. Before the war, it was one of the island's finest hotels,' replied DS Turnbull.

'I gather from the manageress their bookings are down for the summer. She was telling me the owner won't spend any money. She thinks he's either trying to sell the hotel or develop it into some sort of complex of apartments. I don't know why, but I asked her if the open-air swimming pool is still open.'

'And?'

'It has been closed for almost a year. Last April, it was filled with fresh water for the summer season, but within days the chlorination and heating plant packed up. The owner, rather than have it repaired, had the pool boarded over. He never got around to fixing it.'

'If I remember rightly, it is quite isolated, about 100 yards from the rear of the hotel, down at sea level?'

'Yes, it's at the bottom of a steep path that leads from the back garden. The wall is roughly six feet thick on the sea side of the pool, and the changing cabins are opposite, tucked under the cliff.'

'It's a beautiful spot. If I remember, it gets the sun all day.'

'When I realised that the pool was no longer used because the water wasn't being chlorinated, I thought I'd better ring you. About three months ago, you asked us to look for possible sources of contaminated water where the body that was washed ashore in Douglas could have drowned. At the time I thought the hotel's swimming pool was being maintained properly. It struck me last night that the water could now be fetid.'

'Who's the owner these days?' asked George.

'A guy called Jack Tyson. He lives in one of the last houses on King Edward Road as you go from Onchan Head towards Groudle. The house is called *Bay View*.'

'I know it – the big house with its back to the road, so that its front overlooks Douglas Bay. He's got his fingers in a lot of pies.'

'He also owns the Majestic and the Mount Murray hotels,' added the constable. 'All three hotels are rumoured to be white elephants. God knows why he bought them.'

'There are rumours he's into money laundering. Unfortunately, until he hangs himself, there's not much we can do.'

'Do you want me to go and see him?' volunteered the PC.

'No, I'll go. I'd like to find out exactly when the pool was closed and what state it was in when he closed it.'

★

After making an appointment for later that afternoon, DS Turnbull was met at *Bay View* by Mr Tyson's secretary and shown into a large, plush office with a huge bay window giving an unobstructed panoramic view of Douglas Bay.

'Mr Tyson is with a client who is just leaving. He will see you in a minute. Please make yourself comfortable.'

George looked around the office. *Three times the size of mine*, he thought.

He ogled at the view. From the window, he could see Douglas Lighthouse and several Steam Packet ships berthed in the harbour. He could pick out a tidal race sweeping across the bay from the south.

What an incredible view, he thought.

A voice from behind asked, 'I'm sorry to keep you waiting, Sergeant. I'm Jack Tyson, how can I help?'

'I would like to ask a few questions about the Aragon Hotel. I understand you own it.'

'That's correct. What do you want to know?'

'I believe you boarded up the swimming pool last year.'

'The cost of its upkeep was proving colossal. The boiler broke down and needed replacing. On top of that, the cost of oil to heat the water was going through the roof. Fresh water, if not circulated and filtered with chlorine, soon goes foul and becomes a health hazard. On top of that, many of the pool's tiles were loose. It would have cost the earth to put right. I closed it last April. I can get the paperwork if you like.'

'That won't be necessary. Why wasn't the pool drained before you shut it?'

'I took the advice of my foreman who looks after all my properties.'

'Fair enough. However, I would like to have your permission to allow the government health inspector to take a sample of the pool's water.'

'May I ask why?'

'We are trying to determine where someone drowned.'

'And you think he may have drowned in the hotel's pool?'

'I didn't say it was a "he".'

'I just assumed; that's all. He, or she, must have drowned before last April.'

'Unless someone or some persons removed the wooden boards and he, or she, drowned later.'

Mr Tyson nodded his head as if accepting George's proviso. 'I have my men check the pool regularly,' he said defensively.

Strange that he doesn't want to know who was drowned, thought George.

'As long as the health inspector secures the boards afterwards, that will be OK. However, I would appreciate if this could be kept confidential,' he added.

'May I ask why?'

'I am in the middle of negotiating the Aragon's sale to a well-known local resident. Rumours of a drowning in its pool might slow or stop the sale.'

'Can I ask who wishes to buy it?'

'Let's just say he's a famous international sportsman.'

★

Although it was almost five o'clock when he returned to his office, George rang the office of the Government's Science Laboratory and asked for the Chief Scientist, Bill Stead.

'I'll just try his office, but I think he may have gone home,' answered the receptionist.

The phone rang for nigh on a minute. There was a grunt as the receiver was picked up. 'Yes?'

'Bill? George Turnbull. I've a favour to ask.'

'You've just caught me on the way home. I was putting my coat on. Why do you always ask for help at the wrong time?'

George ignored his old pal's sarcastic wit.

'Last November, do you remember analysing water samples to see if we could discover where the body washed ashore near the Palace may have drowned?'

'Go on.'

'Well, we think we missed a possible source and I am wondering if you could get one of your boys to take a sample from the swimming pool at the Aragon Hotel.'

'And give the job priority, no doubt. For you, George, it'll cost you a pint the next time we're together in the Dog's Home.'

★

On Tuesday, George briefed the Super about his visit to see Tyson and how he had asked Bill Stead to urgently analyse samples from the Aragon swimming pool.

'I think we had better look into this at once, George.'

The Super picked up his phone and asked Dolly to get Sergeant Swindlehurst to come and see him.

'Can I tell him what it is about, in case he wants to know?' she asked.

'There's nothing for him to worry about,' replied the Super.

Jimmy Swindlehurst had been a policeman for as long as the Deputy and was the island's senior traffic officer. His new toy was the radar gun that had recently been acquired by the Force. He was enjoying catching the young tearaways who, until recently, had been able to drive at illegal speeds willy-nilly on the island's roads.

He entered the Super's office and saluted. 'You wanted me, sir?'

'Yes, sit down, Jimmy. Your brother has a fishing boat, if I remember correctly?'

'Yes, a fifty-foot trawler.'

'He'll know all about the tides around the island, then?'

'I would have thought better than anyone. Why?'

'Suppose a dead body entered the sea at Santon. Where would it drift to?'

'I don't know, but Harry would.'

'It's a theory we are working on that the body washed ashore before Christmas could have drowned in the disused swimming pool at the Aragon Hotel. The question we want answered is: if it had been dumped in the sea, what direction would the currents take the body?'

'I know Harry's not fishing this week. I can ring him and get him to come and see you, if you wish.'

The Super gestured towards the phone on his desk.

'Harry? It's Jimmy… Yes, I'm fine. How are the kids? Good. Can you come down to the station? The Super wants to know something about the sea's currents on the east side of the island… He'll tell you why when you get here.

'He's on his way, sir. He lives in Hope Street. It's only five minutes away.'

While waiting for the fisherman to arrive, the three officers discussed the success of the new radar trap and its potential to generate income. Ten minutes later, a large man with thick, black, curly hair and a weather-beaten face, wearing a navy polo neck pullover and worn jeans, was sitting with the three policemen.

'The state of the sea around the island is largely determined by two factors,' Harry began. 'Firstly, there is the Atlantic Gulf Stream – it keeps the British Isles relatively warm and enters the Irish Sea through Saint George's Channel. When the Gulf Stream reaches the Calf of Man, it splits so that it flows north on both sides of the island. The second influence is the colder water from the Arctic that flows south past the Outer Isles of Scotland. It enters the North Channel, between Northern Ireland and Scotland. The two warmer currents coming north clash with the colder current at the Point of Ayre. It is the reason why the sea there is always rough. Of course, that's only a generalisation.

There are the tides and weather to consider – particularly the wind direction.'

He paused to allow the Super to ask questions.

'So, if a dead body had drowned in a swimming pool at Santon and was put in the sea, what would happen?' asked the Super.

'It would mostly depend on the tide,' replied Harry. 'When the tide at Port St Mary is on the ebb, the tidal race rushes through the Sound from north-west to south-east at about twenty-five knots, or more. After Spanish Head, it slows as it swings east towards Langness. The current then picks up with the remnants of the Gulf Stream and heads north-east towards Douglas.'

'So a body would float from Santon towards Douglas?'

'It's not that straightforward. For a start, the tides sweep in and out twice a day. The body wouldn't be travelling in a straight line. It could get stuck on rocks or by seaweed. And don't forget it's not necessarily floating on the surface; that depends on its buoyancy. Furthermore, when there is a flood tide at Port St Mary, there is the opposite effect and the body could drift south-west, admittedly slower, away from Douglas. My guess is that the body could be in the water for several months before it might reach Douglas.'

The Super looked at George. 'All this ties in with the pathologist's report.'

'Yes and if Bill Stead's team come up with the goods, then we may have enough evidence to prove the body drowned at the Aragon.'

CHAPTER 17

On Wednesday, George didn't arrive for work until almost lunchtime. 'I've been making enquiries in Onchan,' he explained to the Super. 'I did some delving to find out if anyone remembers Quilliam. It seems he used to stay at the Howstrake Hotel, now renamed the Rembrandt Hotel. Their old records show that the last occasion Quilliam stayed there was in July 1930.

'The hotel's owners, at the time, sold up four years ago and retired. I went to see them. They remembered Quilliam and described him as a quiet and unassuming man. He holidayed regularly with them for about ten years, during which time they never saw him drink alcohol. After dinner, he would sit in the bar, be sociable and make an apple juice last most of the evening or go for a stroll to the funfair at Onchan Head. Apparently, he spent most of his holiday walking. He would take a small tent with him and stay away for two or three days, camping at places as far apart as the Point of Ayre and the Sound.

'It seems several of the hotel's guests were semi-permanent, living there all year round. I've only been able to trace one of them. He stayed there throughout the war and was a bachelor from the Channel Islands who fled here in 1939 – long after Quilliam's last stay.'

'So, the Manx connection between Lemont and Quilliam appears to be at a dead end?'

'It would seem so, at least for the time being,' replied George.

At that point, Dolly knocked and entered the room. 'Excuse me, sir,' she said, speaking to the Deputy Chief Constable, 'but the Government's Chief Scientific Officer wishes to speak to Sergeant Turnbull.'

The Super nodded for George to leave and take the call.

★

'I think you owe me a pint.'

'You've analysed the water already?' exclaimed George.

'Taking the samples didn't take long. Mrs Fraser, the stewardess, was very accommodating; she even gave us a pint before we left. We analysed the samples when we got back. That took a little longer, as we had to repeat some experiments to be absolutely sure of our results. In some cases, we are talking about minute quantities of chemicals.'

'What have you found?'

'We took two samples from each end of the pool. Analysis shows the water is polluted as a result of being stagnant for so long. We compared the results with the water found in the cadaver's lungs and it is practically identical.'

'Would the similarity stand up in court to prove the location of where the body drowned?'

'I doubt it, but the pool's samples have the same minute percentages of chlorine as the cadaver's – quantities of two to three parts per million. There were two other things.'

'Go on.'

'There was some evidence of seawater in the samples, consistent with the sea coming over the pool's sea wall in a winter storm.'

'That could have occurred recently. What was the other thing?'

'The temperature of the pool's water was much warmer than I expected. We took the temperature of the sea; it was barely 7°C. The pool, however, was 15°C.'

'What would cause the difference?'

'The pool is boarded up and the wood acts as an insulator. Because of the pool's sunny position, the boards absorb the sun's rays and stay warm. It explains the amount of flukes in the water.'

'Thanks for that, Bill. I think I owe you two pints, not one.'

★

George resumed his meeting with the Super and told him what he had just learned from Bill Stead. 'The existence of seawater in the Aragon pool's samples, but not in the cadaver's lungs, will be sufficient to cast doubt on whether Lemont drowned there. Tyson said the pool was boarded up last April. The pathologist said the cadaver drowned around September. If he did drown at the hotel's swimming pool, he must have been pushed into the pool, breaking the wooden coverings. They may have been rotten, or there was a gap. He was then prevented from getting out.'

'He may have fallen in by accident and couldn't swim,' warned Bob.

'I don't buy that. Surely, he could have grabbed the wooden boards and pulled himself out?'

'It would have required two people to prevent him clawing out.'

'I agree,' said George. 'Lemont was apparently fit and strong. If he was struggling to get out, there's a chance his fingernails could have got broken as he clawed on the wood.'

'The pathologist's report didn't mention anything about his fingernails; I'll check with Dr Parton. Meanwhile, I think we should look further into Tyson's background. Who do you know in the Government Tax Office?'

117

'Fred Cubbon is the Head of the tax office. However, we will require a warrant from the Deemsters' Office if we are to get access to Tyson's tax records. And I'm thinking we should get one to inspect the boards covering the swimming pool too.'

A phone call by the DCC to the Clerk of the Rolls Office after the meeting ensured the police immediately had the two appropriate warrants.

★

Sergeant Swindlehurst and Constable Rimmer were allocated the task of examining the pool's protective planks the next day.

George met Fred Cubbon in the Government Offices and was led to the department that handled companies' tax returns. He was introduced to Pat Corlett.

'Pat will give you all the help she can. My office is at the end of the corridor. Come and fetch me if there's anything you want,' said Fred.

The files on Tyson's tax records were handed over. There were six substantial files, each in their own semi-stiff covers. Piled on top of each other, they stood well over two feet in height.

George sighed, knowing this was not going to be a quick job. He began looking at the names of the companies and their directors written on the front of each of the files.

The top file appeared to be a holding company, C and W Stone Walls Ltd, whose directors were Christine Tyson, Jack Tyson and Rex Tyson. The other files listed the five companies within the group: Wight Needles, Mount Murray Golf Associates, Aragon Hotel Ltd, Majestic Apartments Ltd and Crescent Properties Ltd.

Being an old-fashioned bobby who kept his nose to the ground, George had heard rumours that large tracts of land had been bought surrounding the Mount Murray Hotel on the Castletown Road. The locals knew the shabby wooden-structured hotel as a white elephant. It had been losing money since the war. His curiosity aroused, he glanced through this file first. The front of the file confirmed Rex Tyson, Jack's son, was the Chief Executive Officer. Draft outline plans showed a complex of one hundred houses to be built on the edge of a new 18-hole golf course with a hotel on the present site of the old one.

Where does the money come from? thought George. *The island already has seven golf courses. It doesn't need another one. This must be money laundering.*

The other folders revealed plans to convert the Aragon Hotel, the Majestic Hotel at Onchan Head and the Crescent Cinema on Douglas Promenade into expensive apartments.

However, it was the Wight Needles file that astonished him. Christine and Jack Tyson were the sole owners of the business. This file was by far the largest. George began taking notes. As each entry in the file was examined, he became ever more amazed. He worked non-stop until six o'clock when a knock on the door disturbed him and Pat coughed, 'You can always come back tomorrow, if you wish.'

'No, thanks; I think I've enough to be going on with. The files have been most revealing,' replied George.

★

The following morning, the Chief Constable met with his two investigating officers.

The Super began: 'I met Dr Parton yesterday afternoon and asked whether our body could have been made unconscious with chloroform or something similar when he drowned. He naturally wanted to know the reason for the question. I said we had a theory that the body may have drowned in a disused swimming pool that originally had some chlorinated water. I sensed he was embarrassed. He explained that chloroform can be formed when chlorinated water degrades in a swimming pool, depending on the micro-organisms present. He explained much of the chlorine escapes into the air, but some chloroform can remain dissolved in the water for up to two years, depending on its temperature.

'"We are talking of minute quantities, however, and nowhere near enough to render a body unconscious," he warned.

'Nonetheless, he admitted the water in Lemont's lungs was not tested for chlorine and he promised to do it straight away. This morning, he rang me to say they had found minute traces – three parts per million. He said the cadaver's samples were sufficiently contaminated with flukes that, if he had drowned in a swimming pool, then the pool couldn't have been properly chlorinated. However, there was no residual chloroform in the cadaver's blood nor was there any evidence of his fingernails having been damaged by scraping wood. He was sure the body was not rendered unconscious by chloroform when it drowned.

'I told him Bill Stead had reported there were small amounts of seawater in his samples. Dr Parton was adamant there was none in his. We agreed the seawater must have entered the pool after the body drowned.'

George began his report on Tyson's business affairs. 'Tyson's fortune appears to have been made by being Britain's sole importer of needles—'

He was instantly interrupted. 'Needles?' asked the Chief Constable.

'Yes, sir; the sort your wife uses to stitch a button on a shirt, the type in Singer sewing machines. He imports all shapes and sizes: industrial needles to stitch leather furniture, tiny domestic cotton needles, medical needles for sutures, and so on. You name it and Wight Needles Ltd is the sole importer. Millions are imported into Britain every year – all through Tyson's company. Because needles are relatively small, his distribution centre in Birmingham, where he employs twenty staff, is not particularly large. He imports the needles from three sources. Fifty percent are made in Morocco—'

'Morocco?' queried the Super.

'Yes, sir; I was surprised too. I was even more surprised that the rest come from either Tunisia or Syria.'

'You're joking?'

'No, sir; I'm not. It all adds up to Tyson being a multi-millionaire. He seems to have been the sole importer since 1947 when the company was founded. He makes a great play of claiming expenses too. His tax returns claim he visits the factories in those countries twice a year.'

'Will you stop there?' asked the Super.

George paused.

The Chief Constable looked at his Deputy.

'There's a pattern emerging,' began the Super. 'Lemont, O'Boyle, Paillole and, now, Tyson have links to either North Africa or the Middle East.'

'What are you getting at, Bob?' asked the CC.

'I wish I knew, but you'll remember O'Boyle said Lemont was a wheeler-dealer. It sounds as if Tyson is too. Is there any chance that Tyson and Lemont are business partners?'

★

Later that afternoon, Sergeant Swindlehurst reported back to the Super.

'By chance, when we arrived at the Aragon's swimming pool, Tyson's foreman was carrying out some repairs. He told us that the 5-ply wood he used initially to cover the pool hasn't been up to the job and he is gradually replacing it with stronger marine plywood. I asked him if anyone had ever fallen through the 5-ply and he told us that he had come across a hole where, as he put it, "it looked as if someone had fallen in at the deep end".

'I asked if he knew who had fallen in and when.

121

'He didn't know and said he found the hole towards the end of September. He has since covered the deep end with the stronger plywood. If there ever was any evidence of a drowning, it's long gone.'

'Do you believe him?'

'Yes, sir; we were at school together. He's as honest as the day is long.'

CHAPTER 18

Friday, 11th March 1960

'Mr Crampton?'

'Yes?'

'Oh, good evening. It's Superintendent Bob Kinley here. I'm sorry to be ringing you on a Friday evening, but I thought catching you at the weekend might be easier than during the week, when I'm sure you're busy at school. You recently helped us get a passport checked with the French Embassy in London. It's in your capacity as the island's honorary French Chargé d'affaires that I'm ringing you.'

'Really? How can I help?'

'It's quite a long story and I was wondering if we could meet sometime so that I can explain our dilemma.'

'It would have to be in the evening as I am busy with mock "O" and "A" level exams at school.'

'That would be fine. Where and when can we meet?'

'Monday evening, if you like.'

'Excellent. How about the Central Hotel on Broadway? It will be quiet in the lounge bar. I'd like to bring Detective Sergeant Turnbull along. Say seven thirty?'

'Can I ask what it is about? I assume the French Embassy was helpful?'

'Yes, it was. This, in some ways, is a follow-up and there's nothing for you to worry about.'

★

The two policemen arrived before the French teacher and were sitting in a suitably quiet corner supping their pints of Castletown Ale when Norman Crampton arrived. After introductions, they offered him a drink and were somewhat thrown when he asked for a glass of merlot.

A Manxman, Norman had graduated from London University in the mid-1930s with a good honours degree in French and German. He spent his year abroad, a compulsory part of his four-year degree, studying firstly at the university in Aix-en-Provence, where he met his future wife, and, secondly, at the University of Freiberg. He married Lissette on 3rd September 1939 – the day war was declared. They moved to the island and shortly afterwards he volunteered to join the Army. He was commissioned into the Army Education Corps with the rank of Captain. His fluency in French and German saw him being transferred into the Special Operations Executive on its formation in July 1940.

At the time, no one had even heard of the SOE, yet alone be aware of its role. When leaving his AEC colleagues, he told them he was being transferred to the Inter-Service Liaison Bureau. 'Whatever that is,' he had joked. But within six months, Norman had found himself in occupied France, near the Swiss border. His role was to work with the French Resistance help RAF aircrew, who had been shot down, to escape. He would plan their return to Britain either via Switzerland or over the Pyrenees to Spain.

At the end of the war, the AEC received its Royal Charter and became the Royal Army Education Corps. Major Norman Crampton RAEC left the Army in 1946. His last job was to organise pre-release courses for soldiers returning to civilian life, for which he was awarded an MBE. He joined the staff of his old school a year later.

'So, what's all this about?' opened the schoolmaster.

'Just before Christmas, a man was washed ashore not far from here—' began the Super.

'Ah, yes; I read about it in the paper,' interrupted Norman.

'Well, thanks to your help, we discovered his French passport was a fake. However, there's a mystery about his profession and how he came to die.'

The Super then summarised what they had learned about Lemont's background. From time to time, Norman asked sensible questions, and when the apparent friendship between Lemont's father and de Gaulle was mentioned, he showed particular interest.

'It's a long time ago,' Norman reminisced, 'but after the liberation of Paris in October 1944, I met de Gaulle some months later. I had worked with the Resistance during the war and de Gaulle made a Cook's Tour of the Maquis to thank them for their sterling work. He struck me as a rather arrogant man, considering we had won the war for them.'

'The problem we have,' continued the Super, 'is that Lemont hinted in his letters that two foreign intelligence officers may have something to do with his death. One of them is a member of the Irish Secret Service and we don't expect you to be able to help us with him. However, the other man is called Paul Paillole. He is a colonel in the Directorate General for External Security.'

'The DGSE – military intelligence,' remarked Norman.

'George and I have interviewed both of them, and we aren't convinced they were telling us the whole truth. Both men cast aspersions on Lemont to such an extent that we didn't believe their stories as there were inconsistencies in their accounts; although neither queried whether our cadaver could be anyone other than Lemont, I'm keeping an open mind. Now that I have read parts of Lemont's draft book on the 1941 war in Syria, and his letters claiming that he knew de Gaulle personally, I am more suspicious than ever that Paillole and O'Boyle could be leading us up the garden path.'

The Super removed the tablet from the bag he had brought and handed it to Norman.

Norman took hold of the object and turned it over. 'It is beautiful, but what is it?'

'Let me show you. But I want your word that you will not tell anyone.'

'You have my word.'

The Super opened the slab and showed Norman the portrait.

'Who is it a picture of?'

'We believe it is a portrait of Mohammed and is 1,300 years old.'

'I was always told there are no portraits of the Prophet. They had all been destroyed over the millennia by the Muslims.'

'Ten days ago, I went to SOAS where its provenance was confirmed. Among Middle Eastern historians, the tablet and its contents are known as The Caliph's Great Seal.'

'This is all very interesting, but what exactly do you want me to do?'

'We need to establish Lemont's bona fides. If we go through the usual channels to find out if Lemont really was an acquaintance of de Gaulle, then Paillole could find out. Is it possible for you to approach de Gaulle directly with your Chargé d'affaires hat on?'

'From what you've told me, you believe Lemont, although working and fighting for the Vichy, remained loyal to the Free French. This alienated Paillole who remained true to the Vichy Government?'

'Yes.'

'But how come Lemont ended up with the tablet?' asked the schoolmaster.

'We're not exactly sure. Have you ever heard of Abdullah Quilliam?'

'No. Who is he?'

'He was of Manx descent and used to come regularly to the island for his holidays in the 1920s and early 1930s. He was a convert to Islam and opened Britain's first mosque in Liverpool. We believe he may have acquired the Great Seal from the last Ottoman Caliph.'

'And somehow Lemont found out about it from Quilliam?'

'No. Quilliam died in London in 1932. Lemont was by then working in the *Deuxième Bureau* in Paris. They could not have met.'

'Interesting.'

George asked, 'Would you like another glass of wine?'

'Yes. That would be much appreciated.'

While George went to the bar, Norman explained his role as the island's Chargé d'affaires. 'I cannot write direct to the Élysée Palace, but have to go through the official channels at the French Embassy in London. There, my letter will be opened by a civil servant, possibly a junior administrator. Even if I stressed that de Gaulle would wish to be informed of Pierre Lemont's death and it was being investigated by the Manx Police, there would be no guarantee de Gaulle would be informed. The letter would probably end up with their security services anyway. On the other hand, I could try writing to his personal address at Colombey-les-Deux-Églises. He'll have a personal private secretary who may just give him the letter if we mention de Gaulle was imprisoned at a German POW camp in World War One with Lemont's father.'

'That would be fantastic if you would do that for us,' replied the DCC.

'It's not a problem, but tell me exactly what you want to know from de Gaulle.'

★

The following day, the island's French Chargé d'affaires, having shown the Super the English translation of the letter that was to be sent to France, posted the letter: Personal for: *The President of France, La Boisserie, Colombey-les-Deux-Églises, France*.

Two weeks passed before Norman received a reply. He read it with interest and gasped when he had finished. He wrote out a translation for the Super and rang him.

'We've had a reply from France.'

'What does it say?'

'I think you'd better read it for yourself. Perhaps we could meet this evening at the Central again?'

'Fine. Eight o'clock all right?'

★

Norman gave the Superintendent the translation.

CONFIDENTIAL

From: Jaques de Yonne, Personal Private Secretary to the President of the Fifth Republic.

Dear Norman,

The President was most disappointed when I showed him your letter – for two reasons. Firstly, that you broke with protocol by writing to him directly, insinuating that all might not be well within the usual channels. Secondly, but much more importantly, he is most upset to hear of the apparent death of Pierre Le Mont, whom the President remembers with great fondness.

The President wishes to discuss these matters further with you and the senior police investigator. Weekends are the only time when it will be possible for you to meet him, and for security and political reasons the meeting will have to be on a purely personal basis – no officialdom whatsoever.

You are, therefore, invited to Colombey on Saturday, 23rd April.

Please inform me when and how you expect to arrive in Paris, the name of the accompanying police officer and your hotel's address. I will arrange for an unmarked car to meet you early on Saturday morning and bring you to the President's residence.

My direct phone number is Chaumont 52010111. Ring me anytime between 0800 and 1800 hours.

Yours,

Jaques

'Well?' asked Norman. 'What do you think?'

'It's unbelievable.'

'We'll have to go.'

'I feel very apprehensive. I've never been to France,' replied the Super.

'If we travel out on Thursday, we'll be back on Monday. I think the best way to go will be by boat and train. In that way, our movements are less likely to be noticed. We could fly back.'

'I agree.'

'Then, leave the arrangements to me.'

CHAPTER 19

Thursday, 21st April 1960

The two Manxmen left Douglas on the 9.00 am boat for Liverpool and arrived in London that evening. The following morning, they sailed from Newhaven to Dieppe and were in Paris by mid-afternoon. Norman knew his way around and agreed to show Bob some of the sights. After booking into their hotel, it was a short, brisk walk to visit the Eiffel Tower before a quick trip on the Metro to visit the Tomb of Napoleon at Les Invalides. That evening, they had dinner at a restaurant near the Moulin Rouge, which Norman remembered fondly from his days as a student.

'It will be fascinating to see de Gaulle's manner toward us,' Norman remarked over their meal.

'Why?'

'I've read the material you gave me, written by Lemont. Although it mentions the 1916 Sykes-Picot Agreement, it doesn't spell out many of the subsequent repercussions.'

'Really?'

'The so-called line in the sand agreement between Britain and France was originally a straight line from Acre on the Mediterranean coast to the Persian border. To the north of the line, France would control Lebanon and Syria; and to the south, Britain would administer Palestine, Transjordan and Iraq. However, by the time the Ottoman Empire surrendered at the end of World War One, the British Army had advanced up the River Tigris to about 120 miles beyond the line. The captured territory included Kirkuk and Mosul.

'Needless to say, the French weren't happy when Britain decided to keep the region that became part of north-east Iraq instead of eastern Syria. It's ironic, but the area turned out to be rich in oil.

'After oil had been discovered in Kirkuk in 1927, the French encouraged the Turks to do their dirty work for them by trying to reclaim the region as part of Turkey. In exchange for French military equipment, the Turks agreed a deal that would give the French exclusive oil rights. The Turkish incursion failed, thanks to extensive bombing by the RAF and its ability to airlift troops, even from as far away as India. As the West's requirement for oil increased, the Anglo-Iraq oil company decided the most economical method to export oil was to run a pipeline to the Mediterranean. Although the route through Syria would have been far shorter, the British Government didn't trust the French. Consequently, a much longer pipeline was built that passed through Jordan and Palestine. In a fit of pique, the French paid Syrian Arab terrorists to regularly blow up the pipeline. Afterwards, they would flee back across the border to Syria and be out of the reach of British troops.

'When the Jews began to be victimised in Germany and Poland in the early thirties, Britain allowed them to settle in Palestine. By 1933, about 10,000 Jews had settled in Jerusalem. During the next four years, as the persecution worsened, the numbers doubled each year, and in 1937 about 100,000 arrived. This was unacceptable to the Arabs, although they were quite happy to sell land at exorbitant prices to the Jews for settlements. Arab terrorists were again encouraged by the French to ferment trouble.

'The root of the problem was nationalism. Britain surrendered its Iraq mandate in 1932. The Kingdom of Iraq, under Faisal, then joined the League of Nations in its own right. The French, however, saw their overseas territories as part of a greater France. They hung onto them for grim death and still do. Algeria is the classic example. The war there with the nationalists broke up the Fourth Republic two years ago. By contrast, we gave up India in 1947, Cyprus last year, and Macmillan's *Wind of Change* speech last month shows the way things are going in Africa. France will still have colonies when you and I are long gone. So you can see the so-called *entente cordiale* is not all it's cracked up to be.

'The politics of the Middle East during the last war was a complicated business. We always had to balance the wishes of the Jews, the Arabs and the French. Things got worse when we decided to create the Jewish State of Israel – something the French, again, exploited. After the defeat of the Syrian Vichy Government in 1941, bickering with the Free French began.

'De Gaulle was resisting change while Britain was pushing France to relinquish its mandates so that Lebanon and Syria would become independent like Iraq. We exacerbated the situation by encouraging the Arab nationalists to make trouble in Syria where we believed the French were dragging their heels.

'Although the Free French were theoretically our allies, the pressure on them to concede to the Arabs eventually became so great that elections were held in 1943, although de Gaulle tried all sorts of tricks to preserve the status quo. Nothing much happened until the war finished.

'By then, the Zionists were agitating for Israel to be an independent state, believing we were also dragging our heels. Extreme right-wing Jews had formed several terrorist groups. The most militant was the Stern Gang. Britain was the piggy in the middle trying to placate both the Arabs and the Jews. As so often in life, if you try to please everyone, you end up pleasing no one. Britain's solution was to suggest granting the Jews a coastal strip on the Mediterranean with a corridor access to Jerusalem. The idea was generally accepted by the Arabs but rejected by the Jews. With the unsung approval of the French, the Zionists began ambushing British police patrols in Palestine and then retreating back to the safety of French Syria. The whole thing came to a head when in November 1944, Lord Moyne, a member of Churchill's cabinet and Minister of State for the Middle East, was assassinated. There is no evidence that de Gaulle was organising the Zionist attacks, but as leader of the Free French, he has to shoulder some responsibility.

'Now that de Gaulle is President of the Fifth Republic, his policy seems to be as imperialistic as ever. I am staggered he has agreed to meet us. It can only mean that Lemont was someone special, whom he held in the highest regard.'

'I expect he will talk in French when we meet.'

'I would think so, although I've been led to believe his English is quite good. When he had meetings with Churchill, for example, Churchill insisted English was spoken.'

'Each as stubborn as the other?'

'Quite.'

★

As arranged, on Saturday morning, an unmarked Citroen DS arrived promptly at 7.30 am at their hotel. The journey to Colombey took two and a half hours, much on the fast RN 4 to St-Dizier before swinging south through local roads. They were greeted by Jaques de Yonne, who spoke in accented English. After the usual pleasantries, he explained that, as the President's PPS, he would be attending the meeting to take notes.

'The President will meet us at eleven o'clock,' he said, 'so you have time to freshen up, and we can have coffee in the library. It would be helpful if you outline what you expect from the meeting. It will, of course, be held in French. I understand

Superintendent that you don't speak our language, but it will be quite in order for Norman to translate.'

When a clock outside the library began to strike eleven, the door opened and the President of the Fifth Republic entered majestically. All three stood. Seemingly towering above them was a man six feet five inches tall with a military bearing, whose presence demanded attention. His long Gallic nose, above a neatly trimmed moustache, seemingly stretched his oval face. Immaculately turned out in a dark navy-blue lounge suit, he strode across the room to meet them.

Jaques reacted first. 'Sir, allow me to introduce you to our Manx Chargé d'affaires, Norman Crampton, and Superintendent Kinley, the Isle of Man's Deputy Chief Constable,' he said in French.

Having been briefed previously on protocol, Norman took one step towards the general, bowed his head and offered his hand. They shook hands and de Gaulle, speaking French, surprised Norman.

'We meet again. Sixteen years ago it was in St-Claude, if I remember rightly?'

'Yes, sir. You came to meet the local Maquis.'

'And you were their liaison officer to help RAF aircrew get back to Britain. How many did you successfully repatriate?'

'Over one hundred, sir.'

'Excellent.'

Turning to his PPS, he remarked, 'I think Crampton deserves a *Légion d'Honneur*. Arrange it, will you?'

'Yes, sir.'

He turned to the Superintendent. Speaking clearly in English, he asked, 'What role did you play in the war?'

'I was a humble policeman, sir. I volunteered in 1939 to join the Royal Navy, but my Chief Constable retained me for the duration.'

'And when did you become a policeman?'

'I joined as a cadet in 1933 and became a constable in 1936.'

'So, you always wanted to be a policeman?'

'Yes, sir.'

The pleasantries over, the President gestured for them to sit. He resumed in French, 'Now I understand you believe that one of my most trusted servants has been murdered and you are suspicious that our DGSE may be hiding something from you. Is that right?' He looked at the Super while Norman translated.

Although Norman was unsure if de Gaulle meant to use the word servant, he made no alterations to the translation as he knew both de Gaulle and Jaques would spot changes.

The DCC replied, 'Yes, sir; that is correct.'

'Fine, then begin at the beginning and tell me why you think the body washed ashore is that of Pierre Le Mont.'

CHAPTER 20

The Super began to describe the events that had occurred since Lemont's body had been washed ashore five months previously. Throughout, RJ realised that he had de Gaulle's full attention. The President seemed to understand what he was saying without the need for Jaques to translate. From time to time, the General would ask questions in French, nod when satisfied with the answers, and then gesture for Bob to continue.

'Have you a photo of the corpse?' he asked early on.

The Super showed him the police photographs of the dead body with its mutilated face, taken on the foreshore and later in the path lab. De Gaulle nodded, neither confirming nor denying its identification.

When shown the artist's sketch, he said nothing. When shown the copy of Lemont's French passport, he paused for several moments before announcing, 'It's a fair likeness of Pierre, but you know French passports are never flattering.'

The policeman thought, *there's something in the manner of his reply. I think he's holding something back.*

The interview was slow and laboured as questions and answers were translated for the Super's benefit.

'Lemont's letters were puzzling for many reasons,' said the Super. 'They were written in a manner that suggested Pierre knew he would be murdered.'

'But why should he write to you?' interrupted the General.

'In his correspondence, he explained that he and I are, or rather were, cousins. His father and my father were brothers – both born in a small village in the Isle of Man. I never knew my father had an older brother. I suppose the disgrace of illegitimacy in those days was so great that it broke families apart.'

De Gaulle nodded silently.

'I think Pierre chose to buy a house in the Isle of Man thinking it would be a safe retreat from his undercover work.'

The General stopped the Super. 'What do you know about his work?'

There was a degree of tetchiness in the General's voice.

'We know from his housekeeper that he regularly left the island for long periods. His income was a regular deposit paid from a Swiss Bank. Furthermore, if he was working in a foreign country, he must have had a network of banks from which to draw cash because there are restrictions to taking Sterling out of the UK. Someone or some organisation must have been bankrolling him.'

'Perhaps he had a private income?'

Although having to wait for Norman to translate, Bob could feel that de Gaulle was stalling from telling him Lemont's role in French affairs.

The Super thought hard before answering. He knew he was skating on thin ice, but this was what he had come to find out. Years of experience interviewing witnesses and criminals had given him a sixth sense when people were withholding information. He could feel de Gaulle was deliberately hampering him. He decided to hit the nail on the head.

'If he had a private income, then where did his money come from? His father was a soldier, his mother the daughter of a warrant officer. Assuming his parents left him the family home, it is highly unlikely there was a fortune sufficient to justify a Swiss bank account. No, he was in the employ of someone who was paying him five times more than me. I want to know why. What did Pierre do that justified him being murdered? If you want us to find the culprit, then we will need to know more about Pierre's background.'

'OK, let's assume you're right. Why exactly haven't you gone through the usual channels? What makes you suspicious about our security services? Why have you come to me direct?'

He's clearly not used to being cross-examined. Perhaps I'd better lay off if I'm going to get to the bottom of this.

'Pierre's letters drew my attention to two men, O'Boyle and Paillole, who were in Syria at the same time as Le Mont. Initially, there seemed to be no reason why Pierre should mention them. O'Boyle is now Head of Ireland's Security Service and is mainly concerned with the threat posed by the IRA, while Paillole is in your DGSE. When they were interviewed, both attacked Le Mont's integrity to the extent that neither my senior detective nor I believed them. What links the Irish G1 to your DGSE?'

'Where did you interview Paillole?' asked de Gaulle.

'He came to Manchester and spun me a yarn that you had personally appointed him to root out Vichy sympathisers in 1941. On the other hand, Pierre claims the same thing in his letters – that you had personally appointed him to work undercover during the Vichy interregnum. Their tasks seem identical. Why use two men to do the same job? Or couldn't you trust one of them? I'm an old dog, Mr President. My nose tells me one of them was lying.'

De Gaulle shifted uncomfortably in his chair. 'What else do you know about Le Mont?'

'This is a picture of a rectangular box that can only be opened if you know its combination. The tablet was hidden in an extremely secure safe that had been buried underground in

Pierre's garage. While searching his library, we found the opening combination inside one of his chess books. The case contains a portrait painted on a wooden slab.'

He paused to show the President a photo of the portrait.

'We believe this is the only image of the Prophet Mohammed, painted in 632AD. The tablet is known among Islamic historians as the Great Seal of the Caliphs.'

'It must be priceless,' the President murmured.

'And potentially fatal,' continued the Super. 'The last Ottoman Caliph to possess the Great Seal was Sultan Mehmed VI. When Ataturk created the modern state of Turkey, the title of Caliph was abolished and Mehmed settled in San Remo where he died in 1926. Today, King Saud of Saudi Arabia claims to be a direct descendent of the Prophet and, therefore, the Caliph and leader of the Sunnis. In Iran, however, the Shias see the Aga Khan as their Head because he claims to be descended from Ali, Mohammed's son-in-law. Both families would pay a fortune to possess the Seal. There is even the potential for the two countries to go to war. How Pierre Le Mont came to be in possession of the portrait we can only speculate, but we believe it is the reason for his death.'

'What else have your inquiries uncovered?'

'Pierre claimed he gave you the Nazis' plans to kill the Iraqi Royal family and replace them with Rashid-Ali when he was working undercover for you in Damascus.'

'Anything else?'

'He described how he came to be shot when his Vichy battalion was trapped at Palmyra.'

De Gaulle nodded thoughtfully for some time.

'I think it's time I put my cards on the table.' He spoke English.

'I knew Jean Le Mont, Pierre's father, was born in the Isle of Man. It is one of the reasons I wanted to meet you. I knew you and Pierre were first cousins.'

The President paused and smiled.

'I had you checked out by my personal intelligence staff. You look remarkably like your uncle, by the way. Normally, I would not entertain a British policeman in this manner.'

'I understand, sir.'

'Jean and I became good friends during our time in captivity during World War One. I privately attended his funeral.

'Pierre stayed here with my family on two occasions. He was an exceptionally bright lad and became one of a handful of confidents whom I could trust completely. The Free French were widespread in the war and I had a hell of a job knowing who I could rely on. I seemed to be flitting from one French colony to another all the time.'

He paused as he remembered his war years.

'One man's spy is another man's patriot. After Pierre's capture at Palmyra and his recovery from his flesh wound, Pierre resumed his role as my Head of Security in the Syrian administration. He kept me in the picture of what was happening. It was far from straightforward. There were tensions between the Arabs and the British over the creation of a state for the Jews; tens of thousands of Jews were arriving every month, fleeing from Germany and Eastern Europe. There were tensions between us and the British over the boundaries of a future Jewish state. The British wanted southern Lebanon to become part of the new Israel. On top of that, the Arabs and the Zionists were at each other's throats as it dawned on the Arabs that Palestine would not only be broken up, but also that the Jews wanted Jerusalem as Israel's capital. In the thick of it all, Pierre had managed to convince Ertrugel that I was sympathetic to the aim of restoring the Caliphate in Syria.'

'Why?'

'I believed that as Caliph in Damascus, Ertrugel would go a long way to appeasing the Muslims and in so doing, we could keep control of the Levant. I was wrong. I had underestimated the lingering hatred of the Arabs for the Ottomans. I appointed

Paillole, after we defeated the Vichyites, as our intelligence officer. He was not privy to my plans for Ertrugel. Pierre began to suspect Paillole was a closet Zionist. I specifically told Pierre to keep an eye on him.'

So what Paillole told us in Manchester was total rubbish.

'What happened to Ertrugel?'

'We held him under house arrest in Acre. He was in his mid-thirties. When the war ended, he was tried as a Nazi sympathiser. On my instructions, Pierre gave evidence that Ertrugel was a victim of circumstances beyond his control. Syria was lost and I wanted to get rid of him. Had he been hanged like most of the Vichyites – well, you can imagine the reaction. Killing the legitimate Caliph would have been asking for trouble. The Americans allowed him to settle in New York despite their Jewish lobby protesting. He still lives there as far as I know.'

'So it is possible that when visiting Ertrugel during those four years under house arrest, Pierre learnt about the Caliph's Seal?' asked the Super.

'I would have thought so. Although now I think about it, it doesn't quite make sense. Surely, if Ertrugel had the Seal when he became Governor of Vichy Syria, he would have announced its existence. Then with the Seal returned to its rightful place in Damascus, the ancestral home of the Caliphs, he would have declared himself the new Caliph?'

'True, except for one good reason. He didn't have the Seal. His father had given it to someone he could trust for future safekeeping.'

'Who?' asked the President.

'Mehmed VI couldn't trust Ertrugel with the Seal. It was too dangerous to give to his teenage son. So, before his death, Mehmed gave the Seal to Abdullah Quilliam.'

'Who on earth is he?'

The Super began explaining the background of Quilliam when there was a knock on the door. A servant entered.

Immaculately dressed in a black suit with white shirt and black bow tie, he announced, 'Lunch is ready.'

The General turned in his chair. 'Please bring it in, Edouard.'

Three tables were brought into the library, and within a minute, several staff had laden them with a variety of finger buffet food, sparkling water and white wine. 'I thought we should have a working lunch. Please help yourselves, gentlemen,' said the President as he led the way to the immaculately laid tables.

Within three or four minutes and reseated with his napkin tucked into his collar and his amply filled plate precariously balanced on his knees, de Gaulle began. 'Now, where were we? I have decided you must find who killed the son of one of my best friends.'

Aha! He's still spinning the line that Lemont is dead, thought the Super.

De Gaulle paused to look at his PPS. 'Jaques will give you all possible assistance from now on. Contact him at any time, day or night. He knows all my personal staff. Jaques will choose the most suitable operative to assist you.'

Jaques nodded assuredly at the policeman.

De Gaulle continued: 'What do you know of the Sykes-Picot Agreement?'

'I know that it was an agreement between France and Britain to split the Middle East into two halves.'

'There was a bit more to it than that. The League of Nations intended that France and Britain should guide the five new countries towards independence over the succeeding twenty-five years. However, both our countries wished to retain them as colonies.'

That's not what Norman said last night, thought the Super.

'The American President, Woodrow Wilson, was a strong anti-imperialist and only brought the United States into the war on the understanding that the indigenous peoples could choose their own destinies when the war was over. The British

Government, however, wished to keep control of Egypt and the Sudan. So to dodge any complaints by the Americans of land-grabbing, the British saw the Balfour Declaration as an excuse to create a Jewish state in Palestine, thereby placating the American Jewish lobby. The British thought a friendly State of Israel would safeguard the Suez Canal's eastern flank.

'The British were selling the Arabs the idea that they would gain economic advantages by the creation of Israel. The British were, of course, being duplicitous as they had promised to create a pan-Arabian state encompassing Syria, Palestine, Jordan and Iraq to Sharif Hussein, the Emir of Mecca and Medina, as early as 1915.

'The peaceful handover of colonies is politically very difficult – knowing when the natives are capable of governing themselves and letting the reins go. I am currently holding a referendum to get the agreement of the French people to give Algeria independence. It's a nightmare.'

He sighed loudly as the Algerian problem, which had become international news, clearly weighed heavily on his mind.

'The days of empires and colonies are over,' he mumbled.

He paused while he reflected on what he had said.

'Now, you may be asking what this has got to do with Pierre Le Mont.'

He waited for the Super to nod.

'Have you ever heard of the *Comité de l'Asie Française*?'

'No.'

'The *Comité de l'Asie Française* was, or rather still is, a powerful group of politicians, civil servants and businessmen who are imperialists to their very core. Georges Picot was one of them.

'For example, they believe we gave up French Indo-China too easily, despite there being no going back after Dien Bien Phu. Money, to misquote the Bible, is the root of all evil; never a truer word than with the *Comité de l'Asie Française*. When the Vichy Government came to power in July 1940, they saw the

Nazis' policy of deporting the Jews as an opportunity for the committee to take over running the French banking system. Consequently, they backed Pétain and began leaking the names of Jewish bankers to the Nazis.

'Within weeks, most of our colonies had come under Vichy control, including Syria. At the time, Pierre along with most of the other diplomats acquiesced, at least on the surface, to the new regime. Years earlier, I had recruited him to the cause of Free France, and he began working for me undercover.

'After the 1941 Iraq *coup d'état* failed, my Free French troops, with support from Australian and Indian brigades, invaded Syria that June and we defeated the Vichy and German troops within six weeks. However, the country still needed civil servants to run it. Those who had reluctantly accepted the Vichy rule were quick to transfer their loyalty back to us. However, there remained a cadre who did not. Pierre's task was to keep an eye on them.'

The President stopped, waiting to see if the policeman had any questions.

The Super asked, 'So when Ertrugel was under house arrest, Pierre was keeping pally with him while at the same time looking after your interests by pretending to be pro-Vichy to anyone who couldn't be trusted, including Paillole?'

'Yes, and when World War Two ended, I gave him a roving ticket to work for my personal intelligence service. He became my rock in Syria until the country's full independence around the end of 1949. Don't look surprised. Running a country is too important for politicians. It is a military operation. I need a covert corps of men whom I can trust 100 percent. Pierre is, or rather was, one of them. My agents are all-powerful. They can bypass my ministers and contact me direct. As you have found out, Le Mont, along with the others, has a numbered Swiss bank account. Their task is highly dangerous and stressful. I have encouraged all of them to have a personal bolthole. Pierre chose the Isle of Man about eight years ago. Others have similar hideaways in Madeira and various out-of-the-way places. Pierre knew his father had been born in your island and wanted to see what it was like. I know he fell in love with its tranquillity.

'His swarthy complexion allowed him to pass himself off as an Arab and, after 1949, he operated mostly in Algeria where his information proved invaluable in helping to make decisions. As a policeman, you won't approve, but there are many instances when my agents can take short cuts that you, confined by the law, cannot.'

'Are you saying that Lemont had carte blanche to carry through assassinations?'

'Although he could go anywhere and do anything, such extreme measures would normally require my tacit approval. I can assure you Pierre never undertook anything like that to my knowledge. The passports you found – did they have any entry stamps on them?'

'Now you mention it, no, they didn't,' replied the Super.

De Gaulle smiled. 'He used his Irish one mostly. If you never found it, then it must have been taken from him when he was killed.'

'When did he last contact you?' asked the Super.

'Jaques, you have his dossier.'

The secretary flicked through a file.

'On Saturday, 13th February – two months ago – he reported he was in Annaba on the Algerian-Tunisian border. On Friday, 9th October last year, he contacted us from the Rif Hotel in Tangiers. Three months previously, he called from the Isle of Man on Wednesday, 1st July. Before that he was in Liverpool on Wednesday, 11th March.'

'Those dates don't tally. You're saying he was alive on those last two occasions when we know he had drowned. And what on earth was he doing in Liverpool anyway?' exclaimed the Super.

'I'm afraid the detail of his reports will have to remain confidential,' replied Jaques.

'OK, I respect that, but isn't Liverpool off his patch? And how can you be sure it was Le Mont if he contacted you by phone?' asked the Super.

'He has to answer correctly at least five randomly chosen questions from the data on his personal file.' Jaques gestured towards Le Mont's thick folder. 'There are potentially a hundred or more possible questions. There is no way anyone other than Pierre can make the correct responses,' replied Jaques.

The President then expanded, 'Without giving any big secrets away, for the past five or six years, Pierre has been following leads that link the Algerian FLN, *Front de Libération Nationale*, the IRA, Mossad and the UDBA—'

'The UDBA?' asked Norman, who was translating.

'Yugoslavia's Secret Police Organisation,' replied de Gaulle. 'Thanks to Pierre's work, I am certain the FLN is acquiring soviet-built weapons from the UDBA, via Israel. Pierre also thought the IRA was getting arms from the same source. Jaques, remind me; what was the gist of his report from Liverpool?'

The PPS rifled through the file. He read silently for a brief moment. 'In essence, he had gone to Liverpool to enquire about someone called Henry Leon. In his later July report from the Isle of Man, he said he was about to accompany a member of the Irish security services to Belfast in order to follow up a possible source of IRA funding.'

'Thank you, Jaques. At the time, I thought no more about the Liverpool report, but who is Henry Leon?'

'Firstly, can I ask Jaques a question?'

'Of course,' replied the President.

'You said Pierre "was about to accompany a member of the Irish security services to Belfast". Did he give a name?'

'No,' replied the PPS.

The Super thanked Jaques and turned to address the President. 'I can only imagine Pierre was in Liverpool because he was researching Abdullah Quilliam, who opened Britain's first mosque in Liverpool.'

'Ah, you had started to tell me about him before lunch was brought in.'

'Quilliam used Henry Leon as an alias. He was made a Sheikh of Islam in 1894. It has been suggested, by an eminent historian of Islamic art at London University, that Quilliam met Mehmed, the last Ottoman Caliph, before the Caliph died. Mehmed may have given the Seal to Quilliam as his son, Ertrugel, was too young to comprehend the responsibilities of becoming Caliph.

'However, getting back to our dead body; our post-mortem suggested the cadaver had been in the sea for up to two months. If Pierre was in Tangiers in October and Algeria in February then our dead man is definitely not Pierre Le Mont.'

'I'm afraid those are your problems, Superintendent. When I agreed to meet you, I must confess that I could not see how your cadaver could possibly be Pierre. But you'll understand that I had to be absolutely certain you were wrong. Your dead body is definitely someone else.'

'I don't suppose you know if Pierre had been circumcised, by any chance?'

'No, of course not; is that significant?'

'It could be. However, the last question I would like to ask is why did Paillole paint such a black picture of Pierre?'

'Paillole, whose mother was Jewish, was appointed by me after I had learnt the British Government was planning to implement the Balfour Declaration at the end of the war and create a State of Israel in Palestine. The richer Jews were fleeing the Nazis and arriving in Palestine in vast numbers throughout the war. The situation was out of control. The British were trying to bargain with me. They wanted the new State of Israel to encompass the southern three quarters of Lebanon. In exchange, they said, the northern quarter could become part of Syria. Syria would thereby have a much greater Mediterranean coastline. I wasn't prepared to play ball. After all, what were they giving me? Fifty percent of the population in Lebanon are Christians – mostly in the south – can you imagine their reaction to finding themselves in a Jewish state? I needed someone on the ground with contacts among the Jews to keep an eye on things. Appointing Paillole was a risk because I suspected he might work both ways, but there are times when that can be advantageous. For example, Paillole denies Israel is in the loop supplying arms to the FLN and IRA. However, Pierre has uncovered an American company, Permidex, being financed by Mossad to train an Algerian right-wing group, called the *Organisation Armée Secrète*, or *OAS*, to assassinate me. It's a dirty world and the reason I have my own modern-day Musketeers.

'However, I have said enough. I'm afraid we'll have to leave it at that. It's three o'clock and I have another meeting in half an hour.'

He looked at his watch and began thanking them in English.

'I'm sorry that it has been necessary for me to converse with you in French, but I have to be sure there is no misunderstanding. I congratulate you, Norman, on the quality of your interpreting. Had you used words with which Jaques disagreed, he would have stopped you. It has been a pleasure meeting you, Superintendent. I don't suppose we'll ever meet again, for I doubt if I'll ever get to visit your beautiful island. I promise, however, that Jaques will keep in touch and will give you every possible help.'

De Gaulle shook hands with his visitors and left the room. It was left to Jaques to take them to their chauffeured car and see them leave. They were back in their Paris hotel by seven o'clock that evening. After they had freshened up, they wandered down to the Seine, where Norman chose a suitably quiet restaurant in a side street. They began discussing their meeting.

'Did you learn anything new today?' asked Norman.

'Apart from how long everything takes when it has to be translated?' joked Bob. 'If we are to believe de Gaulle, then Paillole and O'Boyle lied to us about Lemont. Mind you, I'm not convinced de Gaulle told us everything about Paillole. The explanation of where Lemont's income came from has been cleared up, and the question now is who is the cadaver, if it's not Lemont?'

'And you think the explanation for Lemont being in Liverpool is something to do with Quilliam?'

'The theory that Mehmed gave Quilliam the Seal in 1924 is something I learned from meeting the Professor of Arab History at SOAS.'

'So you think Quilliam may have brought the Seal to the Isle of Man when he was on holiday?'

'Yes. Apparently, he regularly stayed in Onchan. He must have hidden it somewhere safe, and Lemont somehow worked out where it was. As he knew the combination to the tablet from Ertrugel, he was able to open it.'

'So, where do you plan to go from here?'

'To be honest, I'm not sure. Are both O'Boyle and Paillole after the Seal, or just one of them? Neither arrived in Syria until after the defeat of the Vichy regime. By then, Ertrugel was under house arrest. Consequently, they never met Ertrugel nor would have known about the Seal. Did they know about the Seal before we told them?'

CHAPTER 21

Bob and Norman flew from Paris Orly the following morning in an Air France Caravelle to Heathrow, changed aircraft to a BEA Viscount and arrived at Ronaldsway that evening. Periodically, on their journey together, they continued to throw ideas at each other as to what should be the next stage of the investigation.

'I think I'll have to contact the New York Police Department to see if they will interview Ertrugel for us,' mused Bob.

'He might not play ball.'

'When Ertrugel learns that Lemont has been murdered because of the Caliph's Seal, which he disclosed to him, then hopefully he will cooperate.'

'So although you now have doubts about the cadaver's identity, you will tell Ertrugel the body is that of Lemont?'

'Yes. Policing is a pragmatic business, I'm afraid.'

★

The next day, the Super brought BP and George up to date.

'De Gaulle is certain Lemont was in Algeria as recently as Saturday, 13th February. This effectively confirms my growing suspicion that I've had for a while. The body washed up cannot be Lemont.

'I would like George to go to Liverpool as I believe we must find out why Lemont went there a year ago. Was he following up a possible connection between the Seal and Quilliam? If I'm right, there may be someone at Quilliam's mosque who will remember Lemont.'

'I could go tomorrow, if you wish,' said George.

'There's no time like the present,' agreed Bob.

'What was the other development you had in mind?' asked the Chief.

'When Ertrugel was under house arrest in Acre, we know he told Lemont about the Great Seal being given to someone called Leon. What we don't know is how Lemont discovered Leon's real name was Quilliam and where he had hidden the Seal.'

'But wasn't Ertrugel under arrest from 1941 to the end of the war?' queried the Chief Constable. 'Why did it take Lemont nigh on fifteen years to follow it up?'

'My guess is Lemont never gave it any more thought until possibly a year or two ago when something triggered his memory.'

'So what you're saying is that something happened to Lemont while working undercover for de Gaulle, possibly last year, which prompted him to investigate the disappearance of the Seal?'

'Yes, and bearing in mind most of his work for de Gaulle is carried out in North Africa, that's where his stimulus to investigate the Seal's disappearance must have been. We could use Interpol to contact the New York Police Department, but after the Met Special Branch eavesdropping on us, I propose we write directly to the NYPD and ask them to interview Ertrugel. We request they keep the matter confidential as it's part of an ongoing murder inquiry. With luck, we could have a reply back inside a fortnight.'

★

The following day, George caught the early flight to Liverpool. Britain's first mosque turned out to be an unimposing, early Victorian, end-terraced, three-storeyed house. To the side of the front door was a discreet plaque: *Britain's First Mosque – opened by Abdullah Quilliam in 1889.* George tried the door, but it was locked. At the adjacent house a brass plaque read: *Register Office – Births, Deaths and Marriages.* Somewhat puzzled, he entered. In the hallway, sitting behind a reception desk, was a young Asian woman. Her long, jet black hair shone in the sunlight that was pouring through the open door.

She smiled and asked, 'Can I help you?'

'I hope you can,' replied George, showing his ID card. 'I'm Detective Sergeant Turnbull from the Isle of Man Police. I'm making enquiries about a murder and have reason to believe that the victim may have come here last March.'

'What was his name?'

'Peter Lemont.'

'It rings no bells. Have you come to register his death?'

'No,' replied George, laughing. 'Lemont probably expected 8 Brougham Terrace to be a mosque, like I did. I think you misunderstood me'.

'Oh, it hasn't been a mosque since before the war. The terrace now belongs to Liverpool Corporation and this is its register office.'

'Do you know where Liverpool's mosque is now?'

'The only one I know is in Penny Lane.'

'You're not...'

'No,' she smiled. A beautiful beam lit her face, showing her pearl white teeth. 'I'm a Hindu. My family are Indian.'

'I'm sorry, I didn't...'

'That's OK, it happens all the time. My boss, the registrar, may remember your... what was his name?'

'Lemont.'

She picked up her phone and talked to someone. 'Mr Seaton will come down to see you.'

A minute later, dressed in a dark suit, white shirt and black tie, a pale-skinned man, sporting a trimmed, grey beard, descended the stairs into the hall. George thought he was probably in his late fifties.

'I'm Brian Seaton,' he said with a friendly smile as he held out his hand. 'How can I help you?'

George introduced himself.

'Please come up to my office.' He asked his receptionist, 'Could you rustle up a pot of tea for us? I'm sure the DS would appreciate a drink after travelling all the way from Douglas.'

At the top of the stairs, they entered his office which overlooked the main road. He gestured for George to sit down. 'If you can start from the beginning...' and paused.

'I believe that in March last year someone called Peter Lemont may have come here. We think his body may have been washed ashore in the Isle of Man last November, and a post-mortem has revealed he was murdered. Do you remember seeing this man?'

George showed the registrar Lemont's photo that had been copied from his passport. 'If he did come here, I would be grateful if you could tell me the purpose of his visit.'

'Yes, he did come here. I know because it was my youngest son's eighth birthday – the 11th. I'd bought him a Dinky Toy – a model of John Cobb's record-breaking MG and it was here on my desk. Mr Lemont admired it and reminisced that he'd loved Dinky Toys as a boy.'

'What exactly did Lemont want to know?'

'He, like you, had thought No 8 was a mosque. He asked where the mosque is now and I told him it is on the corner of Penny Lane and Dudley Road. It's easy to find – fifteen minutes away by car.'

★

Twenty minutes later, George was met cautiously by a man who introduced himself as the Imam. Although wearing traditional Middle Eastern dress with a white prayer cap, or *kufi*, he was Caucasian.

Definitely English – a Manchester accent, thought George as he introduced himself.

'How can I help?' the Imam asked.

'I have come from the Isle of Man and I'm trying to trace the last movements of a man called Lemont,' George began.

After mentioning Lemont's name and the Isle of Man in the same sentence, his defensive attitude changed and he took George into a side office.

The Imam said he remembered Lemont's visit as he had asked questions about Henry Leon.

'I explained that Leon's real name was William Henry Quilliam and he had changed his name during World War One to Henry Leon because of his views that Muslims must not fight fellow Muslims. His views were tantamount to treason. I told him that after the Great War, Quilliam lived in Woking where he became an Imam at Britain's first purpose-built mosque – the Shah Jahan Mosque. I explained that, although he was originally from Liverpool, he had been educated at King William's College. Mr Lemont then asked me if I'd ever met the great man.'

'And had you?'

'Yes, once. I'd met him when I was in my late teens while studying here at Liverpool University in the 1920s. I'd been to several meetings at Brougham Terrace and met him. He had a powerful presence. He was a great orator and I converted to Islam thanks to him.'

'Did Lemont ask you anything else?'

'He asked me if I'd ever heard of Ertrugel Effendi. I told him I knew he was the son of the last Caliph, Mehmed VI. He then asked me if there was any possibility that Quilliam could ever have met Mehmed or Ertrugel. I replied I had no idea.'

'Did Lemont ask anything else?'

'Only to ask me where the mosque was in Woking.'

★

The following day, George arrived in Woking and was met by the Imam, who was of Asian extraction. 'My colleague in Liverpool rang. He told me you wanted to know if someone calling himself Lemont came here last year.'

'Specifically, did Lemont ask about Abdullah Quilliam and whether he could have met Mehmed VI?' asked George.

'Of course. Please come into my office. Would you like a coffee? It's only instant, I'm afraid.'

'That would be much appreciated.'

While waiting for the kettle to boil, the Imam began, 'I'll tell you what I told Mr Lemont. Abdullah Quilliam lived in Woking for about ten years under the alias of Henry Leon. During that time, I was one of his assistant Imams and got to know him quite well. Most years, he would take a three-month vacation, always to the same place – Onchan in the Isle of Man.

'On one occasion, I asked him, "What's so special about the Isle of Man?"

'He told me he had been to school there and loved walking the island's glens and coastal paths. "I can walk all day and not see a soul," he told me.

'It gave him time to contemplate the meaning of life in a world where eleven million men can get needlessly killed in less than four years.'

'Did he ever mention meeting Mehmed?'

'Yes. It was April 1924 and he went to see Mehmed in San Remo. I remember him leaving. I saw him off from the station. It was Cup Final Day – Newcastle United versus Aston Villa, and pouring rain. He joked as he boarded the train, "The weather will be better in Italy."

'Don't forget, of course, that he was a Sheikh of Islam – the only European ever to be honoured with the title. It had been bestowed on him by Caliph Abdul Hameed II. Wherever Abdullah Quilliam went in the Muslim world, he was received like royalty. He must have met Ertrugel who would have been a teenager when he was there.'

'When Quilliam returned from San Remo, did he mention the Caliph's Great Seal?'

'How do you know about it?'

'It cropped up in our inquiries.'

'He never mentioned it as such; although he told me Mehmed had given him a gift for safe keeping that shouldered an enormous responsibility. At the time, I wondered if it could have been the Seal. A few weeks later, he went off for his annual holiday to the Isle of Man. I was pretty sure he took the gift with him.'

'Did you tell this to Lemont?'

'Yes.'

'One last question: was there anyone with Lemont when he came here, or has anyone else been here asking about him?'

'No.'

CHAPTER 22

Thursday, 28th April 1960

George updated the two senior officers on what had occurred in Liverpool and Woking. 'We now know Quilliam met both Mehmed VI and Ertrugel in San Remo in 1924. Mehmed gave Quilliam a gift, almost certainly the Seal. Only Ertrugel can confirm that. Assuming Mehmed did give Quilliam the Seal, Mehmed would also have told him its opening combination. Otherwise, there would be no point in giving it to Quilliam. Ertrugel's statement from New York will hopefully confirm this.'

'Can I interrupt you there,' said the Chief Constable. 'Late yesterday afternoon, I had a telegram from the New York Police Department. They had arranged to interview Ertrugel today and will send us the transcript by airmail as soon as possible. So we shouldn't have long to wait.'

George resumed. 'Shortly after returning from San Remo, Quilliam came to the island for his annual holiday. The Seal was in Lemont's garage when he left the island last September, so he must have located it when he returned from Woking. However, we still don't know what triggered him to go to Liverpool in the first place. Now, we need to work out how Lemont found the Seal that had remained hidden for thirty-odd years.'

There was silence in the room for a few moments until George suggested, somewhat hesitantly, 'I'd like to play devil's advocate, if I may. There could be a possible explanation for everything.'

'What's that, George?' asked the CC.

'The man reporting to de Gaulle last October and February this year could have been Paillole. Lemont found the Seal when he returned to the island and had the Dotteling safe installed. When O'Boyle visited Lemont in July, Lemont showed O'Boyle the Seal. O'Boyle told Paillole, and realising the value of the Seal, they hatched a plot to kill Lemont...'

'Stop there,' said the Super. 'De Gaulle is 100 percent certain Lemont contacted him on those occasions. There's no way Paillole could impersonate Lemont.'

'I've thought about that,' replied George. 'Paillole works in the DGSE. If he's as clever as we think he is, and is an Israeli agent, he's in the right place to break into de Gaulle's personnel files. He will also have access to some sophisticated Israeli toxins. He used one to kill Lemont and it left no trace in his blood. He then impersonated Lemont to make de Gaulle think Lemont is alive.

'Paillole having killed Lemont, allowed O'Boyle to return to Ballaugh. He broke into Lemont's house and opened the safe in the library; after all, if Jim Ridgeway could open it, so could O'Boyle. At that point, O'Boyle hit a brick wall. Lemont had already prepared for his death by writing you a letter. It spelled out that to access further documents involved going to Qualtrough and Quine Solicitors and the need to know about your chess game. Consequently, O'Boyle couldn't get the keys to open the Dotteling. The post-mortem findings are correct after all.'

'Allow me to summarise,' said the Chief. 'If you're right, then Lemont is our cadaver?' He paused.

The CC continued. 'Last September, after the Manx Grand Prix, Lemont left the island and we know he was alive. If your hypothesis is correct, then Lemont must have met his death before October when, supposedly, he was in Tangiers, but in reality was floating in the Irish Sea. The crux is: could Lemont's personal file, held by de Gaulle, have been compromised by Paillole?'

'The man who contacted de Gaulle in October and February could speak French sufficiently fluently to pass himself off as Lemont. It must have been Paillole,' added George.

The Super slowly shook his head. 'Jaques de Yonne was certain the man who reported-in was Lemont. In their conversation, Lemont had claimed there was a link between the IRA, the Israelis and the *Front de Libération Nationale* – the Algerian National Front. Assuming Paillole really is an Israeli double agent, would he implicate Mossad in order to pass himself off as Lemont?'

'I think he would. In that way he strengthens his impersonation of Lemont. O'Boyle and Paillole are accomplices – it tallies,' said George.

'Gentlemen, this is all very well, but we're missing something,' said the Super. The only way to get the key to the Dotteling safe was from Qualtrough and Quine. The solicitors' office has neither had a break-in nor has anyone tried to pass himself off as me. But, the big problem with your hypothesis, George, is this: was there any sign that someone had searched Lemont's house before us? Answer – no!'

'There was no obvious evidence of a break-in,' agreed the DS. 'An intruder would have had to avoid Mrs Craine who regularly went there to clean and dust the house.'

'We've agreed we're dealing with pros. I believe Lemont is alive, that he did speak to de Gaulle from Tangiers and Algeria. Lemont will remain ignorant about our cadaver until he next makes contact with the General. I believe Lemont went to Liverpool to get as much information as he could about Leon and solve the mystery of where the Seal could have been hidden. He had learnt about the Seal when visiting Ertrugel under house arrest. Ertrugel thought the Seal was given to someone called Leon. When Lemont went to Liverpool, he would neither have known who Quilliam was, nor the Onchan connection. It wasn't until he got to Liverpool that he discovered Quilliam's real name and the Manx link.

'The cadaver has, by pure chance, prematurely kicked off a chain of events. We weren't meant to discover all of this until after Lemont's real death. If O'Boyle and Paillole want the Seal, then they may have been watching us. We cannot rule out the possibility that they have Ballaugh staked out. We must put the Seal somewhere secure. At the moment it is downstairs in the station's safe.'

'Are you worried that O'Boyle may try and break into the station?' asked the CC.

'We can't rule that out. We have opened a can of worms,' sighed the Super.

'Should we move it to the vaults in the Isle of Man Bank?' asked BP.

'I know you've suggested that before, but I think we should keep it here and issue the duty sergeant immediately with a firearm to be kept under his desk. The station is manned twenty-four hours a day. Until this is cleared up, I suggest we close the Athol Street entrance and only use Church Street.'

The Chief Constable nodded his approval.

★

A week later, an airmail letter arrived from the United States. It confirmed the statement had been given voluntarily after explaining to Ertrugel that a body, thought to be Lemont, had been washed ashore and investigations had subsequently discovered a casket containing a portrait in Lemont's home.

Attached to the covering letter was the signed statement made at the home of Ertrugel Effendi on Thursday, 28th April 1960:

I met an English man called Henry Leon in April 1924 when I was about fifteen. My father had invited him to San Remo to ask him to protect the Great Seal of the Caliphs. My father, the last Caliph, Mehmed VI, realised that there was no way I could inherit his title. The Caliphate had brought him nothing but unhappiness, and he did not wish that I should carry the burden of its office.

I was a typical teenager who wanted to be a racing driver like Antonio Ascari, who was winning races in his Alfa Romeo and had just won the Italian Grand Prix.

I attended their meeting, spoken throughout in English. My father was adamant that it was the language of what he called "the future". My father explained the significance of the only portrait of Mohammed to Mr Leon.

'I believe it only right that Ertrugel should know the tablet's history and secret,' my father said. 'Under happier circumstances, my son would inherit my title. However, with the world situation as it is, I fear the split, which has existed for over a thousand years between ourselves and the Shias, can only worsen. There will be wars between the Palestinians and Syrians on the one hand and the Jews on the other. I foresee Iraqi Shias, backed by the Persians, rising up against King Faisal. As long as this division within Islam remains so bitter, possession of the Seal will be a weight around my son's neck.

'You, my friend, will know what to do with the Great Seal – where to keep it safe. Are you happy to take on this critical responsibility?'

'Of course, it is a great honour to be asked,' Mr Leon replied.

My father asked Mr Leon to protect it until such time as a future undisputed leader should emerge to spearhead the faith. After he agreed, my father gave Leon the tablet and showed him how to open it.

'These ten squares must be depressed in the correct order,' he said. 'I found remembering the order of the numbers from 0

to 9 difficult,' he explained, 'so I think of them as the first ten letters of the alphabet: A to J. I was then able to use the letters to make an anagram.'

He took a pen and wrote: BATCHED FIG. Immediately under the letters he wrote the numbers of the squares: 1092743 586. ' I had to change the letter J to a T to make it work.' He depressed the keys in the order written and opened the Seal.

I recall gazing at the picture of the Prophet and thinking his eyes were incredibly mesmeric.

Leon asked, 'What exactly do you want me to do with the tablet? I may not live long enough to see our faith united.'

By that I understood him to mean the unification of Sunnis and Shias.

'Hide it where it cannot be found accidentally, but leave a clue to where you have put it.'

'That's a pretty tall order,' Mr Leon replied.

'It will be safer in England than anywhere else. Use your wits to find a secure haven that will be almost unbreakable to all except a determined researcher of Islam and its history.'

I never saw Leon again. I assumed the Great Seal would be lost forever as I couldn't imagine how anyone could hide the Seal to be both difficult to find and yet possible to uncover.

In June 1940, a few days after Paris fell to the Nazis, I was approached by von Ribbentrop to head up the pending Vichy Government in Syria. At the time, I was a successful businessman exporting French wines and living in Paris. I knew von Ribbentrop well, as he was my best German importer of champagne. He was very persuasive, arguing that my ability to speak fluently in French, German, Italian, English, Turkish and Arabic was useful. He also hinted that he would set up a team to find the Great Seal after they had won the war. How he knew about its existence, I never found out.

At the time, it seemed the war would only last a few more weeks. When he promised to establish me as the Caliph in

Damascus by uniting Syria and all the other Arab-speaking countries into one, it was an offer my ego would not allow me to refuse.

Of course, things turned out differently. After Syria fell to the Allies in 1941, I was held under house arrest in Acre. Peter Lemont would visit me frequently. He had been my senior security officer in Damascus and had persuaded de Gaulle that he could be trusted to work for the Free French. We would spend many hours playing chess, and one day he remarked that there were more positions on a chess board than there were atoms in the universe. I laughed. He said that if a chess position could be made into a lock, then no one could ever unpick it.

The idea reminded me of the day Leon took away the Great Seal for safe keeping. So I told Peter about the Seal, how it would be priceless but at the same time would leave the owner open to grave danger. Thinking that my role for the Vichy Government would lead to my execution, I gave Peter the anagram code that would open the Seal, warning him that any attempt to force the box open would break the phials of acid and destroy both the portrait and Fatima's shawl. I remember him shrugging his shoulders and saying, 'God only knows who Leon is – he'll be long gone by now.'

When the war ended, I was tried as a war criminal, but my lawyers argued I had been purely a puppet Head of the Syrian Vichy regime. Consequently, I was given a suspended sentence and banished from ever entering France or any of its overseas territories.

I am now a successful importer of South American wines into the USA.

Ertrugel Effendi

CHAPTER 23

Thursday, 5th May 1960

'What do we know about Lemont?' asked the Super to his senior detective.

'What do you mean?' George replied.

'Well, for example, is he married? Has he any relatives?'

'Are you wondering if there is a homosexual connection in the three-man triangle?'

'Not really, George. But the O'Boyle-Paillole relationship confuses me. It was something you said the other day about Lemont being the cadaver. Is it possible that Lemont found a lookalike and murdered him, hoping to throw O'Boyle and Paillole off the scent? Lemont correctly guessed that we would trace the body to his house in Ballaugh. We would then follow up Lemont's suggestion to tell O'Boyle and Paillole that he was dead.

'Let's think about this for a minute. Ertrugel's statement confirms Henry Leon was given the Seal, and he must have brought it to the island to hide it. We know he used to stay at the Howstrake Hotel in Onchan and that he would go for walks that sometimes lasted for days. We know he would walk all over the island and spend nights in a tent before returning to Onchan. Where would you hide something like the Seal?'

164

'Bury it in a canvas bag?'

'Yes, but it would have to be in a place where it could be found in the future.'

'But not by accident.'

'Agreed,' replied the Super. 'Practically all the footpaths around the island at some place pass close to the graveyards in the parish churches. Heading north from Onchan, the first would be at Baldrine, then Lonan, and so on. Leon's real name was William Henry Quilliam—'

'I'm catching your drift,' interrupted George. 'After visiting Liverpool, Lemont knew Leon was Quilliam. If Abdullah came across a grave with the name William Henry Quilliam – his full name – then he might bury the Seal in that grave.'

'Unless he found a grave for Henry Leon?'

'Yes, that too,' agreed George.

'There must be about thirty cemeteries on the island. We'll need to search every churchyard. If we find a likely grave, assuming this is what Lemont did, then we might have hit the jackpot. You organise a search for graves marked *William Quilliam* and I'll see the Chief about getting any necessary legal paperwork for exhumations.'

★

After discussing the idea of the search with the Chief Constable, the Super walked along Athol Street to the government offices on Prospect Hill. There he sought the legal aspects of disturbing graves with the First Deemster.

'I can't see a problem, Bob, as long as you don't disturb the coffin. How deep do you think you will have to dig into the grave?'

'I would imagine no more than two or three feet.'

'Coffins are laid at a depth of six feet. You shouldn't be anywhere near disturbing them. Providing you leave the site the way you found it, I can't see a legal reason for any paperwork.

From what you have told me, the Seal was probably buried in the 1920s, so I see no reason for getting permission from the next of kin.'

★

Within twenty-four hours, a dozen constables had found fifty-eight graves inscribed *William Quilliam*. Of these, sixteen gravestones were marked *William Henry Quilliam,* and the Super and George began searching discreetly. Their first trip was to the remotest graveyard on the island at Saint Adanman's Church, Baldrine. There, the headstone was almost impossible to read:

William Henry Quilliam
Died 12th March 1698
Beloved husband of Martha.

There was no evidence that the grave had been attended for a very long time; indeed, the grave had collapsed badly and looked unsafe. Consequently, they moved on to the next cemetery heading north. At Lonan, a few miles south of Laxey, they found:

William Henry Quilliam
Died 9th August 1958, aged 10
Only son of Fred and May
He will be remembered forever.

George realised the grave was too recent, and it dawned on him that the instructions he had given the constables for the search had been insufficient. *Quilliam could only have used a grave where the occupant had died before him.*

'George,' said the Super after seeing the Lonan grave, 'you do realise the grave has to be prior to Quilliam dying in 1932.'

'Yes, sorry, Boss; I've just realised that too!'

'Never mind; it's triggered a thought – Quilliam's father was Robert Quilliam, and he was reputedly a descendent of Captain John Quilliam who was on *HMS Victory* at the Battle of Trafalgar with Admiral Nelson.'

'Yes, and the story is that when lying on the deck after being shot, Nelson asked Quilliam, "How are we doing?" and Quilliam famously replied, "Fair to middling." Captain Quilliam is buried at Arbory Church, next door to where I went to school. I'll bet a pound to a penny that is where Abdullah buried the Seal. He knew the grave is kept pristine as it is maintained by the Royal Navy Association. Every Trafalgar Day, my school had to go to the grave for a memorial service. Shall we go there now?'

'No time like the present,' replied his boss.

George smiled. *If I'd a pound for every time he said that, I'd be rich.*

★

A forty-minute drive saw the two men in Kirk Arbory Churchyard, where George quickly led his boss to Quilliam's grave.

Captain John Quilliam RN
Born 29 September 1771
Died 10 October 1829

The grave was in immaculate condition. Underneath the headstone was a lengthy inscription about the Captain's role at Trafalgar.

'If Abdullah Quilliam used this grave to hide the Seal, then unearthing the possible hiding place shouldn't take long,' remarked George.

After carefully scraping the white marble chippings that covered the grave to one side, they noticed a patch of earth, about two and a half feet square, that appeared to have been disturbed more recently than its surroundings. With their trowels, they carefully dug the patch deeper. At a depth of about two feet, the soil became much firmer.

'So this is where Lemont found the Seal, but what did he do then?' asked the Super.

'Presumably, he took it back to Ballaugh and opened it.'

'And put it in his garage?'

'Yes.'

'But why? Why not leave it here, where it had been safe for about thirty-five years?'

'Because he knew someone else was after the Seal and could work out its location.'

'Exactly! When did Lemont have the safe built in his garage? Do we know?'

George shook his head.

'My guess is it was after finding the Seal. He had the safe built as quickly as possible and then moved the Seal into the Dotteling. We need to find out when the German safe was installed. Jim Ridgeway should be able to help.'

★

The two officers drove back to Douglas and went straight to Jim's shop in Strand Street.

'Jim, do you remember that German safe in Lemont's garage at Ballaugh?'

'The Dotteling?'

'Yes. Can you find out when it was installed?'

'The UK agents for Dotteling are Eurovaults Ltd. They will have installed it. I do occasional business with them. Shall I give them a ring?'

A few minutes later: 'Yes, that's right, Sam; you supplied a Dotteling to a Mr Lemont on the island… when?

'Last year – on 21st May… And who installed it? One of your Dotteling specialists… OK, thanks for your help.'

Jim put the phone down. 'You probably heard all that?'

'Yes,' replied the Super, 'and it proves one thing – Lemont didn't lose any time finding where Quilliam hid the Seal. It was in the Dotteling when O'Boyle stayed with him, prior to going to Belfast.'

'Our theory depends on Lemont showing O'Boyle the Seal. Why?' asked the Super. 'It doesn't make sense, unless he wanted them to lower their guard while he plotted to assassinate them and keep the Seal for himself.'

'A bit fanciful, surely?' asked George.

'All along, we've believed everything Lemont has told us in his letters. Is it possible that he is the fly in the ointment? After all, my father never told me he had a brother, and Hector's aunt never knew she had a sister called Ann.'

'What you're saying is we need to check that a girl called Isobel Kinley was born in Wigan and find out if there was a formal adoption process when she was given to the owners of a cotton mill.'

'Yes. I'm afraid we've been guilty of not checking our facts,' sighed the Super.

★

Back in his office: 'Dolly, get me the police HQ in Wigan, will you?' asked the Deputy Chief. 'Tell them I want to speak with the Superintendent of their division.'

Half an hour later, it was agreed that a police car would meet George the following morning at Liverpool Speke Airport and take him directly to Wigan's registrar of births, deaths and marriages.

★

Forewarned of the inquiry, there was only the formality of signing receipts before George was reading a copy of the birth certificate of Isobel Kinley. A further document showed she was adopted by Gillian and Jacob Blackwell in 1899 and took their surname. George also acquired the death certificates of the Blackwells. Gillian had died of tuberculosis in 1932 and Jacob in 1941 by accidental death.

'Do we know what happened to Isobel Blackwell? Did she inherit the mill from her father? Where is she now?' George asked the registrar.

'There's nothing in our records of her death or marriage,' was the reply.

Outside, George asked his driver if he could help.

'I can't help you there, Guv, but I know someone who might. PC Ramsbottom was Wigan's families' liaison officer for as long as I can remember, until he retired. He's something of a local historian too. What he doesn't know about Wigan society isn't worth knowing. Shall I take you to see if he's at home?'

'Great, let's go and find him.'

★

'Blackwell's factory was destroyed in a German air raid in 1941. Old man Blackwell was killed along with five workers. It was a bad time. By then, their daughter Isobel had been to Oxford University and was teaching at a Midwest University in America. After the war, she sold the bombed-out site to a developer. I guess she's still in America. Sorry I can't be of any more help.'

Before catching the 1400 hours flight back to Ronaldsway, George rang his boss and summarised what he had found.

'That's great, George. See you on Monday.'

CHAPTER 24

Monday, 9th May 1960

George knocked on the Super's door.

'Ah, George, take a seat. While you were in Wigan, I had our registrar of births check for John Kinley and Ann Cregeen. Lemont is my cousin.

'I also checked what you told me on Friday afternoon. PC Ramsbottom was right. Oxford University confirmed Isobel graduated from St Hilda's College in 1926 with a good degree in History. Three years later, she got a DPhil after excavating a crusaders' castle in Lebanon. The college's alumni secretary told me Isobel was a lecturer at the University of Iowa five years ago. Since then, they've lost contact. Why the hell we didn't check all this before, I don't know.

'However, there was another thing. I asked you to check whether O'Boyle had ever flown to the island with Aer Lingus. How did you get on?'

'I contacted the airport's senior controller about what we wanted. He was more than helpful and had one of his staff check the Aer Lingus passenger arrival lists that go back to their first flights from Dublin after the war. However, would you believe, despite the name O'Boyle being so common in Ireland, there has never been anyone with that name on their lists flying to the Isle of Man. But he came up with a brainwave. He suggested I contact Bill Peters, the *Examiner* photographer. Peters privately employs juniors every summer from May to September to meet all the incoming flights and take photos of the passengers as they come down the steps of the aircraft. They then hand the visitors a card and tell them they can buy the print for two shillings from his photography shop in Strand Street. It is a money-spinner, seemingly.'

'And Peters has kept all the photos?' asked the Super.

'The negatives – yes. So I sent young Alan to his studio.'

'DC Kilip?' queried RJ.

'Yes. Firstly, it took him several hours to separate the Aer Lingus pictures from the other airlines. The rest of the day, he sifted through the most recent flights, working backwards, comparing the photos with our description of O'Boyle. He came up with a dozen, or so, possibilities. I examined them and look what I found.'

George handed the Super a print.

'It's a young girl.'

'Yes, but look who is behind her, in the background – the next person coming off the plane.'

'O'Boyle!'

'And look at the next photo that was on the spool.'

'O'Boyle is trying to hide his face with his trilby hat.'

'Exactly. Final proof that O'Boyle was lying when he told us he had never been to the island.'

'Do we know the date when the photo was taken?' asked George.

'Yes, Tuesday, 30th June last year. And that ties in with de Gaulle's assertion that Lemont contacted him from the island on 1st July, when Lemont told him he was about to go to Belfast.

'DC Kilip checked the names on that flight and there were three unaccompanied men: O'Hanlon, Brady and Murphy,' added the Super.

'You could hardly have more common Irish names.'

'He then went back to the Aer Lingus passenger lists to see when these three men left the island. And guess what?'

'What?'

'The man calling himself O'Hanlon had bought a single ticket. The other two returned to Dublin the following week.'

'So how did O'Hanlon get off the island?'

'He must have used the Steam Packet, and they sail to Belfast on Thursdays. Unfortunately, they don't keep a record of names – only the numbers of passengers on each sailing.'

'He could have returned on one of the Dublin sailings,' cautioned Bob, 'but I'm betting on O'Hanlon being our man going to Belfast with Lemont. Nonetheless, we ought to check before jumping to conclusions. We need to know where he stayed. Organise O'Hanlon's photo to be copied and circulated. Possible lodgings where he could have stayed must be checked, and for how long.'

'All the boarding houses are open in the summer. There could be over 300 to inspect,' warned George.

'The Tourist Board will give you a list of approved lodgings. Get sufficient copies of that photo made and get them handed out. We've got seventy PCs on the ground. It shouldn't take too long.'

★

'I'm satisfied we've tried everywhere,' said George to his boss on Thursday.

'O'Hanlon disappeared after he arrived. He didn't stay at any of the approved addresses we were given by the Tourist Board.'

The Super sighed. 'My wife tells me I'm daft at times. I'm beginning to think I'm stupid too. I'll bet he stayed with Lemont.'

'I could ask Mrs Craine. She's not on the phone. I could get to Ballaugh and back in little over an hour. Shall I go now?'

'Yes, there's no time like the present.'

★

'Sir? It's George. I'm ringing from the Raven.'

'I didn't send you to Ballaugh to have a pub lunch.'

George knew the Super's sense of humour, smiled to himself, and ignored the rib. 'Mrs Craine recognised O'Hanlon straight away. According to her, he stayed with Lemont for two nights and they went away together on the first Thursday of July. She didn't know where they went, but Lemont returned alone a week later with his dirty washing.'

'Does she know whether they left the island by air or by boat?'

'She doesn't even know if they left the island.'

'How does she remember it was a Thursday?'

'Thursday is market day in Ramsey. She always goes to do her weekly shopping and meets an old friend for lunch.'

The Super looked at his desk diary. At the front, there was a small calendar for 1959. 'That Thursday was the 2nd July. Is there any way we can confirm if Lemont and O'Boyle were on the Belfast sailing?'

'I shouldn't think so.'

'I'm getting a gut feeling that we could have been barking up the wrong tree. You'll remember O'Boyle telling us Lemont may have been involved in smuggling arms to the IRA. I'm wondering if Lemont and O'Boyle are working together. O'Boyle's ploy of painting a black picture of Lemont was simply trying to put us off the scent.'

'If they are both involved with selling arms to the IRA, then we're getting out of our depth.'

'No, I'm thinking the other way around. Lemont is helping O'Boyle uncover IRA gunrunning. De Gaulle told me Lemont had a theory that both the FLN and the IRA were getting arms from the Israelis. Instead of exporting their own Uzi submachine guns, which would be too risky, the Israelis source the weapons from Yugoslavia. Both Lemont and O'Boyle are investigating the same source of illegal arms. It may be worth me having a word with the Royal Ulster Constabulary. I became good pals with a guy called Jeff Young from the RUC when I was on the senior course at the Police College last year. He's now an Assistant Chief Constable. He may be able to help.'

★

That afternoon, Dolly put the Super through to the RUC HQ in Belfast.

'Jeff, it's Bob Kinley in Douglas.'

'Bob, how are you?'

'Keeping well. When are you coming over to see us? You mentioned you wanted to see the TT.'

'Bob, I'm busier than ever. Dissident Republicans are making more trouble in the border areas. We lost two officers earlier this year, which makes seven officers in the last four years. There's a lot of trouble bubbling up in the countryside. Anyway, how can I help?'

'I'm wondering if you can assist me with a murder investigation.'

'Go on.'

The Super then began outlining the story of the body being washed ashore, the letters that steered them to the identity of Lemont and the lead to O'Boyle.

'Stop there, Bob!'

'What's the matter?' asked the Super.

'Do you know who O'Boyle is?'

'Yes, I've met him. Why?'

'Then you know he's the Head of Eire's Security Service, G1. I have to be careful over the phone. I think we need to meet if I am to help. Can you come to Belfast so we can have a secure confab?'

'Can I bring my DS?'

'Is he PV-cleared?'

'Yes. What about next Monday? There's a flight that arrives at Aldergrove at 0930 hours. We could get the last flight back at 1730.'

'Good – I'll meet you there.'

CHAPTER 25

Monday, 16th May 1960

Jeff met Bob and George in the airport's arrivals hall. Minutes later, a police car was whisking them away from the airport towards the Police HQ in Belfast.

When they arrived at Knock Barracks, both Manxmen noticed that not only did all RUC officers carry side arms, but the station entrance was guarded with men carrying semi-automatic carbines. The ten-foot-high wired perimeter was topped with razor wire. The main building seemed to have an excess of radio aerials of all shapes and sizes on its roof.

Jeff showed them to a minimally furnished room with a table and four chairs. Coffee and assorted biscuits had been provided. 'This room is caged with wire mesh,' explained Jeff after introducing his sergeant, who was to take notes. 'I apologise for it being so spartan, but the mesh prevents electronic eavesdropping from outside. The minutes of the meeting will be classified secret. When you mentioned O'Boyle, Bob, I had to stop you going any further on an insecure line. Let me explain why.

'What you probably don't know is that O'Boyle's appointment was political. When Fianna Fáil won the March 1957 Irish Election from Fianna Gael, de Valera became the Taoiseach. One of Fianna Fáil's aims, written into its constitution, stipulates the unification of all Ireland. Sinn Féin won four seats and agreed to support de Valera providing…'

Jeff paused, thinking how to continue.

'Eighteen months later, de Valera pressured the Head of G1, Tommy Cosgrave – an honest, honourable man from a well-known Fine Gael family to take early retirement. That November, de Valera replaced Cosgrave with O'Boyle – a Fianna Fáil man.

'The security situation began to deteriorate after de Valera's victory. The IRA started a campaign to create trouble in the border areas, thinking they were on a roll. They steered clear of making trouble in Belfast, fearing reprisals against the Catholic population by the Protestant paramilitaries. However, to their surprise, Sinn Féin did badly in the UK General Election last October. Since then, the IRA's operations have been losing some momentum as they realise the unpopularity of what they had been doing.

'Nonetheless, we have lost seven good men during this period. Consequently, we have stepped up security. We now use remote cameras, X-ray machines and infra-red devices to supplement security at the border posts. In known infiltration routes, patrols have been increased and remote automatic cameras installed. We can't cover everywhere of course. There are several farms on the border that have fields in both Eire and Ulster, but we try. This morning, you will have been photographed coming off the plane. There is a rumour floating around that we are soon to detain suspected terrorists, both Unionists and Republicans, without trial. Prisons called "H" blocks are being built, as we speak. They will house up to 500 of the buggers. I would have thought it was illegal, but nothing surprises me anymore.

'Now you're probably wondering where all this is leading. Last July, O'Boyle was photographed coming off the *Lady of Man* from Douglas with someone we didn't know. Is this the man you call Lemont?'

The RUC Deputy Commissioner showed the two Manxmen a photo.

Both officers nodded affirmatively.

'Can I have a copy of the photo?' asked Bob.

'Of course,' replied Jeff.

'Someone met them and they were quickly whisked away by car. Our constable at the docks didn't recognise O'Boyle. It wasn't until a day later that our specialist team identified him, but by then we'd hit lucky.

'Their car was caught in a speed trap by our traffic division as it passed through Dungiven on the A6 towards Londonderry. The car was stopped and the driver had to produce his driving licence. He was warned he would receive a £40 fine. His name is Seamus McNeil and we know him to be a low-life who is often in trouble – drunk and disorderly, that sort of thing. The officer recalled the occasion as he had come across McNeil before. When shown the photo of O'Boyle later, the traffic sergeant confirmed it was O'Boyle in the back of the car. I now know the third man was Lemont.

'The question arises, why were they going to Londonderry? But first of all, Bob, tell me why you are interested in O'Boyle.'

'We thought the body washed ashore at Douglas last November was someone called Peter Lemont, although now we're pretty sure it was someone else. The body had been in the water for about two months, and his facial features were disfigured where it had scraped against rocks. We created an artist's impression of his face, and after an appeal in the local newspapers, Lemont's housekeeper came forward. A search of his property revealed documents in which he named me as the only person he could trust to investigate his death. His letters claimed I was his cousin. His father was my uncle – an uncle I never knew I had. His papers told me to contact two people – O'Boyle and a Colonel Paillole in France's DGSE. George and I have interviewed both of them. They painted a black picture

179

of Lemont that neither of us swallowed. They claimed they knew Lemont in Syria during and after the war. Paillole asserted Lemont was a gunrunner – selling arms to both the Arabs and the Zionists who were at each other's throats.'

'What makes you think they were lying about Lemont?'

'In Lemont's garage, we found a hidden specialist Dotteling safe. When we finally opened it, there was a metal case containing a decorated wooden block. X-rays at low temperatures showed the block was not solid, but a box. Eventually, we found how it could be opened, and inside was a portrait that could be priceless. We believe it is the only picture of the Prophet Mohammed and is over 1,300 years old. Have you ever heard of Abdullah Quilliam?'

'No.'

'He opened the first British mosque in Liverpool in 1889. A sheikh of Islam, he was entrusted to look after the portrait in 1924 by the last of the Ottoman Caliphs, Mehmed VI. Mehmed's son, Ertrugel Effendi, was present when the portrait was handed over to Quilliam for safe keeping.

'Ertrugel became the Vichy Governor of Syria in 1940 when Lemont was the embassy's security officer, but secretly working undercover for de Gaulle. Lemont befriended Ertrugel and learnt about the portrait and its significance. Thirty-five years after Quilliam had hidden the portrait, Lemont worked out where it was. Needless to say, if sold to the right people, it could make millions.

'When I met de Gaulle last month, he told me Lemont had been investigating how the Algerian terrorists, the FLN, are supplied with arms from Yugoslavia via Israel. Lemont had told de Gaulle that the IRA is also supplied by the same route.'

Bob paused.

'I've never heard of Paillole,' began Jeff, 'but I understand your doubts about O'Boyle. Over the years, we've developed a small network of covert officers inside the IRA. Our problem is we can't always trust our own men. The RUC is supposed to have thirty per cent of its manpower Catholic. However, recruiting is difficult and, as of today, only eighteen per cent of our officers are Catholics. There's no way a Protestant could infiltrate the Republican Army, so we have to rely on those Catholics who are prepared to risk not being given away by our men, or even by their own family. It's all very well for the official line being that the Unionist-Republican divide has nothing to do with religion, but I'm afraid it has.

'O'Boyle has come up on our radar several times. It may be that he has some G1 agents inside the IRA and is playing it straight, but he seems to spend a disproportionate amount of time in Londonderry – this is the third time we know he's been there in the last two years. I wonder if O'Boyle is a clandestine Sinn Féinist and is using Lemont to divert arms from the FLN to the IRA.'

Jeff's pause allowed the Super to intervene.

'That's interesting, but after talking to de Gaulle, I would like to think the opposite. Maybe O'Boyle and Lemont are actually working together to investigate why the Israelis are supplying both the IRA and the FLN. Why is Mossad making trouble for the UK and France? O'Boyle slagging off Lemont's integrity only makes sense if he was trying to put George and me off the scent. I think Lemont is alive, but until he reports to de Gaulle, we can't be sure about what is going on.'

'So Lemont has carte blanche from de Gaulle to do whatever he wants, wherever he wants?' asked Jeff.

'De Gaulle has a small worldwide network of agents that are independent of France's DGSE and report directly to him. They use a system of questions to confirm their identity when contacting him.'

'We use a similar system when our undercover operatives contact us in the field. We ask questions randomly from their personal file. Consequently, there are dozens or more questions we can ask if we have any doubts about their bona fide. The questions are not obvious either and have to be answered in a precise manner. Extracting the correct responses to all the possible questions is impossible. If de Gaulle is certain Lemont is alive, then your cadaver is definitely someone else.'

George had said very little to this point. 'Earlier, you said you understood why we had doubts about O'Boyle. Why was that?'

'So much of our work is experience, George. Call it a gut feeling, if you like. I have met O'Boyle twice. We exchange information regularly with the Garda in the south. At neither meeting has he admitted coming to Northern Ireland. Yet we know he has. Why keep that secret from us, if he is above board?'

'So you think he is playing the field both ways?' asked George.

'Until he makes a mistake, we'll never know,' replied the RUC officer.

'Then where the hell do we go from here?' asked the Super.

'It's your case, Bob. My advice would be to see if Lemont has been in touch with de Gaulle since you met him. Also, get a second autopsy. Meanwhile, I'll let you know if I find anything more on O'Boyle. My bet is Paillole masterminds Mossad supplying the arms, with O'Boyle's support.'

The meeting petered out and, after lunch in the police canteen, Bob and George caught an early afternoon flight back to Ronaldsway.

CHAPTER 26

The following morning, the Super had been in his office less than half an hour when his phone rang.

'Bob? It's Norman. I had a telegram from Jaques in Colombey yesterday morning. It came as I was about to leave for school, but it was too late to reach you – your secretary said you'd left for Belfast. Lemont contacted de Gaulle last Friday from Algeria. During their conversation, de Gaulle told Lemont he had met you at Colombey. Lemont was unaware you were investigating his supposed death. The telegram said Lemont will contact you in the next few days.'

'Thanks for that, Norman. Since France, we've discovered more about the Seal and how it was hidden by Quilliam. We're making progress.'

*

An hour had passed when the station sergeant knocked on the Super's door. 'Sir, there's a gentleman downstairs wishing to see you. He wouldn't give me his name. Shall I bring him up?'

'Did he say what he wanted?'

'No, except to tell you he plays the Blackmar-Diemer Gambit.'

The Super instantly shot up from his chair and awkwardly knocked it backwards; it fell over noisily. He fumbled to pick it up.

'Are you all right, sir? You look as if you've seen a ghost.'

The Super coughed to clear his throat. 'I'm fine, thanks. Please bring Mr Lemont up.'

Moments later, a man of his own height and build stood in front of the Super. There was a similarity to one of the Super's younger brothers – dark eyes, a firm, bristled chin and black hair.

'Hello, cousin,' the stranger said with a broad smile as he offered his hand.

Still flummoxed, the Super remained frozen behind his desk for a second or two before regaining his composure. He moved around his desk and they shook hands.

'From your reaction, I gather you weren't expecting me.'

Initially, the Super had seen the family resemblance. Now he was noticing other features such as a straight, long nose, high cheek bones and tanned skin. A picture flashed through his mind of his opponent at the chess board eight years previously. *Yes, this is the guy I played at Ramsey.*

'So, you're Peter Lemont,' the Super remarked.

'That's right, and I gather from General de Gaulle you thought I was dead. That's why I left Algeria yesterday and flew here to explain what's going on.'

'You've come from Algeria in a day?'

'An Air France Caravelle to Paris and a second to Heathrow. An overnight stop in London and a BEA Viscount to the island this morning – all in less than twenty-four hours. Wonderful what can be done these days.'

By now the Super's self-possession and usual *sang-froid* had returned. 'There is a lot of explaining to do,' he began, 'and I'm not sure where we should start.'

'I think the onus on explanations is mine. Can I call you Bob?'

184

'Yes, please do. However, before we start, I think it appropriate if the Chief Constable and my DS, George Turnbull, also listen to what you have to say.'

The Super asked Dolly to fetch the CC and George. While waiting, Lemont briefly explained that he couldn't stay long on the island. 'Things are moving fast in Algeria,' he said. 'The OAS, the *Organisation Armée Secrète*, a right-wing terrorist group, is receiving funds indirectly from Mossad through an American intermediary company called Permidex to pay for an assassination attempt on de Gaulle. You'll appreciate the importance of keeping my ear to the ground out there?'

'Of course.'

When the Chief and George arrived, Bob made the introductions.

'I've had no chance to contact Mrs Craine, but if I know her, Ravenswood will be ready for me anyway. We could go there if you don't want to be disturbed.'

'That's OK. We will use our conference room,' replied the Chief Constable.

The four men settled behind the room's round table and Dolly was asked to purchase sandwiches for a working lunch. 'Bring them in, and then we are not to be interrupted for the rest of the day,' the CC instructed.

'Perhaps I should begin?' the Super asked his boss.

A nod of approval, and the Deputy began.

'Last November, a man's body was washed ashore at Douglas. His face was unrecognisable as a result of hitting rocks. We believed his body had been in the sea for about two months. We asked a local artist to draw a picture of what she considered the man may have looked like. After publishing it in the local newspapers, your housekeeper contacted us. She thought it could be you.

'We searched your home and found two passports. Mrs Craine and your solicitor confirmed the passport photos looked like you. Subsequently, we found the correspondence you had written in case of your death...'

'Can I stop you there? As you probably gathered from General de Gaulle, I work undercover in a small team. My life is nomadic, although mostly spent in North Africa. I decided eight or nine years ago to make Ballaugh my bolthole. I wanted somewhere safe to keep documents pertaining to my work and had the Chubb installed in the library. I had the Dotteling installed in the garage after I found the Caliph's Great Seal. At that point, I decided if I disappeared permanently, and it's a risk I take in this job, then I could trust you to investigate. Hence why I left clues that only you could untangle, such as our Blackmar Gambit game.'

'How did you find out about the Seal?' asked the Super.

'I worked undercover for the Free French during the war. After the Vichy Syrian Government was defeated in 1941, I gathered evidence against those officers who remained pro-Nazi. At the end of the war, my files were used to convict many of the hard-line Vichyites. Most were executed.

'Days after Germany surrendered, de Gaulle called me to Paris to discuss my report on Ertrugel. During Ertrugel's four years under house arrest in Acre, I had visited him regularly. He trusted me, believing I was pro-Nazi and I had built a strong case against him. De Gaulle, having read my report, explained that the execution of the rightful Caliph could backfire on France's ambition to retain control of Syria. Consequently, I redrafted the accounts of Ertrugel's involvement in the Vichy Government. I made great play that he had been a victim of circumstance.

'On my last visit to see Ertrugel, while playing our usual game of chess, I told him I had watered down his involvement with the Nazis and that he might only receive a suspended sentence. Overjoyed that he would escape the rope, Ertrugel told me about the Caliph's Great Seal and its code. He explained the Seal had been given to someone called Henry Leon for safe keeping. I forgot about the story and never thought any more about it. Then a year last March two things occurred by accident.

'It was a beautiful spring day and I decided to go for a walk up Ballaugh Glen. I remembered my father's first wife, Ann Cregeen, came from Glen Dhoo and decided to go and find the derelict village. I asked Mrs Craine where it was, and she admitted she'd never been but told me to turn right at a track opposite the Ravensdale Hotel.

'About an hour later, I was wandering around the ruins and thinking it would be an ideal place to hide something. The thought triggered the story told to me by Ertrugel about the Seal and the impossibility of someone hiding an object that could never be found except by a knowledgeable, determined investigator.

'Funnily enough, there was an old boy with a trowel digging inside one of the delapidated cottages. He stopped scratching the earth and introduced himself as Denis Thompson.

'"I'm an amateur archaeologist and writing a book about Glen Dhoo," he explained.

'I joked, "I thought you were digging for gold."

'"Broken pottery is about the limit, so far," he replied, laughing.

'We stood chatting and he told me he was a history teacher at King William's College. I always have to be careful when socialising so as not to give away my background. However, I told him that my father had married a girl born in Glen Dhoo and he pricked his ears up. "Is your name Kinley?" he asked.

'I was amazed that he knew about my dad and Ann. I told him my father eventually changed his name to Lemont. I said my farewells and left him to continue looking for fragments in the ruins. As I left, he remarked, "If you ever want to know anything about Manx history, I'm your man. You can contact me at the college."

'I decided to do some research about Henry Leon. The only clue I had was that Leon must have been an important Muslim.

After all, Mehmed would hardly have asked him to travel to Italy from England if he wasn't someone special. There are no mosques on the island, so I chose to go to Liverpool. There, and at Woking the next day, I discovered Henry Leon's real name was Abdullah Quilliam and he had been educated at King William's. At Woking, the Imam seemed pretty sure Quilliam returned from San Remo with the Seal and took it with him to the island a little later. I made contact with Mr Thompson when I returned and was told Quilliam regularly holidayed in Onchan and often went on walks lasting days. Initially, I spent a couple of weeks walking the island's footpaths and trails looking for a likely burial site, but to no avail.

'All the time, I was thinking what sort of a clue Quilliam could have left to help someone find the Seal. Eventually, the penny dropped – it had to be in a grave marked *Quilliam*. I decided he must have hidden the Seal in either a grave marked *William Henry Quilliam* or in his ancestor's burial place – Captain Quilliam's grave at Arbory. I searched there and found it. I had the Dotteling built in my garage and removed the Seal from Quilliam's grave when the Dotteling's concrete was set. I marked the Seal's combination in Diemer's book on the Blackmar Gambit, knowing it was the one book you would search more diligently than the others.'

He paused, smiling at his cousin.

'One of the reasons we thought you were the drowned man is that he had a scar on his left shoulder,' said Bob. 'Your notes said you were similarly shot.'

Lemont shrugged his shoulders. 'I can't explain that, except to say my scar is here,' he paused to point to the left side of his torso, 'under my armpit where I had a flesh wound.'

'OK, but why did you tell us to contact O'Boyle and Paillole?'

'I was coming to them. I came across O'Boyle by accident in Algeria during the summer of 1958, two years ago. O'Boyle introduced himself and reminded me that we had met briefly in Damascus in 1949 after the war, but I didn't remember him.

'A few months earlier, in February, Syria and Egypt had joined to become the United Arab Republic. Everything was going Nasser's way after Suez; even the creation of CENTO didn't deter his ambition to build a gigantic socialist Arab state. The UAR was the first step. When O'Boyle and I met, it was a few days after General Qassim's *coup d'état* had overthrown the Iraqi Royal family. It was believed Qassim intended Iraq to join the UAR as well.

'Consequently, CENTO, better known as The Baghdad Pact, moved its headquarters to Ankara.

'Algerian independence was also rearing its ugly head, and the French didn't know what to do. The Fourth French Republic fell that October, and de Gaulle created the Fifth Republic, with himself as President.

'As you can imagine, Israel began to panic at the possibility of being surrounded by a pro-Soviet Arab Confederation. The Jewish banks in America put enormous pressure on Eisenhower's Government to stop what Ben Gurion was calling the potential Arab Holocaust. Consequently, the US gave Israel secret nuclear plans that would allow them to begin building an atomic plant in the Negev Desert. They will have an atom bomb within five years.

'Now, to get back to O'Boyle. He was still in Ireland's G2 service when he introduced himself. He believed there was gunrunning from Yugoslavia to the IRA, funded by Mossad, using fishing trawlers sailing under Spanish flags from Ceuta. I had been gathering similar evidence that the FLN, with Israeli financial support, had been getting Soviet arms. We decided to pool our resources—'

George interrupted.

'So what you're saying is that you and O'Boyle are on the same side?'

'Yes, of course. Why should you think otherwise?'

'He painted a picture of you that wasn't exactly complimentary.'

'He was trying to mislead you. The fewer people who know about what we do the better.'

The Super picked up the thread. 'Look, Peter… yesterday, George and I were in Belfast and we were shown a photo of you and O'Boyle getting off the Steam Packet's *Lady of Man* after he stayed with you last July.'

'Taken by the RUC?'

'Yes.'

'As you can imagine, the situation for both of us is very delicate. Tom is only too aware his appointment as Head of G1 had political overtones, but I'm convinced he's determined to smoke out the IRA. Although the IRA's administrative HQ is in Athlone, the strongest IRA Brigade by far is in Londonderry and that is where he's concentrating his efforts. O'Boyle wanted to show me what he has achieved by getting me to meet one of his undercover agents.

'After getting stopped for speeding near Dungiven, we met his contact in a small village called Claudy. He told us the IRA is getting Semtex and Soviet automatic rifles and planning attacks on the mainland within the next few years. I have since reported this to de Gaulle who, I believe, has warned Harold Macmillan.'

'Why can't O'Boyle warn us himself?'

'He's afraid that if he goes through the usual channels then it could expose his own undercover operatives. There are some extreme republicans inside the Fianna Fáil Government. And, anyway, MI5 might not trust him any more than the RUC.

'However, a direct warning from de Gaulle will be taken seriously. This brings me to Paillole.

'To run the French mandates of Syria and Lebanon required a large administrative staff – over 5,000 personnel altogether, split roughly in the ratio of four to one between Damascus and Beirut. About eighty per cent, mostly in lower grades, were locally recruited – Arabs in Syria, but nearly 50 percent in Lebanon were

Christians. I had been appointed the Syrian Mandate's security officer in 1936.

'In June 1940, after the fall of France, we all had to take an oath of allegiance to the Vichy regime. Over three quarters of us feigned becoming pro-Vichy. But after the defeat of the Vichy Army in the summer of 1941, we happily reverted to de Gaulle's Free French. The problem was that the occupying troops controlling Syria and Lebanon were predominately Indian and Australian. Fewer than two thousand troops were Free French and, therefore, security on the ground remained firmly in the hands of the British. Rumours began to spread that the unification of the Arab States into one large country ruled by King Abdullah of Jordan could become a reality.

'Paillole had arrived soon after the fall of Vichy Syria and became the senior intelligence officer with the same grade as myself. I never got to the bottom of his background. He told me, on one occasion, he had worked undercover for de Gaulle in Marseilles, but I wasn't convinced. Initially, our relationship worked reasonably well, despite the boundary between intelligence and security being fuzzy; it's easy to step on each other's toes.

'By 1943, the number of Jews in Palestine was approaching half a million – getting on for a fifth of the population. Panicking, the British began to increase restrictions on Jewish immigration. Simultaneously, Zionist terrorism increased dramatically, and I noticed Paillole's visits to Lebanon became ever more frequent. My suspicions aroused, I gradually became convinced he had a private agenda: he was helping a group of Zionist extremists known as the Stern Gang.

'Among the Syrian Arabs, there was a split. Fifty per cent wanted a new pan-Arabian empire that had been their dream since World War One, while the other half wished to keep Syria separate from Jordan and Iraq. I was sure Paillole was inciting a cabal known as the *Bureau Noir* that had the support of senior

Syrian civil servants and local politicians in the administration. The *Bureau Noir* was spreading the rumour that the British planned to unite the four countries of Lebanon, Syria, Jordan and Iraq. It was striking fear into the Zionists as well as those Arabs wishing to retain the separate countries.

'De Gaulle was determined to keep Syria and Lebanon as French colonies, but it put me in an awkward position. I was working undercover for de Gaulle, who felt the Syrians were a long way from being ready for full independence, but on the other hand I'd seen how successful Iraq had become when given independence in 1932 under King Faisal.

'By 1944, I decided that Paillole's habit of disappearing, which had been worrying me, needed investigating.

'I set two of my staff the task of following Paillole. They followed him to Beirut, but on two occasions, a month apart, they lost him.

'Realising he was being followed, Paillole had given my men the slip. What he'd been up to, I'd no idea.

'I decided to let him have a couple of trips without a tail. I hoped this might make him careless. My two men roped in their teenage sons to help them. It's well known that when being followed, people don't suspect youngsters playing in the streets. However, the plan was disastrous – all four disappeared. Their bodies were never found.

'There was only one explanation. Paillole was encouraging the Zionists to make trouble in Palestine by supplying them with information and arms. By stirring the *Bureau Noir*, he was making the situation much, much worse – playing both sides off against each other. To this day, I'm convinced the Stern Gang – the forerunner of Mossad – killed my men.

'I believe Paillole was passing information to the Zionists about weak points in Britain's defences in Palestine, hoping this would divert British troops back to Palestine and away from Syria. Whether this was with the direct approval of de Gaulle, I don't know...'

He hesitated.

'I've thought about it many times, and I'm still unsure if de Gaulle knew anything about the *Bureau Noir* or Paillole's role.'

The Super said nothing, but his mind was in overdrive. He remembered de Gaulle telling him that he had appointed Paillole because he had Jewish connections. Paillole's task had been to watch for possible attempts by Zionists to annex southern Lebanon to become part of Israel. He wondered if Lemont knew of Paillole's *raison d'être*.

'Conversely, the British allowed Arab terrorists to attack us in Syria and afterwards give them a safe haven in Transjordan. By creating trouble for us – bombing post offices, that sort of thing, the Arabs terrorists thought they might gain independence quicker. It had started as far back as the late twenties. One such attack in 1935 led to my father being seriously injured and later dying from his wounds.'

Lemont took a break for a moment as he reflected on his father. The three policemen knew that sympathetic silence was best.

'It really was a tit-for-tat situation; ridiculous really, as the attacks became ever more serious. I suspect Paillole's information helped plan the bombing of the King David Hotel, where ninety-odd British civilians were killed. He may have had a hand in the assassination of Lord Moyne. I believe Paillole still works for Israel and is a Mossad plant inside our DGSE.'

Why hasn't de Gaulle told Lemont about Paillole? Doesn't de Gaulle fully trust him, after all? thought Bob.

'The post-war years in Syria were very difficult for France. The UN, particularly the US, was pressing France to relinquish control. After the war, de Gaulle asked me to work on his personal staff. I returned to Paris in 1949, glad to be getting out of the mess.'

'Did you ever mention your suspicions about Paillole to de Gaulle?' asked the Super.

'Several times; on each occasion he smiled at me and touched his long nose with his forefinger. I concluded that he uses Paillole as a double agent and feeds him with false information.'

The Super nodded, thinking, *what a world we live in.*

'O'Boyle came to the same conclusion about Paillole, but by a different route. After O'Boyle arrived in Syria, he became well acquainted with Paillole. Theoretically, Syria was, by then, an independent country. But frankly we had left it in chaos. In 1949 alone, Syria had three different governments.

'Little by little, O'Boyle began to realise Paillole was fermenting unrest. The State of Israel had been formed in 1948, and it did not want to see a strong Arab state on its northern border. As each successive Syrian Government fell, it became clear that the Syrian opposition parties were supplied arms from Israel. O'Boyle believes Paillole was in the thick of it. After all, Ben Gurion was Israel's Prime Minister and had known Paillole since the Stern Gang years.'

'Peter,' asked the Super, 'you still haven't answered our question. Why did you hint that both O'Boyle and Paillole could in some way be involved with your death?'

'In what way?'

'Let me show you the file.'

The Super picked up a file. 'It says here… *you should contact Agent Tom O'Boyle of the Irish G2 when you have finished reading my file. He may put you in the direction of Colonel Paul Paillole of France's DGSE (their Military Intelligence). You will then have to decide what to do.*

'You describe O'Boyle as being in G2, but when you wrote those notes — presumably last year — O'Boyle had moved to be Head of G1.'

Unless you wrote that letter earlier, thought the Super.

'You're quite right. *Mea culpa*, a slip of the pen. I had agreed with O'Boyle that in the case of my sudden demise, a roadmap should be drawn for you. I wanted you to find the Caliph's Great

Seal and keep it safe. It must not fall into the hands of the Israelis. I believe the majority of Jews in Israel want to live in peace with their Arab neighbours, but there is a considerable hard core of extreme right-wing Jews who would stop at nothing to get the Seal. If shown to the world's press and insulted in some way, then God help us all. Israel's atomic weapons wouldn't stop the Islamic world making the second Holocaust worse than the first. O'Boyle agreed to help with the plan.'

'By throwing us off the scent?'

'Yes, he had to cover his own tracks at the same time.'

'So if Mossad did find out about the Great Seal, how would they know you had it?' asked the Super.

'Mossad is actively encouraging the Algerian rebels against the French as we speak. They are supplying arms, training them and suggesting targets; even financing an assassination attempt against de Gaulle. By de Gaulle feeding Paillole with false information, however, the FLN frequently find us waiting for them when they attack what they think is a susceptible target.

'Paillole is no fool and will have told Mossad I have the Seal. The unknown cadaver washed up at Douglas has accidentally ignited a premature sequence of events.'

'You haven't answered Bob's question,' observed the Chief Constable.

'I don't wish to be unkind, but when did you meet Paillole?' asked Lemont.

'About three months ago,' replied the Deputy.

'And you showed him the Great Seal?'

There was an embarrassed silence.

'Exactly,' continued Lemont. 'I'm sure it was done in all innocence, but you gave the secret away to the Israelis.'

The silence was broken when there was a knock on the door.

CHAPTER 27

'I thought I said we're not to be interrupted,' shouted the Chief Constable at the door.

The door partially opened and the pale face of Dolly peered round. Nervously, she whispered, 'Mrs Craine has just rung. There's been a break-in at Mr Lemont's house in Ballaugh.'

The four men looked up.

The first to react was the Super. 'When?' he asked.

'She didn't say but I thought you'd want to know at once.'

By now all were on their feet.

'Of course, Dolly,' assured the CC in an apologetic voice. 'You did the right thing telling us.'

The four men looked at each other.

'We should go to Ballaugh straight away,' said the Super.

★

The Super and George dropped Peter off to allow him to follow them in his hire car. Thirty minutes after leaving Douglas Police Station, the two officers were pulling up at Ravenswood.

Mrs Craine greeted them. 'Wipe your feet,' she ordered. 'I've just washed the hall floor.'

The two policemen looked at each other and smiled but said nothing. She led them into the library. Nothing seemed to be out of place.

'Has anything been taken?' asked George.

'No. I don't think so. I've had a thorough look around, but I've not been out to the garage.'

'Is there any evidence of a break-in: a broken window, a door being forced?'

'No, nothing.'

'Then how do you know there has been a break-in?' asked George.

'There's a distinct smell of eau de Cologne,' she replied.

'I can't smell anything,' replied the DS.

'That's because you're a smoker,' she admonished.

The Super, a non-smoker, smiled and politely asked, 'When did you first notice the smell?'

'This morning. I never noticed it when I was last in – two days ago.'

'When did you arrive this morning?' asked George.

'Just over an hour ago.'

'So the break-in must have occurred in the last few days,' mumbled George.

The Super looked at George. 'Mrs Craine is right. I can smell the perfume too, now that she's drawn my attention to it. It's men's aftershave.'

'I've never tried the stuff.'

'Nor have I, but it's becoming more common and is prevalent in France. I noticed it when I was in Paris – most of the men seemed to use it.'

'They'll be using anti-perspirant next,' joked George.

'They already are.'

'When you two have finished, what are you going to do about it?' asked Mrs Craine.

'Yes, what are you going to do about it?' asked Peter.

The two policemen swung round. Peter Lemont had arrived.

Not waiting for a reply, Lemont gave his charlady a hug and after the usual greetings, asked her if she could go and make them a pot of tea.

'I think George is wrong,' began the Super. 'These smells tend to die away rapidly, which suggests the break-in was recent. I think someone has been here this morning before Mrs Craine came to work.'

George looked at Peter. 'We're dealing with a pro. My hunch is you were followed to the island. It's too much of a coincidence that this has happened now.'

'I disagree,' replied Peter. 'You forget I'm a professional too. No one could have followed me without my knowing. I know detectives are trained to ask, "Why now?", but coincidences do happen. Whoever entered my house this morning was looking for some clue to the whereabouts of the Great Seal.'

He stopped to look at the Super. 'I assume you have it under lock and key in Douglas Police Station?'

The Super didn't reply but placed a forefinger to his lips and moved towards an expensive, stand-alone, walnut radiogram near the window. He switched it on. The others watched, wondering what he was up to.

After a few seconds, the valves had warmed up and orchestral music filled the room. The BBC Third Programme was playing the final movement of *Mendelssohn's Italian Symphony*. The Super turned up the volume.

'Ah,' he remarked, smiling, 'I heard this on *Desert Island Discs* a few weeks ago.

'Whoever broke into your house would not have expected to find the Caliph's Seal. After all, the only people who know about it are O'Boyle and Paillole. Assuming Paillole has informed Mossad, they would hardly come barging in here as they know we are holding the Seal in police custody. I suspect hidden microphones have been planted in the hope that something might be overheard that would give them the lead as to where we have put the Seal. Thanks to Mrs Craine's sharp nose, they now know they've been rumbled.'

The symphony was reaching its climax.

'The Head of the Telecommunications Division of the Post Office is an old school pal, Jimmy Shimmin. George, radio Douglas Station and get the station sergeant to ring Shimmin. Tell him to explain there are listening devices in the house, and I want Jimmy here urgently to find them.'

The Super turned to Peter. 'If Jimmy can estimate the bugs' range of transmission then we may be able to find out where the listener has been eavesdropping. Unfortunately, by now he will have flown the nest. With luck, Jimmy should be here within the hour. Meanwhile, we could start searching ourselves.'

'What makes you so sure there is anything?' asked Peter.

'I agree you couldn't have been followed from Algeria. Whoever has been in the house could have been snooping here for weeks. The question is, Peter, who knows about both the Seal and your address?'

'O'Boyle knows my address, but I would rule him out. That leaves Paillole and the Israelis. They have a worldwide system of sayanims, amateur Israeli sympathisers, whose eyes and ears are everywhere. Even here on the Isle of Man, I'll bet there are three or four. One of them, or all of them, could have been instructed to find my bolthole. It wouldn't take them long to go through the Government's register of property sales. One of them could even be a civil servant. Who knows?'

'I only know of a couple of Jewish families living on the island. But to answer your earlier question about the Seal's location, the short answer is no. It is no longer in the police station. Rest assured it is safe. I discussed with the Chief Constable where to hide it. We both agreed Douglas Police Station was too obvious and that I should find a suitable location. Consequently, only I know where it is located.'

'The fewer who know its location, the better, but you'd better tell me in case something happens,' replied Peter.

'I buried it on my own in front of the large tree...'

At that moment, Mrs Craine entered, carrying a tray with teapot and cups.

'Perfect timing; thank you, Winnie.' Peter smiled as he offered to take the tray.

After she had left the room, Peter remarked, 'Marvellous housekeeper. Don't know what I'd do without her.'

George returned.

'You were a while,' the Super said.

'I was having a smoke when Jimmy Shimmin came through on the car radio. He said he would leave Douglas right away with one of his technicians and should be here in forty minutes.'

The three finished their tea and began searching the library for any surveillance devices. 'If there is a bug anywhere it will probably be behind a book, either on one of the top or the bottom shelves,' Peter suggested. 'Books I use regularly I keep at shoulder height. Most people do, and our intruder would know that.'

★

When Jimmy Shimmin and his technician arrived, thirty-five minutes had passed, but nothing had been found.

'Good to see you again, Bob. This is Geoff Corrin, the brains of my outfit,' joked Jimmy as the two old pals shook hands.

After everyone had been introduced, Jimmy asked, 'The message I got was that you believe the house is bugged. Right?'

'I think it's a strong possibility, although we haven't found anything so far,' conceded the Super.

'OK, here's how it works. Geoff will go outside with his aerial and receiver. Meanwhile, we will go from room to room talking normally. In each room, Geoff's equipment will show if there is a transmission. If there is, he will tell us, and this delicate direction-finder in my hand will locate its position. We will then repeat the process throughout the house. OK?'

The three men nodded affirmatively.

'Good; let's get started.'

Within a minute, the library bug had been located – stuck under one of the drawers in the desk. Approximately the size of a packet of ten cigarettes, the black plastic case had no markings.

'Can you tell where it was made?' asked Peter.

'You'll see there isn't a maker's sign on it,' replied Jimmy. 'However, I'll bet my bottom dollar it was made in Japan. They're not only good at making reliable cars – my Datsun is incredible, it uses no oil – they're light years ahead of us when it comes to miniature electronics.'

Using a small screwdriver, he prised open the box, disarmed it, and asked, 'What room next?'

Within ten minutes, two identical gadgets had been found in the kitchen and the master bedroom. Fifteen minutes later, two more were discovered: both in the garage – one under the driver's seat of the Morris Minor. All were deactivated.

'What range have these things?' asked the Super.

'Geoff will give us a fairly accurate figure from the strength of the signals. Let's ask him.'

'The local geography is the major factor. The hills on both sides of the glen are quite high, so the bug's maximum range of about two miles will only be achieved towards the north, where the valley opens towards Ballaugh Beach. However, there's the complication of the RAF bombing range at Jurby Head.'

'What difference will that make?' asked the Super.

'Although the RAF radar's sweep is directed towards the sea, its secondary radiation will cause local interference. If I was trying to eavesdrop on this house, I would want to be no further away than Ballaugh Railway Station, on the far side of the main road.'

The Super turned to George. 'Use the car radio and call up Inspector Lowey in Ramsey. Tell him to send as many PCs as he can. I want a house-to-house immediately. Someone must have seen a stranger in the village, and a description might help Peter with possible identification.'

After Jimmy and Geoff had returned to Douglas, Peter and the two senior policemen resumed their discussions on the problem of the Caliph's Seal and the way forward.

'As you appreciate, Peter, we're a small force – fewer than one hundred men. The body washed ashore before Christmas has led us as far afield as Paris, Manchester, London, Dublin and Belfast. We've become entangled with the Metropolitan's Special Branch, MI5 and the secret services of Ireland and France.

'Now that we know the cadaver isn't you, where do we go from here? If Paillole is a double agent, it's nothing to do with us. If you are saying you believe Mossad is somehow involved in supplying arms to the IRA and the FLN, then again it's not our problem. If you believe the Seal should remain a secret and never see the light of day – fine. But if you want to return it to its rightful owner then please take it away.'

'The problem, Bob, is that there is no rightful owner, except possibly the King of Saudi Arabia.'

'The King is presumably the leader of the Sunnis?'

'He's about as near to a leader as you can get now that there isn't an official Caliph. He claims he is a descendent of Mohammed. Up to 1922, when Ataturk disbanded the Caliphate, the Seal was something of a mythical object. No one was sure if it actually existed; it had only ever been seen by successive Caliphs.'

'Do you think King Saud is aware of the Seal's existence?'

'I'm not sure.'

'Then, don't you think it's time to give the Seal to King Saud before we get swamped on the island with different groups fighting for it?'

'The problem is that Mehmed made Quilliam promise to keep it safe until such time as the two sects reconciled their differences.'

'That's all very well, but you have to be practical. I don't know that much about Islam, except what I've read recently in my *Encyclopaedia Britannica*. However, there is one occasion every year when the two sects appear to bury their differences and that's at the Hajj.'

'True.'

'Then why not approach King Saud and let him know that you are prepared to give him the Seal on condition that he swears to display the portrait every year at the Hajj for all to see?'

'A nice idea, but rather naïve. For a start, the Seal was never intended to be made public. Rather, it is a badge of office. Have you any idea how many layers of bureaucracy I would have to go through to meet the King? At each layer, I would have to explain about the Seal, and corruption in Saudi Arabia is rife. Widespread public knowledge of the Seal's existence would be potentially disastrous. Idiots would make copies; iconography would become rife. King Saud would have to be persuaded to keep the Seal secret.'

'Surely an approach by de Gaulle is possible? After all, it would present an opportunity for France to strengthen its relations with Saudi Arabia.'

'That might work. I would have to go and see de Gaulle personally at Colombey. My worry is that he may not agree. Then we'd be in the mire. He might demand I hand it over to him, and he would then plan to use it as a pawn in some sort of trade deal. Assuming the bugs were planted by Mossad, and as long as they don't know where the Seal is, then we're always going to have the problem of what to do with it.'

'So, what are we going to do?'

'My only contact in Saudi's intelligence directorate is a minor sheikh called Kamal Adamn. You can never tell whether the

Saudis are trustworthy or not. However, if he saw the possibility of internal promotion then he might be able to catch the ear of the King. It was King Saud who set up their intelligence agency, the Mabahith, five years ago, and Adamn heads up their telecommunications division. He knows I have been watching Mossad, and if I let him know that the Israelis are keen to get their hands on a relic that once belonged to Mohammed's daughter then he might play ball with us.'

'It's worth a try, but you'll have to convince de Gaulle first.'

'I think I can make de Gaulle see the sense in our plan.'

'Meanwhile, George can concentrate on our murdered cadaver. We have a few leads that will have to be checked out more carefully.'

There was a knock on the door and Mrs Craine entered. 'Inspector Lowey has just arrived. I told him you weren't to be disturbed, but he is most insistent.'

'Show him in, Mrs Craine,' replied Peter, 'and, perhaps, you could rustle up another pot of tea.'

Tommy Lowey entered and saluted his boss. 'It doesn't take long to do a house-to-house in Ballaugh,' he began, 'and my five constables have found no one who has seen a stranger in the village. However, there is an isolated, empty single-storey cottage down Station Road, about half a mile beyond the station. Apparently, the old girl who lived there died about three months ago. The locals tell me it was sold very quickly. Furthermore, the new owners had fresh locks fitted to its doors and, rather unusually, bars put over its windows. There is evidence that someone has recently been inside.'

'How do you know?' asked the Super.

'Peering through the kitchen window, you can see someone has left dirty cups lying around on the draining board. Someone left in a hurry.'

'Then there could be fingerprints and, possibly, tyre tracks of a car,' exclaimed George. 'I'll go and look.'

CHAPTER 28

Wednesday, 18th May 1960

Peter Lemont left the island, heading for Riyadh via Paris.
Having contacted Jaques de Yonne, de Gaulle agreed he would
meet Peter at Colombey.

George's team found fingerprints in the Ballaugh cottage that
had no match with their records. Copies of the prints were sent
to the Lancashire Police HQ at Preston to be searched urgently,
although George knew it could be several days before receiving a
result. The tyre tracks left in the mud outside the cottage were of
little use other than that their depth and width suggested a small
saloon such as a Morris Minor. The island's car hire companies
were approached to examine their cars that had been out on
rental. Their tyres were checked thoroughly – to no avail.

'It means, boss,' said George, 'that the car at the cottage must
have been local. That leaves us in a predicament. There must be
a home-grown accomplice, almost certainly a sayanim. Lemont
thought that of the three possible groups interested in the Seal
– the Saudis, the Iranians and the Israelis – only one of them
definitely knows about its location. It also happens to be the only
one capable of having a local agent, although I never dreamt we
had any sayanims on the island.'

'Nor did I,' replied the Super. 'There are so few Jews living here. My guess is that if there's a part-time Mossad agent on the island, the chances are he, or she, will be relatively young. The listening devices in Lemont's house were undoubtedly professional; they didn't get to the island on their own. I have asked the Chief to send photos of the devices to his contacts in MI5. They may be able to shed some light on whether they are the type used by Mossad.

'Ask the airport constable if he noticed anything unusual yesterday. Was someone dropped off in a hell of a hurry from a small car? Check the departures to see if anyone left sooner than their original booking. I've a feeling something has been overlooked.'

★

An hour later, George was at Ronaldsway talking to the airport policeman who had been on duty the previous day.

'Did something like that happen?' he asked the PC.

'Yes, definitely. I was standing outside when a young woman in her mid-twenties arrived in a grey Standard 10. She dropped a man off and began to follow him into the departure hall. I told her she couldn't leave the car at the front of the building as it was a bus stop. She grumbled when she had to drive to the car park.'

'Would you recognise her again?'

'She's not the sort of girl you forget quickly. If I was fifteen years younger…'

'Do you remember the registration of the car?'

'I wrote it down in my notebook.' He withdrew the small book from his breast pocket. 'It was TMN 913.'

'What time was this?'

'About one thirty.'

'The man who got out of the car. Would you recognise him again?'

'No. I had started to approach the woman driver and didn't take much notice of him. But he must have caught the Liverpool flight.'

'Why?'

'There's a lull in departures around midday, and that's the first flight out in the afternoon.'

George entered the airport and headed to the BEA desk. After showing his ID card, he explained what he wanted. The receptionist flicked through the flight records. 'Mr D F Smythe caught the 14.00 hours flight to Liverpool and had originally been booked for today's flight.'

George thanked her and returned to Douglas. His next task was to identify the young, apparently attractive, woman.

★

Having found the owner of the car at the Highway Board's offices, George reported back to the Super.

'The car is owned by Jack Speed. He and his wife run that little sweet shop at the top of Wellroad Hill.'

'I know it. They make much of their own confectionary. My son, when he was younger, used to be very fond of their candy mice that had string tails. I didn't know they were Jewish.'

'Mr and Mrs Speed are both in their fifties and have one daughter, Christina. From some enquiries, I have discovered she is a geography teacher at the Girls' High School. She got an upper second at London University in 1955. She must be our potential sayanim. Moreover, I checked if she was at school on Tuesday.'

'And?'

'She took a sickie.'

'That's no proof she's our man.'

'True,' the detective replied, 'but she holds a driving licence and the tyre marks found at Ballaugh are consistent with a Standard 10.'

'We're going to have to call her in,' said the Super. 'Pay her a visit this evening; ask her the usual questions and tell her we want her to help us with our enquiries.'

'And if she won't play ball?'

'Tell her she has a choice. The easy way: tomorrow, she pretends she's ill, or the hard way: we tell her headmistress the police need to interview her.'

★

The following morning, Christina arrived at the police station to be interviewed. The DS went through the evidence pointing to her involvement with setting up the listening equipment at Lemont's house, the use of the empty cottage, the tyre tracks from her father's car and how she had dropped off her accomplice at the airport when they realised their illegal eavesdropping had been found out.

'Furthermore,' added the DCC after George had finished, 'there are the coffee cups. We have taken fingerprints from them. If you wish, we will take yours to see if there is a match. What do you have to say?'

Although clearly distraught at being caught red-handed, she defended herself stoutly. 'I strongly believe in the right of the Jewish people to defend their State of Israel. I was recruited by Mossad in my final year at university. I was President of the London University's Jewish Society and Mossad learned I intended to come home to teach at my old school. As there were no sayanims on the island, they recruited me. I thought it was a bit of a lark because nothing ever happens here. The enemies of Israel tend to be Arabs and, as far as I know, there are none living on the island.

'Then in the middle of March, two months ago, I received a coded letter from my handler…'

After we'd interviewed Paillole, thought the Super.

'My handler came over and we met. He explained that Mossad had been investigating something to do with selling guns to Israel's enemies. Mossad had checked Manx house sales for the past ten years and was convinced it had found what it wanted. To progress, he told me, it would be necessary to set up a monitoring system to listen in on a remote house in Ballaugh. I agreed to help. My job, initially, was to scout the surrounding area within three miles and look for a suitable listening post.

'The following week, my handler returned and I used Dad's car to meet him at the airport and take him to Ballaugh. I waited in Glen Road while he somehow got inside the house and planted his bugs. He checked that they worked, and I showed him where I thought the best place to listen might be. He agreed but insisted that the cottage needed to be made more secure. He gave me £100 and explained how I was to fit locks on the doors and put bars on the windows. I took him to the estate agents in Ramsey handling the sale, and he began negotiations to buy the property. I assume the sale went through quickly, but I don't know. My only job was to make the cottage safe. I never went into the house in Glen Road.'

'No, but you aided and abetted the illegal bugging of the house. What happened next?' asked George.

'He returned a week later to install an automatic listening device in the cottage. He said he would send someone over weekly to check it out. Somehow, it lies dormant and only switches itself on when it picks up noises in the house. I was not told how to use it. I think you need a password to be able to hear what has been recorded.'

'Were you told why the house had to be observed?'

'No, but I guessed it had something to do with the gunrunning. I was with Dan…'

'Dan?'

'He called himself Dan. I don't know his surname. We just happened to be in the cottage on Tuesday morning when he overheard you in the house and realised you had twigged about the eavesdropping. At that point, we scarpered as quickly as possible. He took the listening device in the cottage with him; it was like a small suitcase. He told me to drive directly to the airport, so he could get away. I guess he has left me in the mire.'

'You're probably right,' agreed the Super. 'Do you know where he flew to?'

'Liverpool.'

'Are you sure?'

'Certain.'

George looked at his boss. 'Liverpool Airport has a surveillance system. It's possible they may have a picture of this guy called Dan.'

'Before you go, Christina, give us a description of him.'

★

A phone call to the Liverpool City Police that afternoon and within twenty-four hours of her interview, Christina had identified her contact.

CHAPTER 29

Monday, 23rd May 1960

'If we're going to identify the cadaver,' said the Super to his Chief Constable, 'then we are going to have to find out why Mossad was eavesdropping on Lemont. There must be more to it than simply getting their hands on the Seal.'

'I agree, Bob. And the only way we're going to do that is to use MI5. Whether my old wartime pal will do us a favour, or not, I don't know. However, I'll ring him at home this evening.'

★

The following morning, the Chief called Bob into his office. 'I talked at length last night with Adrian. He thinks things are going too far to keep this in-house. However, he will be contacting the UK's senior Mossad officer at the Israeli Embassy about now. He tells me he knows him well as there is far more cooperation between our two governments than is generally recognised. In his own words, "If there's something in it for them, they might cooperate." I'm hoping Adrian will get back to me as early as this afternoon.'

After lunch, the Chief called both his Deputy and his Senior Detective into his office. 'The senior Mossad agent in the UK is a man called Michael Rumens. Apparently, my old friend and Rumens had a heart-to-heart this morning. It appears Mossad agents in North Africa have been monitoring Lemont and O'Boyle's movements for some time. Rumens is prepared to meet us face-to-face in order to clear up any misunderstandings. He will fly here accompanied by Adrian with the proviso that any charges we were considering against Christina Speed are dropped.'

'What did you tell him?' asked the Super.

'I said that was acceptable.'

'Fair enough,' agreed his Deputy.

'I'm glad you said that as I know you're a stickler for the rules,' smiled the Chief Constable. 'They will arrive on the morning flight from Heathrow next Monday at 10.30 am. We three will meet them. I thought it would be a good idea if we took them to the Golf Links Hotel. I have booked a private room where we will not be disturbed. The hotel will provide us with a buffet lunch. It goes without saying that we will be in mufti.'

George looked at the Super. He didn't have to say anything, but Bob knew his DS wanted to ask a question. An imperceptible nod was sufficient.

'You said Mossad has been watching Lemont and O'Boyle in North Africa for some time. Were those the exact words used, sir?' asked the detective.

'Yes, why?' replied the Chief.

'Lemont is convinced O'Boyle is on-side, but in our triangle there is the third man – Paillole. De Gaulle admitted to the Super that he was using Paillole as a double agent. Yet de Gaulle knew nothing of the Seal. Clearly, after we mistakenly told Paillole of its existence, he passed the information only one way – to Israel. At that point, Mossad suddenly took an interest in Lemont's house.'

'It explains the how, but not the why,' replied BP.

'That's what I'm trying to say, sir. Is there more to this than simply the Seal? Whatever excuse Rumens gives us next Monday for planting listening devices at Ballaugh, we ought to take it with a pinch of salt.'

★

The three Manx policemen met the two visitors at Ronaldsway Airport. After the Chief Constable had introduced his team, a chauffeured police car drove the two guests and the Chief Constable the short two-mile journey around the edge of the airfield to the Golf Links Hotel on the Langness peninsula. A second car carried the Super and George.

★

In a room overlooking the eighteenth tee at the rear of the hotel, the Super gave a summary of what had occurred since the body was washed ashore the previous November. He included his meetings with de Gaulle, O'Boyle, Paillole and Jeff Young. Both the visitors listened intently while taking notes; and an hour had passed before the questions began.

Not unexpectedly, it was the Mossad agent who had the most to ask. His initial interest concentrated on identifying the cadaver. He examined the picture that had appeared in the local newspapers and the photos taken by the hospital photographer. After seeing the copies of the passport photos, he asked, 'Can I see the body?'

'What? Now?' asked the Chief Constable.

'Yes, now,' replied Rumens.

The Chief looked at his watch and around the table. 'Lunch is due to be served at 13.30,' he replied. 'It's not quite twelve noon. It will take about an hour and a quarter to go to Douglas and return.'

'I would very much appreciate it. I have a feeling I know who this man is, but I would need to see the body to be certain.'

213

The Chief looked at his Deputy. 'Bob, will you go with Michael?'

'Of course. Hector will relish breaking the speed restrictions. Perhaps you could ring Dr Parton to have the body waiting in the mortuary when we arrive.'

★

Touching three figures on the rise to the Mount Murray and down the Richmond Hill, the car arrived at Noble's Hospital thirty minutes after leaving the hotel. Dr Parton was waiting in the hospital foyer and was introduced to Michael.

It took only a few moments for Michael to be sure. 'The shoulder injury confirms who this man is,' he said to the Super. 'Have you ever heard of the Palmach Squadron?' he asked.

'Funnily enough, I have,' replied the Manxman. 'The Squadron is mentioned in Lemont's history notes on the Allied assault on Syria in 1941. The Palmach consisted of Jewish volunteers who helped our forces against the Vichy and Nazi troops. They acted as interpreters and used their specialised knowledge of Palestine's geography to help the invasion.'

'This man is Isaac Begin, and was in the Palmach. He is, or rather was, the brother of one of our most prominent politicians.'

'Bloody hell!'

'He was shot during the battle to capture Palmyra. He survived, of course, and joined the Stern Gang after the war. He was one of our best agents in North Africa until he disappeared about eight months ago. I think we can return to the hotel now, and please tell your driver that we're not going to a fire.'

On the return journey, the Super carefully phrased the question he had wanted to ask since Michael had revealed the cadaver's identity. 'If you are so certain the dead man is an important politician's brother, then surely you must have initiated a worldwide search for him after his disappearance?'

'We did, but it had to be kept secret. We could hardly advertise that our possible future president's brother was a Mossad agent, could we?'

'So, where does Dan fit into all this?'

'He traced the link that tied Isaac to Lemont and O'Boyle.'

'Was it Dan's decision to bug Lemont's house?'

'Yes.'

'You know Lemont and O'Boyle met briefly in Syria?'

'I do. Lemont and Isaac were in the same unit that attacked Palmyra.'

In that case, Lemont must have recognised Isaac when he saw the photos of the cadaver, but he told us he had never seen him. Unless, of course, it's Rumens who is lying.

The Super began speculating the possible implications of Rumens lying. Ideas, some plausible, others not, were rife in his mind by the time they returned to the hotel.

★

The others had waited a little over an hour, during which time they had strolled up the seventeenth fairway to see the gulley hole, where golfers have to drive the ball 175 yards over the sea to reach the fairway. The clear visibility on the warm, sunny day allowed the walkers to see the Welsh mountains to the south.

'Well, how did it go?' asked Adrian when they resumed their meeting.

'As I thought,' the Mossad man replied. 'The body is Isaac Begin – the brother of our possible future prime minister.'

'Oh, my God!' exclaimed the Chief Constable.

'It's all right,' assured Michael. 'Menachem Begin knows only too well the risks we take in our profession and was warned months ago of his brother's disappearance. However, I don't suppose anyone expected him to turn up in the Irish Sea.'

It was Adrian who then asked his wartime friend. 'How near are you solving the murder?'

The Chief Constable looked at George to answer.

'As the Super has already said, the body did not drown in the sea. We recently undertook a detailed examination of a disused swimming pool at a hotel not far from here. The hotel's pool had been boarded up for over a year with plywood. If Isaac Begin did drown there, then he was alive when he came to the island and was somehow tricked to the pool's edge. Some of the planks covering the pool could have been uncovered before he was pushed in, or else the plywood may have been rotten. We found no evidence of a struggle on the body.'

'It raises the question,' said the Chief, 'what attracted Begin to the island in the first place?'

'There is just one tenuous connection,' suggested George.

Adrian and Michael looked at him to continue.

'The hotel is owned by a businessman who has links with both Morocco and Syria. His name is Jack Tyson. Our best guess is that Begin must have been tracking the importation of illegal weapons by Tyson.'

Michael slowly nodded his head as if accepting George's hypothesis. He then asked, 'Is there any chance I could go to the pool after lunch?'

CHAPTER 30

The two police cars drew into the Aragon Hotel's car park at 15.00 hours after the buffet lunch at the Golf Links. The reception area was unmanned. George rang the bell on the foyer's desk. Moments later, a middle-aged, rotund woman in her fifties, wearing a black dress, appeared. Her face showed surprise at being faced by five, tall, well-dressed men.

She asked no one in particular, 'Can I help you?'

'Yes,' replied George. Showing his ID card, he introduced himself. 'I'm Detective Sergeant Turnbull.'

Then, gesturing with his hand, he introduced the senior officers standing behind him. 'This is Chief Constable Powell, Superintendent Kinley and two gentlemen from London. We've come to look at the swimming pool.'

'I expect that will be all right. Mr Tyson isn't here.'

'Don't worry. The search warrant used by Sergeant Swindlehurst last March is valid for three months. There's no need to bother Mr Tyson,' replied the DS.

The Super thought, *nice one, George. The warrant is no longer valid, but she won't know.*

'I'm Mrs Fraser,' she said as she ushered the five men to the hotel's rear entrance.

'If you go down the path through the garden, you'll see the back gate. That'll lead you to the pool.'

George directed the others to the zig-zag steps that led down the cliff to the swimming baths. Built at sea level, the pool was some fifteen yards below the hotel's garden. Everything looked in a sorry state. The crazy paving surround was badly cracked, uneven and dangerous. The changing cubicles, situated on the landward side, were either without doors or had their doors hanging at angles due to missing hinges. Some of the plywood covering the pool showed signs of rot. The air of dereliction was depressing.

'This must have been a beautiful place at one time,' commented Adrian.

'It was,' confirmed George. 'After the war, there was a time when the hotel would be full for nine months of the year. Now, I doubt if it ever gets half full, even in August.'

'So you think Isaac could have drowned in this pool?' asked Michael Rumens.

'Yes, but we're unsure on details,' admitted the DS.

'I'm not convinced this is the place,' replied Michael.

The Manx officers looked at him to explain.

'Isaac was an experienced officer. He had been in the Palmach, the Stern Gang and was in Mossad for over ten years. He was an expert in self-defence. His training taught him to the point where it becomes instinctive to smell danger. He would never have allowed himself to be surrounded down here with thugs capable of killing him. This place is such an obvious trap. Just picture it. He gets hit on the head and is unconscious while some wooden boards are removed. He's thrown in the pool. The boards are rapidly replaced. Sorry, I can't buy it.'

Somewhat peeved, the Super asked, 'What do you think happened?'

'Your pathologist said he'd been in the sea for about two months?'

'Yes, and a body put in the sea here in September would take about that time to drift north to Douglas, six or seven miles away. It then came ashore during an exceptional easterly storm. The timing is about right. Furthermore, the water in Isaac's lungs is consistent with him drowning in this pool,' replied the Super.

'That's fine, Bob; but after drowning, why was Begin thrown into the sea? Why not bury it somewhere where it could never be found? If Isaac was killed here, and it's a big if, then the assassin either deliberately wanted the body to turn up on the island or, more likely, thought it would never be washed ashore.'

The two men looked at each other; each waiting for the other to amplify their explanation.

RJ broke the silence. 'The PM showed he had eaten fish before drowning.'

'He could have eaten that anywhere.'

'There was no evidence of pre-mortal injuries, or alcohol having been consumed.'

'That figures. Isaac was a teetotaller. I think the answer lies with the Great Seal.'

'Go on,' encouraged Bob, thinking, *at last, he's admitted the Israelis are interested in the Seal.*

'Since Mohammed died, Islam has been run for 1,300 years by the Sunnis. However, the Shias have always believed the Caliph's Seal is rightfully theirs. And where are most of the Shias? In Iran. Responsibility for this murder lies with SAVAK – the Shah's 60,000 strong security forces.

'SAVAK must have found out about the Seal and followed Isaac when he was investigating the Seal's location here on the island.'

So that's the reason they came here. They want to blame the Iranians for Isaac's murder and stop them getting the Seal.

'Isaac's partner was Dan, and although they worked separately, they would have regularly updated each other on their caseloads.

When Isaac disappeared, Dan would instinctively have followed up what he was doing. The fact that he quickly recruited a Manx sayanim suggests Isaac had told Dan about Lemont and the Manx connection.'

And he got that from Paillole, thought the Super.

'So what you are saying is that Iranian agents may be on the island too?' asked the Super.

'I wouldn't be surprised, although they clearly didn't get anything out of Isaac; otherwise, they would already have shown up at Lemont's house. I'll have to report to Tel Aviv that we've found Isaac's body and arrange for it to be brought back to Israel as quickly as possible.'

The Chief Constable cautioned Michael. 'Now we have a positive identification, there will have to be a coroner's inquest. Are you prepared to give evidence and state who the cadaver is? I'm thinking of the press making a big story about your possible future prime minister's brother being washed ashore in Douglas Bay.'

'In Israel, Begin is a fairly common name.'

'Then, there's the fact that he didn't drown in the sea,' added the Super.

'Need that be mentioned?'

'I will have a word with Dr Parton. I think he could be persuaded not to mention it,' replied the Deputy.

'Assuming all goes well with the inquest,' began Adrian, 'do you intend to investigate how Isaac Begin ended up on the island?'

'Our resources are severely limited,' replied the Chief Constable. 'If he was murdered by SAVAK, could Dan have any extra information that would help us?'

'Dan works mostly in North Africa. I have no way of knowing where he is at the moment. However, I should be able to make contact with him through Tel Aviv. Would you like me to get him to make contact with you direct?'

'That would help us to decide where we go from here, and allow us to release the body to you much quicker,' replied the Chief.

The five men returned to Ronaldsway Airport, and the Manx policemen saw Adrian and Michael catch the 16.30 hours plane back to London.

CHAPTER 31

Monday, 6th June 1960

The following week, the Chief Constable received a phone call from his friend in MI5. 'The Israelis are nothing but efficient,' Adrian laughed. 'Already they have agreed for Dan to tell you all he knows about the Seal, how he thinks Isaac was murdered and how his body came to be washed ashore. You should hear from Dan in the next day or two, providing you agree not to prosecute him for bugging Lemont's home.'

'If it helps to get this business cleared up, then that goes without saying,' replied BP.

★

Three days later, the Douglas station sergeant was astonished when at 9.05 am, a tall gentleman with the characteristics of a well-bred Arab entered the station. Sporting a trimmed beard and wearing a dark, lightweight suit, the stranger, in his mid-forties, asked in accented English, 'Can I see Chief Constable Powell, please?'

'Have you an appointment, sir?' asked the sergeant as he noticed the manicured hands leading to the man's broad shoulders. He portrayed an air of weariness as his eyelids looked heavy.

Perhaps he didn't sleep very well last night, thought the sergeant.

'No, I haven't an appointment,' he replied. 'I arrived late last evening having flown here from Malaga via London.'

The sergeant's face registered surprise. Temporally unsure as to how to treat the stranger, he decided not to leave his desk unattended. He called for a constable from the back room. 'Hold the fort for a minute,' he ordered the PC. 'I'll go and see if he is free, sir,' he said to the traveller. 'Who shall I say wishes to see him?'

'He knows me as Dan.'

A minute later, the sergeant had reappeared and asked the stranger, 'If you'll follow me this way, sir.'

Dolly stood as Dan was ushered through her outer office into the Chief's inner sanctum, where he met both the Chief Constable and his Deputy. They introduced each other while Dolly was making coffee.

'I understand from Michael Rumens that you wish to ask me some questions about why I have been coming to the Isle of Man,' Dan began.

'We're particularly interested in two things,' replied the Chief Constable in a voice that conveyed authority and demanded honest replies. 'Firstly, how did Isaac Begin come to be murdered and washed ashore and, secondly, how does that relate to the Caliph's Great Seal and Peter Lemont?'

Dan paused before answering. 'As you are probably aware, Mossad is a worldwide intelligence organisation of about one thousand professionals who are sworn to defend the State of Israel from its enemies. We are backed by a worldwide team of approximately twenty thousand amateur sayanims who are our eyes and ears. They lie dormant for much of the time but are more active in the Middle East.

'At the end of World War Two, Ertrugel Effendi, former Governor of Vichy Syria, received a suspended sentence for his part in plotting the invasion of Iraq. The leniency meted out was the result of a direct plea to the court from Lemont, who was acting on behalf of de Gaulle. Consequently, Ertrugel was granted asylum in the USA with certain restrictions. Several sayanims were appointed to discreetly keep tabs on him. We knew he was the only son of the last Ottoman Caliph and had been pro-Nazi when he was a wine merchant in pre-war Paris. As such, he remained potentially an enemy of Israel. He was something of a playboy, with the usual weaknesses for wine and women. One of our New York female sayanims volunteered to befriend him. As she got close to him, he would occasionally let things slip that were useful to us. He told her on one occasion that when he was young, he had been present when his father gave the Caliph's Great Seal to someone called Henry Leon. Previous to this, Jews generally believed the Great Seal was simply a legend.

'The information was passed back to Israel and the story was investigated. Research, recorded on our files, shows that we discovered Leon's real name was Quilliam, that he had opened Britain's first mosque and been made a Sheikh of Islam. However, in 1950, we – Israel and Mossad – were still in our infancy. There were more important things on our Government's mind and the file was archived.

'Although many of the Vichyites were hanged after the war, Lemont's role in preventing Ertrugel being punished was not forgotten. It raised questions that were never properly answered, such as why de Gaulle had intervened on Ertrugel's behalf. After Lemont left Syria in 1949, he went to work on de Gaulle's personal staff. A decision was made to keep track of him. He built a reputation of being a slippery customer who occasionally vanished – sometimes for as long as a year. However, one thing became clear – he was a dedicated Gaullist.'

That's interesting, thought the Super. *I'll bet it's been Paillole who's been keeping track of Lemont.*

'After defeating the Arabs in the 1948 war, it became obvious there would always be friction between us and our neighbours. An Egyptian group, the Muslim Brotherhood, which had been formed in the 1930s, began to foment trouble wherever and whenever it could. After Nasser ousted King Farouk in 1952, things worsened considerably. Many of us, who had immigrated to Israel after World War Two, were fluent Arab speakers and were recruited by Mossad. I was French and had worked in Algeria before the war. After training, I was initially assigned to monitor the Muslim Brotherhood in Benghazi; they were particularly strong in eastern Libya.

'We were trained to work individually but always with an adjacent agent to watch each other's backs. By corresponding regularly, we could, if necessary, take over each other's investigations. Isaac became my partner in 1955.'

As Dan stopped to take a sip of his coffee, the Chief Constable took the opportunity to ask, 'Was your HQ always kept informed of what you were doing?'

'We had neighbouring areas. Isaac worked in Tangier, while I'd moved back to Algeria. We would meet on a regular basis. The border between the two countries is very porous. There are things which HQ might not wish to know, which allows us to take short cuts.'

'Carry out assassinations?'

He didn't answer but moved on quickly. 'After a while, you begin to think the same way as your partner. If both of us agreed to inform Tel Aviv, a report would be sent via a circuitous postal route through a friendly country, such as France. Remember, Israel has no formal diplomatic relations with any Arab country as none of them recognise our existence. A letter posted to Israel from Libya, for example, would never reach its destination. It would be opened, its contents analysed, and attempts made to find the sender.

'In early October last year, Isaac and I met in Fez. Isaac had picked up that arms were arriving in Morocco from Yugoslavia.

The guns were then smuggled across the border into the Spanish enclave of Ceuta. He thought the weapons were being delivered to the Muslim Brotherhood through Spain. He had decided to follow the scent. That was the last time I saw him. We always kept in touch by regularly sending each other innocent-looking tourists' postcards every few months. When January arrived and I'd heard nothing, I knew all was not well.

'I moved to Malaga, having acquired a Spanish passport from our HQ. It allowed me to move freely and get digs in Ceuta. I tried to make contact with our only sayanim there, but he'd disappeared. I made extensive enquiries about Isaac, but no one had seen him. I took a job as a porter in the docks so that I could keep an eye on the shipping movements—'

'Can I stop you there for a minute?' asked the Super. 'You know Isaac was found washed ashore on 21st November?'

'Yes, but let me continue. By mid-April, I hadn't seen anything suspicious. I was beginning to fear that I would never find out what happened to Isaac. Our headquarters were getting tetchy. Tel Aviv agreed to give me another month. My orders were to return to Algiers at the end of May. Then on 9th May, I saw a large Spanish trawler load heavy boxes into their hold and sail west towards the Atlantic. It felt wrong somehow. Why use a fishing boat with a refrigerated hold for a cargo that clearly wasn't frozen goods? I caught the next scheduled ferry back to Malaga. I wondered if the cargo could be Isaac's guns destined for the Muslim Brotherhood. From the Malaga office of our Chargé d'affaires, I immediately signalled a description of the boat with its distinctive red and yellow forward wheelhouse to HQ and asked for our Spanish sayanims to be alerted and monitor the trawler's movement.

'The Gary Powers incident had occurred on 1st May, as I'm sure you'll remember. There was nothing else in the press. The US was immediately banned by the Pakistani Government from using Peshawar as its base for U-2 flights. Turkey did likewise, closing its NATO base at Incirlik. Unknown to me, our Government had reacted quickly. Under the guise of a gesture of friendship, our Prime Minister, Ben-Gurion, had immediately offered Eisenhower unlimited use of our Ramat David Air Force Base for their U-2 flights across Eastern Europe.

'Having received my urgent message about the trawler, our Government requested the Americans monitor its movements. Two USAF maritime aircraft were allocated. One quickly spotted it, and by refuelling at a NATO base near Madrid, the two C-45 Expeditor reconnaissance aircraft took turns to follow the trawler, and guess what?'

'What?' asked the Chief Constable.

'The trawler sailed across the Bay of Biscay, entered the St George's Channel and into the Irish Sea. At that point, the American aircraft were at the limit of their range and had to turn back. Our central staff had been receiving updates of the trawler's position hourly, and an urgent sayanim alert went out to cover the Irish coastline. The trawler sailed into Wexford Harbour. There, two sayanims were able to photograph what happened next.'

'I don't suppose...' began the CC.

'Yes, I'm coming to that. They are not very good quality as they were faxed from Dublin to Tel Aviv and back to me in Malaga.'

Dan opened his briefcase and took out a small wad of photos. He handed them to the Chief Constable who immediately spread them out on his desk.

CHAPTER 32

'That's O'Boyle!' the Super exclaimed. 'What the hell was he doing there?'

'You might well ask,' replied Dan. 'Is there anyone else you recognise?'

The Super examined the pictures carefully. 'No, I don't think so,' he replied.

'What about him?' asked Dan, pointing to a man standing in the background.

'No, I don't know him.'

'Are you sure?'

'Yes, why?'

'His name is Jack Tyson. He arrived at the quay in the same car as O'Boyle.'

'Really? I've never met him, but my DS has interviewed him. He owns the Aragon Hotel where Isaac was drowned, although Michael Rumens had his doubts. He believed Isaac would not have allowed himself to be trapped in such an obvious place.'

'Michael has briefed me about that. All these photos were taken from some distance away, but these…' he paused to take a further wad from his case, '…show the boxes being unloaded.

You will see the smaller ones were put aside while the heavier crates were loaded onto a lorry.'

'When was this?' asked the Deputy.

'Sunday, 15th May.'

'Just over three weeks ago?'

'Yes, and you'll see in this photo that all the smaller boxes were repacked in the ship's hold. Our sayanim reported the whole unloading and reloading took less than an hour before the trawler left and headed out to sea with Tyson on board.'

'So it's reasonable to assume it sailed to the island,' remarked the Chief Constable.

'Yes, with a hold half full of needles,' smiled the Super. 'Tyson is using the needles to hide gun-running for the IRA.'

'There's another thing,' continued Dan, 'this is apparently a regular run. Our sayanims made some enquiries in a pub on the quay. They were told the trawler appears every couple of months with a similar cargo. The bigger boxes must be the arms that Isaac thought were coming from Yugoslavia but are going to the IRA, not the Muslim Brotherhood. My theory is that on a previous trip, they used the refrigerated hold to store the frozen body of Isaac. It could then have been tossed overboard in the Irish Sea.

'His body could have been in a deep freeze for months after he was murdered in Ceuta. Goodness knows how long it would take to defrost, or what effect that would have on its deterioration and buoyancy in the relatively warm sea. After all, ice floats on water.'

The Super nodded slowly. *They're determined to make out that the cadaver is Begin in order to retrieve it before we find out how he died. They must think we're daft; asking us to believe he drowned in freshwater in North Africa, was frozen, and brought here to be dumped.*

'That's all very well, but Isaac was drowned — it's an unusual way of murdering someone. His gut was infected with schistosomes of some sort that are common in North Africa, and I assume they would survive the body being frozen. But I can't believe Isaac would be murdered in Ceuta by drowning and then frozen to be dumped in the Irish Sea, unless, of course, he had been given a drug that induced a catatonic stupor. At some time, he was given a meal before being drowned in freshwater in the Isle of Man – an even more preposterous idea.

'It might happen in Edgar Allan Poe stories, but let's move on. The Wexford photos suggest the guns were for the IRA, and O'Boyle's presence proves he's somehow involved. We know O'Boyle visited the island last July and stayed with Lemont before they went to Belfast. Lemont assured us that O'Boyle had managed to infiltrate the IRA, although our RUC contact had grave doubts. I'm wondering if O'Boyle has managed to pull the wool over Lemont's eyes.'

'I think you can be assured Lemont is kosher. The one thing about de Gaulle's musketeers is they are handpicked very carefully. All are unquestionably loyal to de Gaulle.'

Why is he trying to convince us that Lemont is squeaky clean? Paillole didn't.

Dan continued. 'I suspect Lemont's trip to Belfast with O'Boyle was with the best of intentions. Lemont needed to be convinced that O'Boyle is onside before he can prepare a folder for de Gaulle on IRA rearmament.'

How does he know that? He could only have gleaned that from Paillole.

'This brings me to Lemont's connection with the Great Seal. We set up surveillance on his house in Ballaugh because of the Seal's importance to Israel's security and not wanting the Iranians to get it.'

'Wait a minute, you said earlier that Mossad had filed and forgotten the Seal,' interrupted the CC.

'We had, but that was ten years ago. Frequently, information in this game is discovered by chance. A junior accountant in Mossad's HQ was caught speeding with his girlfriend one evening in Tel Aviv – showing off his new car. Nothing unusual, you might think. However, an observant traffic cop, while filling out the paper work, wondered how a junior civil servant could afford a Ferrari. He made some enquiries and found that the administrative assistant owned a sea-view apartment overlooking the Charles Clore Gardens in the Jaffa area of Tel Aviv – about as swanky and expensive an area as you can get. He was observed closely over the following weeks and was caught red-handed passing on information to Iran's Intelligence Service. One of the documents he had copied was our file on the Seal.'

'So, that's how the Iranians know about the Seal being given to Quilliam by Mehmed in the 1920s?'

'Yes, and, of course, the Iranians knew of the Seal's historical significance. They will be currently trying to find it. We know they have followed up the Quilliam lead and have been to Woking as recently as last week. It's only a matter of time before they come to the island; if they're not here already.

'Then in March earlier this year, you visited SOAS and met Professor Mickleman...'

'Yes,' replied the Super, wondering what was coming next.

'You informed the professor that you had found the Seal at Lemont's home and that you thought Lemont had been murdered.'

'Don't tell me... the professor is one of yours?' asked the Deputy Chief.

Dan ignored the question. 'We knew Lemont was alive, not dead as you thought. So it was decided to set up surveillance on Lemont's home in Ballaugh in case SAVAK showed up. I was given the job. My first visit to the island was to meet Christina.'

'Lemont has gone to Riyadh to see if he can reach King Saud and persuade him to bury the Seal in either Mecca or Medina,' said the Super.

'If that information leaked out, then there could be a Holy War.'

'Unless, of course, the King agrees to bury it under the Kabbala,' replied Bob. 'Its position there would give it equal proximity to both Sunnis and Shias when they are at the Hajj, which is roughly what Mehmed asked Abdullah Quilliam to achieve. Lemont is convinced your Government wants to get its hands on the Seal so that it can gloat when showing it to the world's press.'

'I can assure you Lemont is wrong. The reason we decided to watch Lemont's property is the exact opposite. We won the Arab–Israeli war in 1948, but there will be more wars to come. The one thing we can't afford is to unite the Arabs against us. As long as Egypt, Syria, Saudi Arabia and Iraq continue to squabble over who should lead the Arab world, then we will be safe. Our aim is to keep them disunited, believe you me. Capturing the Great Seal of the Caliphs and showing it to the world is the last thing we would want. Israel is far safer if its location remains a secret forever.'

CHAPTER 33

Friday, 10th June 1960

'George, have you got any further with Tyson's accounts?'

'I've been through them again, but I'm not an accountant. I sat with Pat Corlett for a whole day; she certainly knows her stuff. Now that she's fully aware of our suspicions, she saw some irregularities missed previously. Tyson appears to be importing less than he's selling. Pat thinks he has a second set of books, but that needn't necessarily be illegal.'

'How can that be?'

'She thinks Tyson could be passing some needles through an account in the Irish Republic. He then brings the extra needles to the Isle of Man. There are no customs barriers between the Isle of Man and Eire.'

'So Tyson is using the island as a backdoor to the UK market?' asked the Super.

'Yes, but as long as he informs the Irish tax authorities that he's importing the needles from abroad, strictly no Manx tax laws are being broken.'

'Have you heard any more from the Birmingham City Police?'

'I have chased them up and am still waiting. Fraud squads are not racehorses.'

'Chase them up again, will you?' asked the Super.

'Then go down to the Harbour Board. The coastguards should know if a Spanish trawler landed anywhere on the island around the 15th May. Meanwhile, I'll contact the island's Chief Customs Officer, to see if he knows anything. I'll also talk to Jimmy Swindlehurst's brother again. I want to know how close a trawler could get to the Aragon's swimming pool at high tide.'

'You're wondering if a trawler can get close enough to unload its cargo.'

'If I'm right, then Tyson could be landing his bloody needles at his hotel. It might also help explain how our cadaver came to be drowned in the Aragon pool.'

'So you're certain it wasn't Begin who drowned there?'

'I can't believe he was either drowned in North Africa, after eating fish, and kept frozen until being dumped in the Irish Sea, or given a drug and brought here in a stupor. Can you? Dan implied eavesdropping at Ballaugh was to discover if SAVAK had found where Lemont lived, as they wanted to prevent the Iranians getting the Seal. I don't buy that either. I think their story is a desperate cover-up to get the cadaver back to Israel before we discover something about how the body died.

'If the Israelis are mixed up in trying to create trouble in Northern Ireland, then why did they show us the photos of O'Boyle and Tyson? What do they expect to gain?'

'By supporting the IRA in Northern Ireland, the Israelis are hoping the British Government will resort to using detention without trial. They'll have picked up the rumour about "H" blocks. Then, when we criticise their policy of building illegal settlements, they can tell us to put our house in order first,' suggested George.

'I would like to believe Lemont is telling us the truth that he and O'Boyle are preparing a case for de Gaulle to alert the British about IRA rearming. But there is something niggling me that I can't put my finger on.'

'About Tyson's role? He must be the banker between the gunrunners and the IRA?'

'Ever since I took Rumens to Noble's Hospital, it's been puzzling me how he knew the body had a shoulder injury. If you had a scar hidden under your clothes, I wouldn't know. Why should I? And I probably know you a damn sight better than Rumens knew Isaac. I think we should get BP's friend in MI5 to find out if Begin ever had a brother. I know it sounds far-fetched, but telling us the body is Begin's brother can only be a convenient way of rapidly getting the body back to Israel. What if the body is an IRA member, or even an Iranian? Having used something to paralyse him, why drown him and then throw him into the sea? It doesn't make sense. If they wanted the body to be found, they could have engineered a car accident.'

'So what are we going to do with our cadaver?' asked George.

'Leave it in the mortuary until we're satisfied we know who he is and who is responsible. I'm afraid it's back to square one. We know, from the infestation in his gut, that the cadaver spent some time in a Mediterranean climate; that he had been circumcised; that he had been shot in the shoulder at some time; and that he looks like Lemont. What else do we know?'

'The only Manx connection is Tyson, who has a business in Morocco… and who, by chance, has an infested swimming pool where our mystery man could have drowned.'

'OK, let's get cracking. This case has already taken too long. Come back as soon as you have anything.'

★

On Tuesday morning, the Chief Constable called his two case officers together. 'Adrian has confirmed that Menachem Begin doesn't have any brothers. He asked me why we suspected Rumens may have been lying and I told him about the photos that showed arms being imported to Ireland on a Spanish trawler.

He promised that he would look into it and would give us all the help he could to determine the body's identity. Now tell me, what's new?'

The Super began: 'Jimmy Swindlehurst's brother has confirmed that on a spring tide the seawater comes within two feet of the top of the Aragon's swimming pool wall. A fifty-foot trawler weighing about thirty tons has a draft of only eight feet and could easily be manoeuvred near to the wall. He told me there was such a tide on 16th May. So it's possible that Tyson could have unloaded undeclared goods that way.'

'And you're convinced our cadaver drowned in the pool's freshwater, possibly on a previous trip?' asked BP.

'Our body must have been alive at the pool immediately before he drowned. The important question is why are the Israelis so desperate to retrieve the body?'

'To prevent us from finding out who he is,' answered the Chief.

'And to prevent us finding out how he died,' added Bob.

After a short reflection, BP asked, 'What have you found out, George?'

'The Birmingham City Police's Fraud Squad came back to me about Tyson's warehouse. It is situated in a hangar on an old airfield on the eastern edge of the city. They have checked with Birmingham City's council, and Tyson pays the rates regularly. They have asked the UK tax authorities for details of Tyson's tax returns but have not yet received a reply.

'I returned to our Treasury and talked over Tyson's tax returns with Pat Corlett, yet again. Unless his outgoings and lifestyle are clearly disproportionate to his income, there is little she can do. The tax people can only initiate a fraud investigation if there are strong grounds. Superficially, everything appears fine. She did accept, however, that Tyson could have illegitimate businesses just about anywhere.'

'Anything else?' asked the CC.

'The coastguards assured me there hasn't been a trawler unloading anything like boxes of needles at the five ports where they have officers. I visited the Aragon Hotel and spoke to Mrs Fraser again. I asked her if she remembered a fishing boat coming near the swimming pool wall.'

'And?'

'She asked me, "When?"'

'I replied, "Any time."'

'Her exact words were, "On Thursday, 10th September last year, Mr Tyson was here with three men whom I'd never seen before. After their lunch, they went down to the pool. I assumed they were there to inspect the pool with a view to reopening it. I never saw them leave as I was busy. The hotel was almost full that week."

'I asked her how she remembered the date so accurately.

'She told me it was the day Eddie Crooks won the Senior Manx Grand Prix. He is, apparently, married to her cousin.'

'Thoughts, Bob?' asked the Chief.

'The date is two months before the body was washed ashore – within the accuracy of Dr Parton's estimate date of death. I'm more convinced than ever there is a link between Tyson and the dead body. I know Dr Parton was sure the body hadn't been drugged when it was drowned, but if the Israelis are involved, we're dealing with some pretty dark people. Your friend Adrian has promised to help in any way he can. He must know if there is research into undetectable toxins at our chemical and biological weapons research laboratories at Porton Down in Wiltshire. I'm wondering if he could get someone to do a second autopsy, take blood samples, or whatever.'

'I'll get on to him as soon as we're finished.'

★

Minutes after the meeting finished, the Chief Constable was talking to his former wartime colleague.

'The problem, Ben,' explained Adrian, 'is this sort of research is highly classified. In theory, all the work is directed towards finding antidotes to biological weapons, not to developing them. However, it stands to reason you can't do one without the other. You can't develop a smallpox vaccine without cultivating smallpox viruses on which to experiment. The other problem is that Porton Down is under the aegis of the War Office and I'm in the Home Office. I'll have to go through official channels to reach someone who may, or may not, be willing to help. I'll get back to you as soon as I can.'

★

After lunch, the Chief Constable's phone rang. 'Ben, it's Adrian. I've spoken with Dr Roland Raines. He's Head of Porton's Virology Department. I've explained your problem of how could a body be drowned without leaving any evidence of a struggle. He seemed very interested and would like to examine the body, but was defensive about who could be present when he carried out what would effectively be a second post-mortem.'

'I don't follow.'

'He insists only he and a colleague from Porton Down can be present; no one else, not even the hospital's pathologist.'

'It's an odd request.'

'Apparently, they will wear some sort of protective clothing and carry out the examination inside a special tent. Afterwards, the laboratory will have to be extensively cleaned and decontaminated.'

'That sounds extreme, but if it will help us, I see no alternative. When can he come?'

'They will fly up to RAF Jurby from Wiltshire in an RAF aircraft on Thursday.'

'I'll get Superintendent Kinley to explain what is going on with Dr Parton and arrange for Kinley to meet them off the aircraft.'

★

The RAF Anson arrived shortly after 10.15 hours and was directed to a remote part of the airfield, some distance from the main camp. The Super was driven by PC Duff in the Austin Westminster to the Anson's rear door. The two scientists descended and introduced themselves.

'We have a fair amount of equipment,' the doctor said. 'It won't all fit into your car.'

'That's all right. I have arranged for your equipment to follow us in the Black Maria, if that's OK.' the Super replied.

Dr Raines nodded approval, and the Super hailed a black van that was waiting a short distance away.

An airman in RAF flying kit began unloading the sealed cases onto the tarmac. The Deputy was surprised at the amount of gear that Dr Raines had brought. Without having to be told, the airman helped the PC driver load the police van.

On their forty-five-minute journey into Douglas, Dr Raines apologised for the secrecy of their investigation. 'You will appreciate that untraceable toxins, if that is what we are dealing with, can either be chemical or biological. If they are the latter then every possible precaution has to be taken to prevent their release into the atmosphere.

'Now tell me more about this case.'

'...and that's about all we know. We will arrive in a few minutes and I have asked Dr Parton to meet you so that he can brief you on what he found in the original post-mortem.'

CHAPTER 34

When the two doctors met in the hospital's foyer, they looked at each other with astonishment. It was Dr Raines who broke the silence. 'Weren't you a year ahead of me at University College Hospital?' he asked.

'I thought your face was familiar,' replied Dr Parton. 'You haven't changed in what... twenty years?'

'I try and keep myself fit by playing squash whenever I can. What did you do after graduation?'

'I went straight into the Royal Army Medical Corps. After three weeks officer training, learning how to handle a knife and fork, press my own trousers and return a salute, it was off to Rangoon in Burma. I was just in time to get bombed by the Japs,' replied the Manx pathologist. 'After the fall of Rangoon in March 1943, I found myself retreating north with everyone to India. It was a bloody shambles. And you?'

'Similar, except I was posted to Egypt and ended up in Iraq where there was nothing but dates, damned flies and dysentery.'

'And when you left the Army?'

'I specialised in virology at Birmingham, taught at Leeds University for ten years, and ended up working for the government,' replied Roland.

'I came into pathology by accident, finding myself the only one available to do the job in Imphal and decided I wanted to specialise. It was better than dealing with malaria, diarrhoea and trench foot. I went back to UCH. Remember old Doc Davy? He was a wonderful teacher. I came here to the island after training and have never regretted it; I get plenty of fishing and golf. The island is a wonderful place to work and live.'

The Super made his excuses to let them catch up. 'Look, if you two don't mind, I'll leave you to it. Give me a call when you're ready to return to RAF Jurby.'

'That's fine, Superintendent. We should be no longer than three or four hours.'

★

When Dr Raines' assistant had completed setting up the precautionary equipment, including the tent in which the autopsy was to be undertaken, the two men from Porton Down donned their protection clothing. 'You can watch if you wish, Tim, through the observatory window. The tent is not soundproof, so we can talk and I am happy to answer any questions you may have as long as the information is not classified. I think you will understand the need for care as we go along.'

'Are you telling me there could be an infection present in the body that requires all this equipment?'

'I won't know until I find it. There may be nothing, but what we're looking for, if it's there, is not going to be easy to find. Your results suggested the corpse drowned in tepid freshwater, which means that when the body entered the sea, he was already dead. I am looking, therefore, to see if a toxin was used that rendered him unconscious before he drowned.'

'I did all the standard tests,' replied Dr Parton.

'I'm afraid those tests won't find the sort of substances we're looking for. For example, did you test to see if the body had been subjected to radiation?'

'No, of course not.'

'There is a nasty radioactive substance, both soluble and tasteless, called thallium trihydrophenol, that would have rendered him so ill and weak in less than thirty minutes that he could not resist anyone holding him underwater. It could have been slipped into his food. If it was used, there will be a slight radioactive residue in his brain.

'At Porton Down, we do not undertake research into undetectable toxins used as assassination tools. My work is primarily developing vaccines to fight biological weapons such as plague, smallpox and anthrax. There are several overseas governments, however, that do. The leaders in the field are Israel and South Africa. Needless to say, they deny their interest, but we get to hear about them. We do our best to research how the toxins work and whether there are any antidotes.

'For example, there has been a rumour that a botulinum has been developed by Israel that induces a catatonic trance. As you know, the brain controls everything we do, including telling us when to go to sleep. The theory is that the Israelis have produced a protein that, if taken orally, tells the body to go to sleep. Again, if there is a residue to be found, it will be in the cadaver's brain.

'It's a nasty world out there. So you can see why we have to take precautions. We don't know what we're dealing with half the time.'

Dr Parton watched as Roland removed the brain from the cadaver. He examined it with a Geiger counter. 'There is no trace of radioactivity,' he said, 'so I can only assume we're dealing with a non-radioactive chemical or a biological toxin.'

He proceeded to cut small samples of the brain cells and place each in separate test tubes. His assistant, after spinning the tubes in a centrifuge, added various chemicals. The assistant

242

then examined each under a microscope, occasionally drawing his boss's attention to the results. Almost two hours had passed without much comment between the two pathologists.

Roland approached the observatory window. 'Tim, did you examine the endocrine system and pituitary gland?'

'No, I had no need to.'

'True, but you know what I'm thinking. The results so far show no signs of a chemical being used. I think this man ingested a biological material that partially blocked his endocrine signalling. It slowed everything down to the point that he would be helpless to defend himself. What were the contents in his stomach? How recent was his last meal?'

'If I remember rightly, he'd eaten grilled fish with new potatoes and fresh peas about an hour before dying. He'd also drunk several glasses of water.'

'No wine or beer?'

'None.'

'In that case, I'm going to remove the pituitary gland and examine it.'

Fifteen minutes later, both men from Porton Down were examining the gland under their powerful microscope.

'I'm sorry about this, Tim, but there are signs that it has been attacked by something. I am going to have to take the brain back to my laboratories where I have the right equipment to examine it properly and find out how the damage was done. Is that OK?'

Tim nodded and the two men began placing the organs into various glass jars. Soon afterwards, the tent and the equipment were subjected to a vaporised dousing that Tim thought smelled like a powerful mix of bleach and disinfectant.

★

A phone call to the police station had the squad car and the Black Maria arriving at the front of the hospital within ten minutes.

'The hard work now begins, trying to find out exactly what has been used,' smiled Dr Raines to the Super. 'I will confirm as soon as possible that your body was somehow rendered partially or wholly unconscious by an agent that was administered about an hour before he drowned. I will not be able to reveal the exact agent used, for security reasons, but it was undoubtedly not chemical. Rather, my money is on it being an organic toxin added to whatever he ate. Dr Parton tells me the dead man had recently eaten fish. I will be able to confirm the exact list of stomach contents, right down to how the fish was cooked. You should then be able to trace where his meal was cooked.'

'Thank you, Doctor. You have just helped us get much closer to tying up the case.'

★

The two scientists were escorted back to RAF Jurby by the Super and, after seeing them away, he returned to Douglas Police HQ and sought out his DS.

'George, I want you to go down to the Aragon Hotel and see Mrs Fraser again. She said there were three men with Tyson on the day that the trawler may have arrived. She remembered the dining room being busy. Can she remember what the four men ate? Show her our artist's picture of the cadaver and the RUC's photo of Lemont and O'Boyle getting off the *Lady of Man*. Ask her if she recognises them from the pictures. Ask her if it was possible for one of them to have slipped something into our unknown man's drink. Get a written statement from her.

'Even if we don't know who the cadaver is, I have a hunch we are now much nearer to finding what killed him, where he died, and how he died.'

CHAPTER 35

Friday, 17th June 1960

'Mrs Fraser claims she doesn't remember what Tyson and his three friends had for lunch. I formed the opinion she was lying and someone had warned her to keep quiet. Throughout my questioning, she was overly nervous. However, grilled plaice and lemon torte were on the menu that day – I made her check the hotel's menu files. She also didn't recognise the sketch of our cadaver's face, or O'Boyle. Again, I felt she was lying.'

'Maybe she'll change her tune when we call her as a witness and she realises she's under oath.'

'I asked her for a list of visitors staying at the hotel that week. She was reluctant to give it to me, but some gentle leaning produced the guest book with their addresses. They all live on the mainland, and possibly not all of them were having lunch that day, but it could be worth having them interviewed.'

'I agree. How many names have you got?'

'Seven couples and two singles living as far apart as Edinburgh and Gloucester; nine addresses altogether. Apparently, lunchtimes are popular with locals who pay cash. Tracing them could be more difficult.'

'Give me the residents' details. I'll contact the appropriate police forces and fax our artist's sketch together with the photograph of Tyson that was in the *Examiner* last year, when he won some sort of award for industry. I'll stress this is a murder inquiry; and with luck, we'll have statements by the end of next week.'

★

Just over a week passed before statements began to arrive at Douglas Police Station. The first, from Durham, was vague: couched in terms such as *possibly* and *unsure*. Three of the statements were from couples who admitted they had stayed at the hotel, but had always lunched out.

However, a statement from a couple living in Manchester said they had lunch sitting at a table next to four men who had consumed three bottles of red wine and gradually become more and more boisterous. Both the husband and wife, who were holidaying on their silver wedding anniversary, recognised the man in the artist's sketch. They noticed he had only drunk water throughout the meal and overheard him being called Ahmed by the man in the *Examiner* photograph. The husband, who gave the statement, was a retired Army Warrant Officer and, in a covering letter from the police sergeant who took the interview, he was described as a *reliable witness*. The ex-WO particularly remembered the name Ahmed as it triggered his memory. He had served in Lahore from 1934 to 1937 before the partition of India. *There, Ahmed was a common boys' name*. It had struck him as odd that the gentleman was probably a Muslim but looked too pale to be Pakistani – maybe more southern European.

The statement continued: *I served in Egypt in the war and would have sworn Ahmed was a Gippo.*

After a while, two of the men became abusive to Ahmed and we left early without a pudding as we felt uncomfortable. We subsequently

246

complained to the manageress, Mrs Fraser, and she gave us a free bottle of wine that evening.

The Super thought, *Mrs Fraser was lying when she said that she couldn't remember the incident.*

The other diners' statements were similar to each other – remembering a table with four men that had progressively got noisier as they consumed more wine. Three of the statements thought the picture and the photograph *could be* of two of the men.

★

Two days later, a letter arrived for the Deputy Chief Constable, postmarked Salisbury; he opened it with hopeful expectation.

We have exhaustively conducted tests on the samples of your cadaver's brain and glands. For security reasons, I cannot disclose exactly what agent was used to overwhelm him. However, the toxin damaged his pituitary gland and endocrine signalling system. The consequent symptoms would have been consistent with him being drunk. The organism also affected his muscles to weaken him. The result would render him unable to react to physical restraint. The substance was definitely not alcohol. The toxin is colourless, tasteless and odourless. I believe it was taken by mouth. A few drops in a glass of water would have been sufficient. It was, in itself, not the cause of death as its effects would wear off after several hours.

Such a substance could only originate from a country where such toxins are being covertly developed: Israel, South Africa and America.

Fifty minutes before drowning, he had eaten grilled fish, new potatoes and garden peas. Afterwards, he had had a lemon torte dessert.

If you require further information, please contact me direct on the number at the top of the page.

The Super took the letter into George's office.

'I think we are approaching the stage where we have enough information to charge Tyson with aiding and abetting the murder of our man, Ahmed. However, first we must find out who he was and what he was doing on the island, as well as identify the other two men. Have we found out any more about Tyson's business arrangements in Birmingham?'

'The Birmingham police grew tired of waiting for the UK tax authorities and obtained a search warrant to inspect Tyson's business transactions. The books show the names of the firms who purchase his needles. Tyson sells his products to either wholesalers, who packet up the needles and sell them on to small retailers, or he sells them to big corporations, like Singer and Woolworths. The figures and sums appear to match with the returns he makes to the Manx tax authorities,' replied George.

'I think it may be time to delve deeper. What bank does he use?' asked the Super.

'His holding company, C and W Stone Walls Ltd, uses the Isle of Man Bank in Athol Street.'

'Harry Totton is the manager, isn't he?'

'Yes. Do you know him?' asked George.

'Not well enough for us to bypass the proper channels. I'll go and see the Deemster. The close link with Tyson to the murdered man will get us the necessary warrant.'

★

Next day, Bob and George sat in the general manager's office. 'I understand the legality of the search warrant, Bob, but can I ask exactly what it is you expect to find? Then perhaps I can help. As you can see from Mr Tyson's files on my desk, they are large. He has many accounts – one for each of his companies as well as three personal ones held in our Onchan branch.'

'To be honest, Harry, we're not sure what we're looking for – except for whether his outgoings are greater than his income.'

'You mean is he evading tax in some roundabout way?'

'There's a bit more to it than that. He may be importing illegal goods to the UK through Ireland from Morocco that are not being recorded in any books.'

'And you think there may be a clue somewhere in his bank accounts?'

'Yes.'

'Major account holders, such as Mr Tyson, who frequently either send sums abroad or receive money from overseas as part of their import/export businesses, have a personal banker who keeps a watch on such accounts. Our bank has two such trained accountants. Erica Eyres looks after Mr Tyson's affairs. Shall I get her to come in?'

'Do you trust her to keep our inquiry confidential?'

'Definitely; she's a chartered accountant and been trained by the UK tax authorities. She's been with us since she returned from university.'

'OK.'

Less than a minute after making an internal phone call, Erica, a fair-haired, broad-shouldered young woman in her early thirties wearing a blue and white striped cotton summer dress appeared. Mr Totton introduced her to the two policemen and explained their purpose.

'I inspect his company accounts every time there is a transaction; typically, that's three or four times a week,' she explained. 'All monies going abroad from his accounts pass through the British Government's handling agents, Cox's and King's. In Mr Tyson's case, he is allowed £1,000 per transfer before the British Treasury carefully scrutinise its destination or origin.'

'Cox's and King's?' asked George.

'Yes, I should have explained. They are a branch of Lloyds in Pall Mall that handles UK companies' overseas transactions.'

'So, as far as you can see, there is no room for irregular sums being transferred to hidden accounts?'

'No, not on his company accounts, but I don't examine his private accounts,' she replied.

'Why not?' asked the Super.

'The sums involved are generally not large enough to justify inspection, unless the account becomes overdrawn. His personal accounts are held at our Onchan branch,' she replied.

'You told us,' said the Super, addressing the general manager, 'that Tyson has three private accounts. Is that unusual?'

'No, not really. There can be several reasons for having more than one account – such as when an account is used for a specific purpose.'

He paused briefly.

'Perhaps he is paying for his son's education through university.'

'And is this the case for Tyson?' pressed the Deputy Chief.

'I don't know. Erica, ring Onchan and talk to the manager. Ask him to cast his eye over those accounts, will you? Meanwhile, I'll get these gentlemen coffee.'

A few minutes after Erica had left, a thermos of coffee arrived with some assorted biscuits.

The three men chatted about England's prospects of completing a 5-0 whitewash in the test matches against South Africa after England had recently won by an innings at Lords. Twenty minutes passed before Erica returned.

'Have you found anything?' the manager asked.

'Mr Tyson appears to use his first account for general everyday tasks, such as paying utility bills, withdrawing cash, and so on. The account's income is the same each month and comes from his general purpose company account. Account number two is used to pay his wife and his son their monthly salaries. Again, its income comes from his general purpose company account. However, account number three is more interesting.'

'Why?' asked Harry Totton.

'Because its income is regular and comes from the Bank of Ireland.'

'So?'

'Because, sir, the sum is always £1,250 monthly.'

The two policemen looked at the manager to explain the figure's significance.

'There is an automatic trigger on accounts that receive £1,000 or more from abroad. However, since Ireland is within the Sterling zone, that sum is not illegal—'

Erica immediately interrupted. 'It might not be illegal, sir, but it's one hell of a coincidence, don't you think?'

'Why?' asked George.

'The monies going into his other personal accounts come from his company account, but this sum comes from Ireland. The rumour is that Ireland is going to devalue its currency. Its economy is in a mess. There is talk of creating a Punt worth 17s 6d; that's 12.5% less. Perhaps Tyson is ahead of the game,' explained Erica.

'And what is the money in this account used for?'

'It is syphoned off into his various company accounts in small variable amounts – generally around £250 monthly.'

'Have you got the name and number of the account, and which branch of the Bank of Ireland?' asked George.

'Of course,' replied Erica.

'Then if you don't mind, Harry,' said the Super, 'we'll take the details of these transactions and investigate further. Thank you, Miss Eyres. You've been most helpful. I'm sure you realise there is a lot of evidence to be gathered in an inquiry of this sort. It may be that you will be called as a witness at some future date.'

CHAPTER 36

'Where is the Seal now?'

'In a safe place.'

'I want to see it before I show it to the King.'

'You'll have to trust me that it's not a fake.'

'You're asking me to take a lot on trust.'

'We've known each other for many years, and I've never lied to you before.'

'There's a first time for everything.'

'True, but look at the facts. I've come out here at the hottest time of the year to see you. Why? I'd hardly have done that if all I had was some dubious piece of junk with a weak provenance. The Seal is genuinely 1,300 years old. Carbon dating at three of the world's leading universities proves that it is the original and only portrait of the Prophet. I've told you how it was given by the last Sunni Caliph, Mehmed VI, to Abdullah Quilliam for safe keeping on condition that both the major sects of Islam were given equal access to it. There is only one time in the year when that can be done – at the Hajj. The portrait would at least remain on Saudi soil for all time and avoid worsening the divide between Sunni and Shia.

'Ask yourself what's the alternative? The Israelis get their hands on it – unthinkable. Worse – the Iranians find it. You must take me to see King Saud.'

'That's not easy. The King's younger brother, Faisal, is Prime Minister and the power behind the throne. Their relationship can be described as difficult at best. Strictly speaking, I am in the Government's Ministry of Communications and should go to Faisal with this information. The Seal has the potential to create enormous political divisions within my country, let alone other countries.'

'But it is the King who sees himself as a direct descendent of Mohammed and therefore, the de facto Caliph. Surely it will be his decision to bury the Seal beneath the Kaaba, not his brother's?'

'If everything you've told me is true…'

'It is…'

'Then the Seal is priceless.'

'Except that it is also worthless. Anyone known to possess it becomes a marked man. That is why Abdullah Quilliam buried it so that it remained hidden for about thirty years until I worked out where he had put it.'

'And now you won't tell me where it is?'

'I can't.'

'Or won't?'

'That too.'

'You realise that your position here is very tenuous?'

'Meaning?'

'Meaning that I know you are a French spy. If we were to detain you and apply pressure to find the Seal's location, it could be very uncomfortable for you.'

'If that is a threat, then you must take me for a fool. I really don't know its present location. I have entrusted the Seal to someone with whom I would trust my life. Furthermore, before coming to see you, I took the precaution of visiting the French Embassy here in Riyadh to announce my presence. Not only do

I have a diplomatic passport, but I made it clear that if I didn't return to the embassy this evening then the documentation, lodged with the French ambassador, was to be taken to the King. Before leaving Paris, I fully briefed President de Gaulle and gave him the original file containing photographs of the tablet and its contents. He agreed the only satisfactory solution for the long-term safety of the Seal is for it to be ceremoniously given to your king with a small number of the world's press, such as Reuters, in attendance. The President believes King Saud will be delighted to see the Seal buried beneath the Kaaba. Meanwhile, your prime minister would get to know the full story and how you tried to interpose your will in preventing the portrait getting to its rightful resting place. General de Gaulle has agreed to set a timetable to hear from the King. If not met, then he will personally contact King Saud and the whole story will come out.'

'Do the Iranians know where the Seal is?'

'I don't think so, although they probably know of its existence.'

'You realise it has the potential to start a war between ourselves and Iran?'

'Exactly. Would you want that?'

★

A day later, Pierre Le Mont, accompanied by the French ambassador, was introduced to King Saud in the presence of his chief ministers. After listening to the story, the King asked, 'Where was the Great Seal radiocarbon dated?'

'I sent imperceptible pieces of the Seal and fragments of Fatima's hijab to three universities immediately after I acquired the tablet last year; neither university knew the other two were also dating the same material, nor did I disclose where the materials came from. By using official French Government letter-headed notepaper, I was able to assure the universities that payment for their work would come through an official French account. No one queried this as the return address was to my office in General de Gaulle's official residence, the Élysée Palace. Their results were identical within the accuracy of the dating process. The Sorbonne, Cambridge University and the Massachusetts Institute of Technology all agreed the wooden tablet is late 12th century; it is constructed from a Palestinian olive tree of that period. The cloth was much earlier – 7th century. I have brought you their original replies, which you may keep. My department has certified copies. Finally, a specialist at the Sorbonne in dendrochronology, the dating of wood by examining its growth rings, has examined the back of the portrait and confirmed the wood was grown in Lebanon between 570 and 620AD. This is his report. There can be no doubt the portrait of Mohammed is genuine.'

'Incredible. As a boy, my father told me that the Caliphs had a jewelled dagger that was handed down through the generations. He also told me that a portrait of Mohammed had disappeared in the 17th century when the Ottomans came to rule the Islamic world. Now you tell me it has been found and Abdullah Quilliam kept it safe by burying it in his ancestor's grave. What a remarkable story. Where is this island anyway?'

'Midway between England and Ireland, Your Majesty.'

The King looked at his brother. 'Well, Faisal, what do you think?'

'I think President de Gaulle must be asked to come on a state visit with the Seal and witness its burial beneath the Kaaba.'

'There is another possibility.'

'Go on.'

'The portrait is put permanently on display in the Prophet's mosque in Medina. After all, that is where the Prophet lies,' suggested the King.

'My worry is that it would encourage idiots to make copies and icons. Abu discouraged that in 632 and I don't think it is a good idea. However, there is no reason for it not to be sealed in a casket and buried with the Prophet.'

'Hmm… I'm not sure we should disturb Allah's messenger from his slumber… No, we'll do as you say and bury the portrait under the Kaaba.'

CHAPTER 37

As Bob and George walked back to the police station from the bank, they discussed their next move.

'We're going to have to get the cooperation of the Irish Garda to find the source of Tyson's money,' said George. 'The danger is O'Boyle hearing about our inquiry.'

'It's not going to be easy,' replied the Super. 'The only contact we have is Gerry Brady. If we don't handle this carefully, it could backfire on us.'

'I agree, but did you not get a feeling that there was no love lost between Brady and O'Boyle?'

'Police and security services have always been mutually suspicious of each other. Even if Gerry was to help, it's unlikely he could get access to bank records in Ireland without a judicial court order. O'Boyle would pick it up on the bush telegraph and realise what we're up to. Everything we've got is rather tenuous: the link between Tyson and O'Boyle, the lunch at the hotel, and no hard evidence that Ahmed was murdered in the swimming pool. We don't know who Ahmed is. We only suspect why the Israelis lied to us and want the body back. George, we're out of our depth and all because a bloody body was washed ashore last November.'

'Boss, don't be so despondent. We know the Great Seal was given to Quilliam for safe keeping, that Lemont found it and is trusted by de Gaulle. We have a photo to prove there is a link between Tyson apparently importing needles and O'Boyle receiving arms from Ceuta. The tax records show Tyson deals with Moroccan companies and his payments from Ireland are unorthodox. It's not all bad.'

The Super nodded. 'Come into my office and let's talk this through over a pot of Dolly's tea. That coffee in the bank was terrible.'

★

'Assuming Ahmed was at the Aragon on 10th September, he's been AWOL nine months. Someone must have missed him. What can his job have been?' began the Super.

'If he's not Israeli, Irish, or French, then what country could he be working for?' asked George.

'The Muslim Brotherhood? The retired warrant officer from Manchester thought he was Egyptian,' replied Bob.

'Both Lemont and Dan said the arms came from Yugoslavia. Could Ahmed have been a Yugoslavian policeman investigating illegal exports?' asked George.

'If he was working for the Yugoslavian Government then, surely, they would have initiated a search through Interpol. Isn't it far more likely that he was a gunrunner accompanying the arms to ensure the Yugoslavs received their money?'

'But why come to the Isle of Man?' asked George. 'Surely, he could have received the money in Ireland when they unloaded the arms in Wexford and flown back to Europe from Dublin?'

'Maybe not. Go and get the witness statements again, will you? Let's look at how the retired WO described the other two men at the table.'

George left the Super's office and returned minutes later.

The Deputy rapidly perused the statements and removing one, handed it to his DS. 'Does *gaunt face and reddish hair* remind you of anyone?' he asked.

'The witness could be describing O'Boyle.'

'George, I'm getting too old for this game. We should have thought of this before and sent a photo of O'Boyle to Manchester at the same time as we sent the others. I think we need to fax O'Boyle's photo to the Manchester police and see if our army man recognises him, don't you?'

★

'Dolly, get me Commissioner Brady in Dublin, will you?'

Several minutes later: 'He's on the line, sir.'

'Gerry, Bob Kinley in Douglas.'

'Hi, Bob, what can I do for you?'

'We're still following up on our inquiries into the body washed ashore in Douglas. It has opened a can of worms and I need to speak to you on a delicate matter that has cropped up. I'm afraid I can't even mention it over the phone.'

'Can't you give me a clue as to what it's about?'

'I'd rather not. Could George and I come and see you next week?'

'Do you want me to forewarn anyone that you are coming?'

'No, most definitely not.'

'Then let me know what flight you'll be on and I'll arrange accommodation at the Gresham Hotel as before. I'll take the day off – it'll mean we won't be bothered by anyone.'

'That would be fine. The stay will only be for one night.'

★

'Manchester Police have been most helpful,' said George. 'The ex-WO is certain one of the men at that lunch was O'Boyle.'

'Look. We are as certain as we can be that Ahmed drowned in the swimming pool that afternoon. Porton Down says he was rendered incapable by a toxin before drowning. I'll bet my bottom dollar that it was O'Boyle who slipped him the Mickey Finn. Paillole, with his Mossad connections, had given the quick-acting toxin to O'Boyle in case there was a disagreement over the money owed to the Yugoslavs. The WO's statement said things got heated at the dining table. Perhaps O'Boyle panicked. It proves beyond any doubt the link between O'Boyle and Paillole.

'Falling into the pool could have been an accident, but drugging him wasn't. O'Boyle probably had plans to dispose of Ahmed secretly. But it all went wrong when he drowned and they threw him over the sea wall. An ebb tide took him out to sea. We still need more evidence, however. Who was the fourth man? If Gerry Brady can get us the evidence to prove O'Boyle and Tyson are linked in the money trail, then we may have ample evidence to charge Tyson and O'Boyle with Ahmed's murder; even if we're still not certain who Ahmed was.'

★

On Wednesday, 6th July, the two Manx policemen arrived at Dublin Airport and were met by Gerry.

'Because you wanted to keep this low-key, I thought we should go somewhere quiet. The Botanic Gardens are on the way into town and there's a nice café in the conservatory. It'll take fifteen minutes to get there.'

They were soon sitting at a table, in an almost empty café, with a large pot of coffee and a pile of toasted teacakes.

'You'll remember,' began Bob, 'that O'Boyle's name cropped up when we discovered documents in the home of Lemont, who we thought was washed ashore.'

Gerry nodded.

'Well, since then, Lemont has turned up alive and kicking.'

Bob went on to explain what had happened since their last visit to Dublin, including meeting Mossad personnel who claimed the cadaver was one of their agents.

'It turns out Lemont is one of a dozen, or so, worldwide undercover intelligence officers who work directly for de Gaulle. The bizarre thing about the letter, which he addressed to me personally, was it had been written on the assumption that we would not find it until he was dead. He justified his actions by explaining that he was my cousin —who I never knew existed.'

'But why did he mention O'Boyle?' asked Gerry.

'Lemont mostly operated in North Africa and two years ago met O'Boyle, who remembered him from Syria. O'Boyle told Lemont that he suspected arms from Egypt were being sent to Morocco, where they were being illegally exported to Ireland. Egypt and Syria had recently joined together to become the United Arab Republic and Nasser was hoping to stir up more trouble for the UK, after successfully nationalising the Suez Canal. Worried by this development, Mossad began to check out the situation. This photograph was taken at Wexford three weeks ago by an Israeli sayanim and shows O'Boyle watching the unloading of crates from a Spanish trawler.'

'Hang on,' exclaimed Gerry, 'are you making out that Mossad is now monitoring how the IRA are buying arms and believes O'Boyle is some sort of mastermind?'

'To be completely honest, we're not sure, but I'll fill you in as best as I can. We are now sure O'Boyle was present in the Isle of Man on 10th September last year. A reliable witness saw O'Boyle having lunch with a Manx businessman called Tyson. Also present was a man called Ahmed who we believe is our cadaver. He may be Egyptian or, possibly, a Yugoslavian arms dealer. Tyson, we suspect, is acting as the banker between the arms dealers and the IRA.'

'So you're saying O'Boyle is a traitor working for IRA?'

261

'The evidence is building up that way. We think Ahmed was working for the arms dealers and was making sure they received their payment. An argument broke out and O'Boyle slipped an untraceable toxin into Ahmed's drink that rapidly rendered him incapable of resisting physical force. In the fracas, he fell into the hotel's swimming pool and drowned. They panicked and threw him over the pool's wall into the sea.'

'O'Boyle wouldn't have access to an untraceable toxin,' said Gerry.

'We've no proof, of course, but when we interviewed him last January he freely admitted he knew someone called Paillole who is a Mossad agent.

'We know Tyson gets paid regular monthly sums from the Bank of Ireland. We believe the money is his percentage cut of the IRA transactions. At the Aragon Hotel meeting last September, something went wrong which led to Ahmed's death. The incredible thing is there appears to have been no reaction from the gunrunners to retaliate.'

Gerry had listened intently, nodding occasionally as if the Super's explanation was making sense. He had paused to finish off the teacakes and pour himself another coffee. He stretched backwards in his chair and stared at the conservatory ceiling. Several moments passed in silence.

'Bob, what I am about to say must go no further. Our government security services have classified this information as top secret. Understand?'

The Manx policemen looked at each other and nodded.

'O'Boyle is dead.'

CHAPTER 38

'…and I think you have just told me who killed him,' added Gerry.

'When?' asked Bob.

'About a month ago. Someone broke into O'Boyle's home in the middle of the night. A single shot through the forehead with a 9mm silenced Makarov – a professional hit undoubtedly. His wife always slept in a separate bedroom. She was woken by what she called a "dull thud" and went to see what had happened. As she opened her bedroom door, she saw a dark shape run past and down the stairs. There was no evidence of a forced entry. The assassin had picked the locks on the doors and expertly disabled the alarm system. O'Boyle lived in a large detached house in half an acre of grounds near Portmarnock Golf Course, not far from his office. Needless to say, there were no witnesses and everything has been kept under wraps. Inquiries are ongoing, but the killer will be far away by now.

'To date, the investigative team have been barking up the wrong tree – thinking the assassination was some sort of internal matter. The fact that the Makarov is commonly used by the Soviet and Warsaw Pact armies, however, did puzzle them.

'Your story suggests O'Boyle was in the pay of the IRA and it looks as if someone has been selling them Soviet equipment.'

Gerry paused, finished his coffee, and asked, 'Am I right in thinking you would like me to find out where Tyson's monthly payments come from?'

'Yes.'

'I think we can do that off the record. My wife's brother is the manager of the Bank of Ireland's main branch in Lower O'Connell Street. Did you bring any details of the payments – a reference number, perhaps?'

'Yes,' replied George, withdrawing a sheet from the file he was carrying and handing it to Gerry.

'I'll give Con a ring and see if he's in his office. Then we can go into town and get the information you want before lunch.' He left the table, walked to the young lady behind the café's counter and showed her his Garda identity card.

'I want to make an urgent call,' he said.

She nodded and pointed to a phone behind her counter. She was able to stretch the cable for him to make the call from the worktop. Two minutes later, he thanked the waitress and returned. 'No problem, Con will have the necessary details for us when we arrive. It'll only take us fifteen minutes to get there.'

★

The bank was an impressive Victorian, white marble building, with a double-storey arched entrance that led into a large hall decked with, perhaps ten, light oak partitioned cubicles on the right-hand side, each manned by male bank clerks wearing white shirts with emerald green ties. The whole effect was impressive, more so when a young woman in her mid-thirties, wearing a two-piece, emerald green suit with a white blouse, rose from her desk on the left-hand side opposite the booths. She walked to

Gerry, smiled and said, 'Good morning, Mr Brady; the manager is expecting you. Please follow me.'

Gerry smiled, thanked her and nodded for the Manxmen to follow him.

Con O'Connor was introduced by Gerry and they sat down in a panelled room that matched the light oak in the public reception hall.

'I've followed a trail for the payments made to the Isle of Man Bank. It's quite interesting,' he began. 'The money leaves an account at this branch on the last Friday of each month.'

'And the name of the account?' asked George, who was taking notes.

'Quadrifoil Needles.'

'An odd name.'

'It's a four-leaf clover.'

George nodded, apparently satisfied.

'The money trail is fascinating. We receive a transfer for the same amount from our branch in Limerick. The name on that account is Trifoil.'

'Three-leaf clover,' offered George.

Con smiled and nodded. 'Limerick receives the money from the Allied Irish Bank in Ballina, County Mayo.'

'Don't tell me,' said George. 'Duofoil.'

Con nodded again. 'They get it from a post office in County Donegal – a place called Raphoe. And that's where the trail ends. And, yes; the account is called Monofoil. How the money gets into the Raphoe post office, we don't know. I suspect it is deposited as cash. All I can say is that Raphoe is very close to Derry. It seems the trail has been designed to hide the source, and it succeeds.'

'I wouldn't be surprised if the post office is run by the IRA solely to launder money. We believe they have several such outlets in both Mayo and Donegal,' explained Gerry to his police colleagues.

'So it's reasonable to assume the money came from Londonderry,' summarised George.

'Bob, there's one other thing you may want to know,' added Con.

'Go on.'

'Apparently, the money regularly transferred from the Donegal post office to the Allied Bank in Ballina doesn't all get sent to our Limerick branch.'

'Really?'

'My colleague, in our Limerick branch, was told that three times as much goes to the Bank Harpolim in New York.'

'An Israeli Bank?'

'Yes, it's the oldest Jewish bank – founded in New York in 1920. The account there doesn't have a name, just a number.'

'You know what I'm thinking, George?' said the Super.

'Tyson is the intermediary banker between the IRA and Mossad.'

'And his cut is 25 percent.'

The Super thanked Gerry's brother-in-law. 'Well, Con, thanks for all your help. If you ever fancy a holiday in the Isle of Man, please let me know and we'll make sure you are looked after properly.'

★

'I think after all that hard work,' smiled Gerry, 'we deserve a special lunch. I'm going to take you to one of my favourite places – Bray. You may have heard of its famous vicar; it's about twelve miles away. The crab sandwiches at the Harbour Bar are second to none.'

'I remember seeing a film about the Vicar of Bray before the war, starring Stanley Holloway,' recalled Bob. 'The daft thing is that the original Vicar of Bray lived in Bray, Berkshire.'

'Ah, well, we Irish like to concoct good stories,' laughed Gerry.

The two Manxmen nodded appreciatively and spent the next forty-five minutes admiring the views as Gerry drove sedately along the coastal road heading south, pointing out places of interest. On their left, the Irish Sea was a dull grey-green on the sombre day. By contrast, on their right, the light green of the Wicklow Mountains shone relatively brightly.

The sandwiches, suitably swilled down with several rounds of Guinness, turned out to be everything Gerry had said. As liquid consumption increased, formality decreased. It allowed conversation to delve deeper into the problems surrounding O'Boyle.

'The second PM on our cadaver was conducted by a Porton Down pathologist who specialises in virology – finding defensive vaccines for plague, anthrax, that sort of thing. His report suggested the toxin used to incapacitate Ahmed could have come from Israel. I don't suppose your CID found anything unusual when they searched O'Boyle's house that could link him to Mossad?'

'You're looking for evidence that O'Boyle had access to the toxin used. If anything was found then I haven't heard. The lead detective, immediately after the shooting, but before the G1 boys took over, worked for me briefly. I could ask him if you like. I think he was pissed off when the security boys took the investigation from the Garda's hands. If you like, we'll pop into our HQ on the way back to your hotel.'

The detective greeted his former boss warmly and, after being introduced to Bob and George, listened to the theory about the possible O'Boyle-Mossad link.

'My team did a thorough search of both his home and office. We found nothing to link O'Boyle to either the IRA or Mossad. That doesn't mean he was innocent.'

★

The following morning saw Bob and George return to the island on the early Aer Lingus flight. After dropping passengers off at Ronaldsway, the regular daily flight carried on to Blackpool.

They were greeted by a jubilant Chief Constable as they entered the police station. 'While you were away, Bob,' he said, 'the RUC's Deputy Commissioner, Jeff Young, rang. He wanted to tell you that he'd heard O'Boyle had been assassinated and the Irish are trying to keep it secret.'

'Yes, we were told in Dublin.'

'But what you could not have been told is that one of Jeff's covert officers had mentioned Ahmed. Somewhere in Donegal last summer, the Derry Brigade was shown the capabilities of a shoulder-held surface-to-air missile by a Bosnian Yugoslav, called Ahmed. However, the amount wanted by the Yugoslavs was considered prohibitive – £100,000 each.'

'So the IRA didn't buy any?'

'The IRA's general council met in Athlone. A meeting was arranged at a neutral venue to discuss whether a compromise price could be agreed.

'The undercover officer didn't know where the meeting was held, but Jeff wondered if it was at the Aragon Hotel. Possibly realising they were disturbing other diners, the four men went down to the swimming pool to continue haggling. Things got out of hand. Ahmed fell through some rotten plywood, couldn't get out and drowned. Not knowing what to do, the other three pushed him over the pool's wall into the sea.'

'Did Jeff find out anything else?' asked the Super.

'The unknown fourth man that day was the IRA's chief accountant. He has a team of something like a dozen clerks. One of his clerks is Young's undercover agent. Since O'Boyle's murder, the IRA man has gone into hiding. Presumably, the IRA is concerned there will be more revenge killings. What I don't understand, however, is why did it take nine months for the Yugoslavs to seek revenge for Ahmed's death?'

'The gunrunners must have told Ahmed to attend the Aragon meeting. When he disappeared, they probably thought he had run off with their money. Consequently, they began looking the wrong way. It wasn't until the cadaver's sketch appeared in the Manx papers in January that they smelled a rat. It has probably taken them three or four months to discover who was at the Aragon lunch and plan their revenge,' answered the Deputy.

'What you're saying, Bob, is Tyson could be the next to be assassinated; after all, he was there too. The last thing we want are Yugoslav thugs on the island determined to kill him.'

'If they're not here already,' commented George.

'And, presumably, Tyson will not have heard of O'Boyle's murder,' added the Super. 'I think we'd better get up to his house on King Edward Road at once and see if he's OK. George, tell PCs Callow and Brew to draw their sniper rifles and follow us as soon as possible.'

CHAPTER 39

The Austin Westminster left Douglas Police Station at noon driven by PC Duff. In the front passenger seat sat the Super and in the rear, DS Turnbull and the station sergeant, Stanley White. All four carried .38 Smith and Wesson revolvers. The two best police marksmen, PCs Lenny Callow and Johnny Brew, followed ten minutes later in the Manx Force's pursuit car, an MGA. They had received permission from the Deemsters' office to carry publicly and use, if necessary, the station's Lee-Enfield sniper rifles.

The Austin touched 70 mph as it raced along the promenade, passing the Palace Theatre and Ballroom where the cadaver's saga began. Two minutes later, as the car was rounding the left-hander at the Douglas Bay Hotel, PC Duff had to break hard and skid to a standstill in order to avoid hitting a motorcycle that was coming towards them and cutting the corner. The Ariel Arrow two-stroke, bellowing clouds of blue vapour from its twin exhausts, swerved and missed the car by inches. It never slowed, however, and carried on towards the promenade.

'Bloody idiot,' yelled the Super. 'He must have been doing 60 mph around the bend. Did you catch the number plate?'

'No, sir,' replied Hector. 'But that could be the motorbike reported stolen last night in Port St Mary.'

Restarting the car, the remaining one-mile journey, that passed one of Tyson's hotels, the Majestic, took a further two minutes. At 1215 hours, PC Duff rang the doorbell of Tyson's house, *Bay View*. There was only silence. He rang again and they waited. The constable looked at his boss. Nothing was said. A nod was sufficient for the door to be tried. It opened. All four policemen removed their revolvers' safety catches. A further nod and the Super entered first – his Smith and Wesson at the ready. The large hall was empty; there was no sound.

'Something's not right,' said the Super. 'Stan,' he ordered his sergeant, 'you and Hector take upstairs. George, we'll start in here.' He gestured to the closed door on the right.

The Super stood to the left of the door while George cautiously opened it. Everything was still. They stood side by side in the doorway.

What they saw could not have been expected. The sight was gruesome.

In front of them, on the far side of the room, slumped with her back over the large desk situated in front of the panoramic window was a motionless woman. Her legs were spread apart, welcoming the two policemen to "come and have me". Her head was slumped backwards on the far side of the desk, staring at the window that was splattered with dozens of droplets of blood. To their left, a second dead woman lay peacefully on the floor, lying in the foetal position.

Police training immediately kicked in. Without saying a word, the men split. George examined the woman on the floor and recognised her as Tyson's secretary, whom he had met three months earlier. Kneeling over her, he confirmed to his satisfaction that she was dead – a single shot to her forehead with what he guessed was a 9mm weapon. He rose to look at his boss, who had turned distinctly pale.

'My God, what sort of a bastard would do this?' asked the Super.

As George approached the second woman, he saw why his boss was so upset. The woman, whom he didn't recognise, had not only been shot in the chest, but a further bullet had been pumped into her vagina from where blood was still seeping.

'I could be wrong, but I think she was pregnant – perhaps five months?' asked the Deputy Chief. 'I think we may find this is Tyson's wife,' he added.

They both stared for several moments in silence at the horrific sight.

The Super asked, 'Where the hell is Tyson?'

'There is no one upstairs,' replied Sergeant White.

The two senior men swung round. Standing in the doorway were the Sergeant and PC Duff, both mesmerised by the scene in front of them. At that moment, they heard the MGA screech to a halt on the driveway outside. Seconds later, the two PCs, with their rifles, entered the room.

'This was done only minutes before we arrived. The only person we've seen was on that motorbike. He must be apprehended straight away. Stan, stay here and ring Noble's Hospital. Insist an ambulance and the path-lab boys get here urgently. Tell them what has happened. You're in charge. I can rely on you to do the right things... oh, and ring BP. Put him in the picture.

'Hector, that motorbike...'

'The Ariel Arrow?'

'Yes, we need to catch him. Where do you think he'll be heading?'

'My guess is he forced either Mrs Tyson or Tyson's secretary to tell him where Tyson is – almost certainly he's going to the Aragon Hotel to kill Tyson. The bike was stolen in Port St Mary. That's where he must have landed on the island by boat. By now, he'll be halfway to the hotel.'

'I agree,' said the Super, glancing at his watch.

'Lenny, how quickly can you get me to the Aragon in the MG?'

'Less than fifteen minutes.'

'Let's go. There's not a moment to spare. George, Hector and Johnny, follow us. The bastard has got over ten minutes' head start.'

★

With its blue light flashing and its bell ringing, the open-topped MG sped south along the two-mile promenade, rounded the Steam Packet's buildings and up the North Quay. The car took the Old Castletown Road and headed for Santon village. Fourteen minutes after leaving the double murder scene, the MG began to slow in order to turn sharp left up the single track, one-mile-long drive to the Aragon. When the MG was thirty yards from the turn, the motorcycle that had nearly caused the accident previously, exited the lane. The rider used his left leg like a speedway racer to help his sharp turn.

'That's the bastard who shot those women,' yelled the Super over the engine noise. 'Stop a minute.'

Lenny did as he was told, wondering why they had stopped.

The Deputy Chief got out and walked to the rear of the MG.

Seconds later, the Austin arrived, pulling up behind.

'The biker has just left a minute ago. Lenny and I are going after him. You three go up to the hotel. Radio us and let me know what you find. If Tyson has been shot, then Hector, take charge. George and Johnny, follow us. I'll bet the bugger is heading for Port St Mary, hoping to make his getaway.'

The Super jumped into the MG. 'As fast as you can, Lenny. Time is critical if we're to stop him.'

They hit 100 mph heading down the straight into Ballasalla. Standing at the T-junction in front of the Whitestone Hotel was the local PC. The MG slowed and the Super yelled, 'Which way did the Aerial motorbike go?'

The PC stood to attention and saluted. 'Towards the airport,' he shouted and, not knowing of the murders, he began to wander across the road to talk to his boss. To his surprise, the MG had accelerated away in a puff of smoke before he had taken two steps.

The car slowed past the airport; the Super searching for any sign of the bike. There was nothing, and as the MG began approaching Castletown, a message crackled over its radio.

'George here, sir. Tyson is dead. One shot to the forehead. I've left Hector in charge and we're about ten minutes behind you.'

'Thanks, George. We've passed the airport and we'll soon be on the Castletown bypass heading for Port St Mary.'

★

Seven minutes later, the MG slowed as it entered Port St Mary and turned left for the port. As they reached the Albert Hotel, at the head of the quay, the two policemen saw a fifty-foot trawler had cast off from the pier and was making to sail out of the harbour. On the ship's deck, the Super saw the motorcyclist they had been chasing since Douglas – the dark leather jacket, navy coloured roll-neck sweater and blue jeans were identical. There was a gap where the boat had been moored on the pier. The Aerial Arrow was parked above the empty berth.

'Drive down to the end of the pier; quick, Lenny,' ordered the Super.

It took the MG no longer than fifteen seconds to rush down the 150-yard pier before it screeched to a stop and the two policemen jumped out. The trawler was now fifty yards behind them, but already travelling at four knots and increasing its speed.

'Police – stop,' yelled the senior man.

The trawler took no notice and began edging away to its port side in order to distance itself from the policemen.

'Lenny, take out the man at the helm in the bridge house.'

The former Korean War sniper, who had served in the King's Liverpool Regiment, didn't hesitate. Kneeling behind the MG's bonnet and using the car to steady his aim, he fired two shots in rapid succession. The glass in the wheelhouse shattered, and the silhouette of the man at the wheel slumped forward and disappeared. However, the boat neither reduced its speed nor changed its course. Instead of swinging right at the end of the pier and heading towards the open sea, it continued straight towards the rocks that guard the west end of the harbour. Moments later, the trawler came to a grinding halt as it hit the rocks below the Bay View Road Hotel.

'Keep the boat covered, Lenny. If anyone shows his head, fire a warning shot. If that doesn't stop them, shoot to kill. I'll run around to cover their escape from the other side of the harbour.'

'Aye, aye, boss.' The enthusiasm of his reply showed Bob that Constable Callow was enjoying using the skills that he had been taught in the Army ten years previously.

The Super ran around the head of the quay towards the narrow lane, known locally as the Underway. He knew it would give him control of the land side of the wrecked ship and thereby prevent anyone escaping over the rocks. At that moment, the Austin Westminster arrived. George and Johnny Brew jumped out. 'Follow me,' the Super shouted.

During the brief sprint up the Underway, there was sporadic gunfire; the higher-pitched "ping" from Lenny's Lee-Enfield was matched by the lower "thud" of an automatic sub-machine gun. A thumbs-up signal from Lenny across the harbour indicated to the Super that no one had escaped from the trawler. Crouching below the three-foot-high seawall that bordered the path from the rocks, the Super positioned his two men to ensure all possible avenues of escape were covered.

'Throw down your weapons. Come out with your hands up,' yelled the Super as he raised his head above the wall.

There was a short burst of shots. The Deputy fell backwards. A concentration of shots in the chest was all that was required to end a promising career.

'Christ,' gasped George, who was crouched nearby. 'They've bloody well killed the Super.'

CHAPTER 40

George shouted across the harbour, 'Lenny, can you hear me?'

'Yes, Sarge.'

'Johnny?'

'I can hear you, Boss.'

'I'm going to run up the narrow path behind me to the High Street and make a phone call. I'm implementing *Operation Bromet*. For Christ's sake, neither of you let anyone escape. Shoot to kill, if necessary. Now give me some cover.'

Having calculated it would be far more dangerous to run back along the Underway to the police car's radio, George ran the ten yards to the bottom of the steep path that led up to the High Street where he intended to use the Isle of Man Bank's phone.

Operation Bromet had initially been planned for just such an occasion. Soon after becoming the island's Lieutenant Governor in 1945, Air Vice-Marshal Sir Geoffrey Rhodes Bromet KCB, CB, DSO discovered the island's police, fire brigades and coastguards rarely, if ever, practised for large-scale emergencies. During World War II, Bromet had planned RAF Coastal Command's operations against the German U-boats.

'Planning is everything,' he had told the island's senior officers in 1946. 'In the words of Baden-Powell, "Be Prepared".

'What would you do if three armed gangsters held hostages during a bank robbery?' he'd asked the senior officers of the island's emergency services.

'What would you do if a cinema caught fire and the audience was trapped inside; or if a ship was wrecked on the island's most dangerous rocks at Bulgam Bay?

'It's no use sitting on your asses and wondering what to do. Time is of the essence and you must be able to implement a well-practised plan within minutes.'

The outcome was that plans were drawn up for every conceivable crisis, and Bromet oversaw the proficiency of the emergency services' training. Not until satisfied did he stop. Thereafter, exercises were undertaken every six months in different locations and different weather conditions.

George reached the top of the path and ran across the road to the bank. He knew *Operation Bromet* backwards and within a minute was talking to the island's only senior full-time army officer: Major Horton, in the Royal Artillery Territorial Army Centre at Port-e-Chee Meadow on the outskirts of Douglas.

'Peter, implement *Operation Bromet, Armed Siege* – immediately.'

He then rapidly outlined the situation.

'I'll have five armed men there within forty-five minutes,' promised the Major, 'and I'll bring a grenade launcher. My number two, Staff Sergeant Higgins, is with me and has been listening. He will take responsibility for implementing the rest of the operation and co-ordinate communications with the other services.'

The well-rehearsed routine ensured further police, ambulance crews and fire brigade units – many manned by volunteers – would be called into action. Noble's Hospital in Douglas would be put on standby.

'The bastards who did this are going to pay for it,' said George to the bank manager as he finished his phone call. 'I want one of your clerks to man the phone and come and get me if anyone rings back. OK?'

'Yes, of course.'

★

When George returned to the harbour's edge, the scene was pretty much as before. 'Brew, has there been any movement?' the DS asked.

'No, Boss.'

'The Army will be here soon with more armed men, and Major Horton is bringing a grenade launcher.'

'I hope he remembers to bring the tear gas grenades. That will smoke the buggers out. How many men do you think are in the boat?'

'About the last thing the Super mentioned was that Lenny had shot the skipper, so there is probably only two of them in the hold; one of whom has killed four people today.'

The commotion had begun to draw spectators to the head of the quay – 150 yards away. Fortunately, they appeared to have sufficient sense not to come any closer, although George wished he had spare manpower to control them. The harbour was unnervingly quiet. Even the seagulls had fallen silent, perhaps having had the sense to disappear. As far as the two police snipers could see, nothing moved on the boat.

Thirty minutes had passed since George had returned from the bank. 'Lenny, are you awake?'

'Of course, Sarge.'

'I'm going back up to the High Street and will wait for the Army to arrive. They should be here soon.'

'OK, I'll give you cover.'

Johnny Brew, twenty yards further along the pathway, nodded to the DS that he was also ready for George to make a dash for the narrow path.

Reaching the High Street, George walked up to the junction of Bay View Road with Park Road. He only had to wait five minutes before an army Bedford 3-tonner appeared. He waved it to stop.

'I've got four men in the back,' explained the Major, who was sitting in the passenger seat. 'Where do you want us?'

'Go down to the quay and take a sharp left into the Underway. Tell one of your men to keep the sightseers back. Send another two up the pier towards the MG, where they'll see PC Callow with his sniper rifle. Tell them to take cover in suitable positions where they can watch the trawler. Bring the truck up the Underway as far as you can. You will see the trawler stuck on the rocks ahead of you to your right. Be careful when you get out. Whoever they are, they're armed and accurate. Position yourselves behind the low wall and calculate the elevation of the grenade launcher to hit the ship's bridge. I assume you've brought tear gas canisters?'

'Of course, as well as fragmentation grenades, just in case,' he smiled.

'See you down there,' replied George, and he ran back down the path to the Underway.

Three minutes later, Major Horton and his men had arrived as instructed, unloaded, and were crouched behind the low wall near George.

Without being asked, the Major unfolded a portable periscope rangefinder and raised it so he could see over the wall. 'The trawler is exactly thirty-six yards away,' he said as he closed the instrument. 'Do you want me to shoot the canister through the broken windows of the wheelhouse?'

'If they come out firing at us, my two snipers have been told to shoot to kill.'

'I know one of them has killed the Super, but shouldn't you use the megaphone to warn them first?'

'I suppose you're right,' George replied reluctantly.

He picked up the army loudhailer, protruded it over the top of the wall and as he did so, several bullets ripped through its trumpet. Nonetheless, George ordered them to come out with their hands in the air.

'This is a final warning before we fire tear gas,' he yelled. His voice was badly distorted by the fractured megaphone.

There was no reply.

'OK, Peter; go ahead.'

The Major fired the launcher. There was a dull "thump". A second later, there was a louder crash.

Ten seconds passed before a yell came from the shipwreck. 'We're coming out. Don't shoot!'

However, as the two men, dressed in dark leather jackets, emerged from the tear gas that was spreading over the wreck, they opened fire from their hips with Soviet RPD automatic machine guns. One of the men turned to his left and began to fire at the not inconsiderable number of onlookers 150 yards away. He fell dead as Lenny's shot smashed through the back of his skull. His colleague ignored the loss of his accomplice and continued running and firing towards where George and Major Horton were crouched. He reached a further five yards before he, too, fell – Johnny Brew's aim at his forehead accomplished its purpose.

The silence was suddenly deafening after the turmoil of the previous half-minute. Independent police investigators from the Staffordshire Constabulary would later find that almost seventy rounds had been fired harmlessly by the two Soviet automatic weapons. By contrast, just four rounds had been used to kill the three criminals. George and the Major rose slowly from behind the wall and surveyed the scene. Smoke was pouring out of the bridge house and had started to drift away on the offshore breeze towards Carrick Bay and the open sea. In front of them, lying face down and motionless on the rocks, the two gunmen were still holding their weapons. The sight must have resembled that which had occurred at San Vicente, Bolivia in November 1908 when Butch Cassidy and the Sundance Kid had also attempted to charge overwhelming firepower.

George, the hero of the hour, controlled the ensuing events for the rest of the day in a dream. One ambulance took the dead skipper and the two killers to Noble's Hospital mortuary, while the body of the Super, accompanied by two police motorcycle outriders, went in a second vehicle. Once the tear gas had cleared, the police photographer took dozens of photographs inside the trawler, while a supervised search found two 9mm pistols, boxes of ammunition and maps of the island.

Several government science officers began the painstaking task of taking blood samples, sketching where bullets were found and measuring their angles of projection.

Hector at the Aragon Hotel, and Sergeant White at Bay View, supervised the same thorough procedures that had to be followed. The consequent strain on the island's resources meant that these three dead bodies could not be removed until the following day.

The task of informing the Super's wife fell to the Chief Constable who, knowing his own wife and Mrs Kinley were close friends, had taken Mrs Powell with him. The Chief took personal responsibility to organise the funeral. Full honours were given; uniformed police lined the route to church for the hearse, with the Manx Police flag draped over the coffin. Motorcycle outriders led the cortege. Such was the respect of the locals for the Super that not only did traffic stop, but pedestrians as well – men raised their hats as the coffin went past. The Chief Constable gave the eulogy to a full church.

★

A week later, a local inquiry was held under the chairmanship of the Lieutenant Governor with the island's two Deemsters. It took evidence and concluded that the local police had behaved in an exemplary fashion. The UK Home Office, however, insisted an inquiry should be held by an independent police force. Several months later, the Chief Constable of the Staffordshire Force confirmed the findings of the earlier inquiry and recommended that both the Super, posthumously, and DS Turnbull be awarded the Queen's Police Medal.

The investigation into the trawler's origin and the identity of the three men was coordinated by INTERPOL from its HQ in Lyon. Its French Secretary General was charged personally by his President… 'to get to the bottom of who killed the Manx Deputy – a friend of mine.' No government claimed either the return of the three bodies or responsibility for the boat. The three men were buried in Rushen Churchyard in unmarked graves. Their names remain a mystery. Police forces from Spain, Morocco, Tunisia and Libya were asked to investigate, but no countries claimed the ship as having been registered with them. It was subsequently broken up for scrap.

CHAPTER 41

Friday, 8th July 1960

Peter Lemont returned to Paris from his visit to Saudi Arabia. He briefed President de Gaulle that the Saudi king was prepared to have the Seal buried beneath the Kaaba, where it would remain for all time. The Saudis wanted de Gaulle to make a state visit to highlight an ongoing trade deal when the Seal could be handed over. The incident at Port St Mary had occurred the previous day, but not being news of international importance, there had been no publicity in France.

On the 3rd September 1960, General de Gaulle made a state visit for the one and only time to Saudi Arabia. He had not visited the Middle East since 1941, after the defeat of the Vichy-controlled Government in Syria. Despite France's subsequent questionable attempts to prevent Syria and Lebanon becoming independent countries, de Gaulle was warmly received by King Saud. After several hours of discussion between the King and de Gaulle, it was agreed that the world's press should play a low-key role; an announcement was made that the visit was to agree a trade deal exchanging oil for forty Dassault Mirage fighter aircraft.

Much behind-the-scenes diplomacy had resulted in an agreement that the real *raison d'etre* – to bury the Great Seal beneath the Kaaba – be kept secret, with certain provisos. When de Gaulle presented the Seal to King Saud at his palace in Riyadh, the French President ceremoniously removed the tablet from a specially made stainless steel case that was locked by a ten-digit alpha-numeric code and gave the Seal to King Saud.

The President handed the combination of the Great Seal to the King, who opened it. The King unwrapped the Seal from Fatima's black silk hijab and stared at the Prophet's portrait for seemingly a long time. The room, with the minimum of Saudi and French officials in attendance, was silent. De Gaulle, towering above the King, looked distinctly awkward. Several minutes passed before the King, with his eyes welling up, whispered, '*Merci bien*.' He wrapped the portrait carefully in Fatima's headscarf. He lifted it carefully to his mouth and, with tears streaming down his face, kissed it gently before replacing it in the Seal. He handed the Seal to de Gaulle, who placed it in the steel container. King Saud thereby became the last person to ever see the portrait. It had been agreed that the steel container's combination would remain known only to de Gaulle. The next day, the King and de Gaulle saw the steel box buried beneath the Kaaba, witnessed by only a handful of senior Saudi officials and Jaques de Yonne. It was then covered with six feet of concrete.

Despite millions of Muslims having since attended the Hajj and each having walked around the Kaaba seven times, not one was aware that they were within a few yards of the Prophet's prohibited portrait.

EPILOGUE

After removing the Seal from Captain Quilliam's grave in Arbory Churchyard, Lemont had taken it back to his home in Ballaugh. It was the summer of 1957. He'd spent the previous winter asking questions of several Imams he'd met in Morocco as to whether they'd ever heard of someone called Henry Leon. One Imam told him the story that his father, also an Imam, had converted Henry Quilliam to Islam when he'd wintered there for health reasons in 1877. His father, he related, was proud that Quilliam took his father's name – Abdullah. Many years later, he told Lemont that, after opening Britain's first mosque, Quilliam returned. World War One had begun and Quilliam had to escape prosecution because of his views that Muslims should never fight other Muslims. Quilliam stayed with the Imam's parents for many months before returning to Britain, through Ireland, using the false name – Henry Leon.

When next on the island, Lemont visited the Manx Museum in Douglas. Considerable research was necessary to reveal the story of Quilliam's Manx connections and his love of walking the numerous byways, paths and glens when holidaying at Onchan.

On discovering Quilliam's forebear was Captain Quilliam RN, it was a small step to guessing the Seal's location in the officer's grave at Arbory Churchyard.

He'd opened the tablet, having remembered the combination – BATCHED FIG – given to him by Ertrugel Effendi during the war.

He'd been amazed at the wonderful condition of a portrait that was 1,300 years old but realised it was artistically rather crude. His degree at Montpellier University in the History of Art had not only taught him to recognise the quality of a painting but had honed his skills in drawing copies of the great masters: Matisse, Dali, Picasso, and so on. He knew the secret of getting the portrait's eyes so that they followed those who walked past. Copying the portrait was easy. He knew where to lay his hands on hard cedarwood and make paint using poppy seed oil with pigments such as ultramarine and lead white. An old black hijab was found on his next visit to North Africa.

Getting proof of the Seal's historical authenticity proved easier than he'd expected. A visit to the Élysée gave him access to official letter-headed writing paper. Claiming to be writing on behalf of the President of the Republic, he was able to fool the three universities to radiocarbon date the minute samples he sent them. Payment, he assured the universities, would be made from an Élysée Palace account.

Over the next two years, whenever he was home, he would sit in his library, carefully crafting a copy of the portrait. By Easter of 1959, he was ready to put his plan into action. Carbon dating would prove his copy was a fake, but already having the authentications from the three universities, this didn't worry him. He had planned when to switch his copy with the original. It wasn't necessary for him to replicate the hardwood case, which he considered to be the most superlative example of intricate Islamic Golden Age workmanship – easily al-Jaziri's finest work. His fake copy of Mohammed's portrait would be placed in the Seal at the right time.

He buried the original painting and Fatima's hijab inside a waterproof stainless steel container at a location that only he knew. He sold Ravenswood, returned to working undercover in Algeria and infiltrated the OAS. On 22nd August 1962, an unsuccessful attempt was made to assassinate Charles de Gaulle. Its failure was in no small way due to Pierre Le Mont.

Over the years, the consequences of Ahmed's body being washed ashore have largely been forgotten, except by those Manx policemen who were so intimately involved.

The genuine prohibited portrait languishes safely somewhere in Glen Dhoo.

ADDENDUM

Monday, 1st June 632 AD, Al-Masjid, Arabia

'Your father is dying, Fatima. The fever has gripped him and he is in terrible pain.'

'I know, Abu. Is there nothing we can do?'

'We have done our best. Allah has decided he wants Mohammed to sit with him in paradise after he has tasted death. Keep bathing him with lavender oil and cool water. He must begin his journey washed and clean to meet Allah. I fear it is only a matter of days.'

'There ought to be a portrait by which to remember him, Abu.'

'I agree, and last week, I asked Ali Miraj to come and paint a portrait of him. We will then have a historically accurate and authoritative picture of him for all time. He is coming from Mecca and should be here tomorrow.'

'I want Ali to paint my father the way I would always wish to remember him.'

'Miraj knows that; it will be done.'

★

A week later, Mohammed passed away, leaving a multitude of followers in what is today western Saudi Arabia. Leading the mourners was Fatima – Mohammed's favourite daughter from his first wife, Kadija. All Mohammed's three sons had predeceased him. In her arms, she held the portrait of her father. It had been painted over the previous days on specially imported Lebanese cedarwood, chosen for its fine grain and resistance to disease. Accompanying Fatima at the front of the mourners was her husband, Ali Talib.

Mohammed's father-in-law, Abu Bakr, with his daughter, Aisha, followed immediately behind. Aisha was Mohammed's third and preferred wife; his remaining wives followed towards the rear of the cortege.

Thousands of his followers lined both sides of the coffin's route to mourn his death and witness his burial in the small village of Al-Masjid that would someday grow into the city of Medina.

'We will build a dome over his grave, fit for our leader,' whispered Ali Talib to his wife. 'It will rise to the heavens and be the highest building in Arabia.'

'I would like the dome to be coloured green, his favourite colour,' she replied.

Ali looked at his wife. She was already showing the same symptoms as her late father. *I am afraid you may never live to see it completed*, he thought.

His fears were proved correct. Fatima hardly saw the project begin. She died two and a half months later. The site chosen would eventually become a great mosque but not have its dome painted green until 1837 by the orders of the Ottoman Sultan, Caliph Mahmud II.

As the mourners left the burial, however, many began to discuss Mohammed's portrait.

'I could swear,' said one to his friend, 'that the Prophet's eyes were looking at me as Fatima passed by.'

'Impossible,' replied his friend. 'I was on the opposite side of the funeral procession's path and the Prophet was looking at me.'

The subject of discussion among the dispersing crowd was the same: how could the "Most Praiseworthy" have been looking at everyone at the same time? The ambiguity could not be explained by the masses except by resorting to the supernatural powers of the "Servant of God". The converted would talk about the mystery for generations to come, and the portrait would pass into the folklore of Islam.

★

Soon after Mohammed's funeral, a meeting of the elders was held to choose the leader of the new faith – the first Caliph. Rapidly, a schism arose between Abu Bakr and Ali Talib, who were the frontrunners. Both curried favour from Fatima.

'Flattery will get you everywhere,' she said to them.

Unfortunately, what Fatima thought had begun as light-hearted rivalry soon turned nasty. The elders, led by Umar, the leader of the most powerful tribe from Mecca, favoured the older candidate, while the younger followers, but less influential, claimed that Mohammed had nominated Ali to succeed. The meeting ended in acrimony with most swearing allegiance to Abu Bakr – the Sunnis – while Ali's followers refused to recognise him. They were to become the *Shiah-Ali* – the followers of Ali, or Shias.

★

Abu Bakr imposed his authority without delay.

Firstly, he ordered the Army to supress various rebellious tribes in Arabia. The plan, which had been initiated by Mohammed, was to expand the new faith, by attrition if necessary. Less than a year after Mohammed's death, under the generalship of Khalid ibn Walid, the Army of Islam conquered and converted all of the Arabian tribes, including those in Yemen, Oman and Bahrain. Abu Bakr's ambitions did not stop there. Mesopotamia fell to Khalid's Army and formed a buffer from the powerful Persian Empire to the east.

Secondly, Abu Bakr set up a committee of converts, chaired by Umar, to collect all the verses and lessons taught by Mohammed and have them written down. The document was to become the Koran. Although there were no specific references to portraits of the Prophet being banned, Abu Bakr and Umar agreed that the practice of iconography should be discouraged. As a result, Arabian art grew around sophisticating the written word. Portraits of Mohammed were destroyed in Sunni mosques. However, Ali Talib had retained Fatima's portrait, and the destruction of pictures of the Prophet was not carried out by the Shias for some time.

★

In August 634, Abu Bakr fell sick and was not to recover. To avoid dissension, he nominated Umar as his successor and to become the second Caliph. Under Umar's political guile, the Islamic Caliphate began expanding. It would eventually grow over the next one hundred years to become one of the largest empires of all time and stretch from North Africa to Persia. The Umayyad Empire laid the foundation for 700 years of stability in the Middle East. Umar divided the territories into provinces with their own governors, introduced an official language – Arabic – created a banking system, built universities and created a postal service. Laws were enforced by magistrates – all were equal under the law.

Umar's armies conquered the land as far west as Libya and as far east as Persia. In the summer of 636, his army marched north towards Syria and, under the command of Khalid, they defeated the Byzantines at the Battle of Yarmouk. The five-day battle, considered by many historians to be one of the most decisive battles of all time, secured the Levant and Syria as part of the Caliphate. By then, the Koran had been written and was recognised as the living word of the Prophet.

Umar was assassinated in 644 by a Persian slave. A committee of elders, one of whom was Ali Talib, appointed Uthman, the Head of the Umayyad clan, as the third Caliph. He continued the development of the Caliphate along the North African coast as far as Morocco and, with a powerful navy, much of Spain came under his control.

★

In 656, Uthman was to die in a rebellion. Living in Medina, Ali Talib was persuaded to become the fourth Caliph. Armed with Fatima's picture of Mohammed, painted twenty-four years previously, he believed he had at last acquired his rightful inheritance – the position of Mohammed's successor. However, political expediency was not his forte.

Against the advice of his cabinet, Ali Talib moved his residence to Kufa, on the banks of the Euphrates, believing he could manage his empire more efficiently as the city was geographically central within the Caliphate. Mesopotamia had been the battleground for hundreds of years between the Eastern Roman Empire and the Persian Empire. As a result of the continuous unrest, the Mesopotamians had embraced the new faith of Islam, believing it would lead to the stability they so desperately wanted. They had been instrumental in encouraging Ali Talib to move to Kufa.

Ali then began to replace Uthman's Sunni governors with his own Shia followers. The result was that dissent grew across the Caliphate. Within months, an uprising began.

'Ali, there is trouble in the Levant, Syria and Egypt. The governors appointed by Uthman have declared independence from the Caliphate,' announced his most trusted aide and cousin, Omara bin Hanza. 'Your appointees to those regions have been executed publicly and the people are mutinous.'

'Don't they understand that all I am trying to do is to reunite the two paths of our faith?'

'I am also getting reports that Aisha, Mohammed's third wife, has called a meeting of Umar's followers at Basra.'

'She's too clever for her own good – always telling us what to do and what not to do. Just because she's Abu Bakr's daughter, she thinks she should run the place.'

'There may be 10,000 followers with her. She is preaching the heresy that you are not punishing Uthman's murderers because you supported the assassins.'

'That's a lie.'

'Yes, but they believe her. We must raise an army and crush her. We have 6,000 troops and can sail down the Euphrates and be there within days.'

'And that proves Allah sanctioned my move to Kufa. We must leave as soon as possible.'

What took place during the days leading to the battle, known as The Battle of the Camel, is unclear. Ali did not want to fight Aisha as he knew his plans to unite the two sects hung in the balance. His army camped outside Basra before the battle. Initial negotiations with a delegation from Aisha had stalled the previous day. During the night, however, rebel forces, believed to have been sympathetic to Uthman's assassins, attacked Ali's sleeping troops. In the ensuing chaos, Ali could not control his men, and the subsequent fracas spilled over to become a bloody battle the next day. As many as 5,000 soldiers are thought to have died. The battle ended when Ali's soldiers killed Aisha's camel on which she had been sitting, controlling her troops. Ali met Aisha, pardoned her, and an uneasy truce ensued. The outcome was Aisha retiring from public life to live quietly in Medina.

The Sunnis came to see her as the choice wife of Mohammed and call her "The Mother of the Believers". The Shias, on the other hand, reviled her for defying Ali and, although banished to Medina, suspected she continued to undermine Ali's attempts to unite the faith.

★

Ali was murdered in 661 while at prayers in the mosque in Kufa. His succession, according to Shia tradition, passed to his son, Hassan. But the Sunnis had different ideas. Muawiya, the powerful governor of the Levant and Syria, who had been appointed by Uthman, had never accepted Ali as Caliph. Consequently, Muawiya flatly refused to pay homage to Hassan. With his army, easily the strongest in the Middle East, Muawiya declared himself the fifth Caliph and marched into Mesopotamia. The split between Sunni and Shia had become permanent.

★

Muawiya initially corresponded with Hassan to try and persuade him to accept the *fait accompli*: Muawiya's 60,000 trained troops opposed Hassan's Army, numbering fewer than 10,000. Muawiya was sufficiently savvy to realise that if his army had smashed Hassan, then another Talib family member would replace him. Although Hassan never accepted the Umayyad family's rights to the Caliphate, he agreed a truce after eight months of negotiations providing that he, Hassan, would succeed Muawiya as the sixth Caliph.

Consequently, at their last face-to-face meeting, Hassan temporarily handed over Fatima's painting to Muawiya. By then, it was the only picture in existence of the Prophet.

'My father, Ali Talib, believed this picture of the Prophet was ordained by Allah to be the only portrait of Mohammed. You will see as you walk past the image that his eyes follow you. Wherever you are, Mohammed is watching you. As Caliph and leader of our faith, you now possess the power of Mohammed through this depiction of the Almighty's messenger.'

Hassan predeceased Muawiya, which gave Muawiya the excuse to adopt the Shia hereditary system of succession: namely, the line of Caliphs would, in future, be the eldest son. The Umayyad dynasty, based in Damascus, would last for a further ninety years. Its empire would stretch from Spain to the border of India. With a population of over sixty million, it would go down in history as geographically the fifth largest empire of all time. Christians and Jews peacefully coexisted side by side with the Muslims – provided they paid their taxes and thereby showed their acceptance of the Sunni State's laws.

However, the Caliphate's vast territory was difficult to administer, and it began to splinter into different factions with corruption becoming rife. The Army, mostly Arab soldiers, grew tired of far-flung postings year after year as uprisings spread. Three major rebellions were particularly crucial. They came from the geographical extremes of the empire: in the south – the Shias of Mesopotamia, in the west – the Berbers of Morocco, and finally, the powerful Abbasid family in the north of Persia.

On his death bed in 680, Muawiya spoke to his son: 'Yazid, you are about to inherit the Caliphate. With the position comes great responsibility. I have tried to get you ready for this day. You can recite the holy verses and have visited Medina and Mecca on pilgrimage. However, I have one last secret. You must guard with your life this picture. It is Fatima's portrait of Mohammed and is your badge of rank. It is the only portrait of the Prophet and is wrapped in the hijab worn by Fatima at her father's funeral. No one but the Caliph must be allowed to look into the Prophet's eyes – you must keep it with you at all times.'

The transfer of power to Yazid infuriated the Shias, who were now led by Talib Ali's second son, Husayn. He considered the succession as breaching the truce agreed by his brother with Muawiya. Hassan had died in 670 believing his brother would inherit the title from Muawiya in lieu of himself. Husayn led an army to meet Yazid. At the Battle of Karbala, on 10th October 680, Husayn was killed along with his infant son and most of his family. The dominance of the Sunnis was total.

★

The Berber revolt, which had been fermenting for some years, didn't come to fruition until 740. The Berbers, ethnically a mix of Afro-Moorish descent, as opposed to being of Arabian ancestry, defeated the Umayyads who thereby lost Morocco and parts of Algeria. The campaign, at the extreme edge of their realm, dragged on for years and weakened the Umayyads' resources so that within ten years their empire would collapse.

★

Historically, the most powerful clan opposing the Umayyads were the Abbasids. Originally from the Red Sea area, they had drifted to northern Persia and believed they had a direct hereditary line from Mohammed. In 747, led by Abu Saffah with a 10,000-strong army, they overthrew the Umayyad Governor of the province of Khorasan in northern Persia. Abu Saffah's Army then advanced west towards Damascus and, after successive victories, controlled considerable parts of eastern Syria and northern Mesopotamia. Total victory came at the Battle of the River Zab, near Mosul, on 25th January 750 when, despite their army being outnumbered by three to one, the Abbasids routed the Umayyads.

The last Umayyad Caliph, Marwan, fled from the battlefield to the Levant with his badge of office – the picture of Mohammed. Chased by the Abbasids, Marwan eventually ended up in a small town in the Nile delta where he was killed after a short battle. The portrait was captured unharmed and, having been briefed of its significance, the Abbasid general, Abdallah ibn Ali, gave it to an escort party of his most loyal troops. He placed the portrait inside a sealed container and ordered that no one was to look at what was locked inside "on pain of death." The sealed case was taken back to Iraq and returned to Abu Saffah, who became the first Abbasid Caliph.

The Abbasids made Baghdad their capital in 762, and it would become the most important city in the world for almost 500 years. In order to keep a semblance of central authority, a system of viziers, or ministers, with local emirs, was set up. The regional emirs, often politically corrupt, became ever more powerful, and the role of the Caliph gradually weakened to that of a ceremonial and religious head of state.

After establishing good relations with China, where paper had been invented, the world's first paper mill was built in Baghdad and the "Golden Age" began. Great advances in science, mathematics, engineering, literature and philosophy came about as universities were built throughout the Caliphate. The library in Baghdad would eventually hold half a million texts. An interest in automatons flourished as imported machines were brought back from China. Water clocks fascinated the educated elite, and by 1200 AD, Ismail al-Jazari had invented the crankshaft to make reciprocating pumps. He constructed silver trees with birds that sang and flapped their wings to adorn the Caliph's palace and amuse the harem.

In 1201, the Caliph, al-Nasir, who had ruled for twenty-one years, demanded al-Jaziri's presence at his palace.

'I have a job for you,' al-Nasir said.

'What is it, Your Excellency?'

'It is secret. If you disclose the task I am to give you, then you will forfeit your life. Do you wish to proceed?'

'I am yours to command.'

'Since the death of the Prophet, almost 580 years ago, the Caliphs, beginning with Ali Talib, have possessed the only picture of Mohammed. It is our badge of office that makes us unique.'

'I didn't know there were any portraits of the Prophet.'

'All were destroyed except one – the one painted by Ali Miraj days before Mohammed died, and carried by Fatima at his funeral. Since Muawiya, it has been held exclusively by the reigning Caliphs to show we have ultimate authority. It was handed to me by my predecessor Mustadi, wrapped in Fatima's hijab. I think it is high time it was protected. A container is required with some sort of lock that only successive Caliphs can open.'

'I will need to see the picture to measure its size.'

'No. I will show it to you wrapped inside Fatima's headscarf. That will have to do.'

'Very well. Can I take its measurements?'

Al-Nasir handed him the wrapped wooden portrait. Al-Jaziri produced a ruler from his bag and measured the dimensions carefully. On a pad, he began drawing a sketch of a flat case.

Pausing, he asked, 'Do you wish to adorn the case in any way?'

'You can show me some designs as you proceed.'

'My first thoughts are that I would make the box and lid with Bethlehem olive wood.'

'Why olive wood from Palestine?'

'It is exceptionally hard and resistant to disease and warping. Olive trees grow to an old age and I will need a large plank to make the container from a single slab. The internal hinges and lock could be made of brass.'

'Only gold is good enough for Allah's messenger.'

'Gold is too soft. After a short time, the moving mechanisms would wear and become unreliable.'

'Very well, I bow to your judgement.'

'I suggest the lid, base and four sides are decorated with mother-of-pearl and coloured glass.'

The Caliph nodded approval.

'I would like to cover the underside with inlaid nacre squares. Under certain squares, I will attach a rod that penetrates the container's base. Pressing the squares will give the impression they are all sprung. However, only depressing the right squares in the right order would release the mechanism to open the lid.'

'Excellent! How many squares will need to be pressed?'

'I would suggest ten, Your Majesty.'

'Will that be sufficient to keep the tablet secure?'

'It would offer over three million possible combinations.'

'There is an extra requirement. If someone tries to break open the cabinet by force then I want it to self-destruct.'

Al-Jaziri looked at his leader – the most powerful man in the world. He thought for some time and carefully phrased his reply.

'Would you be happy if it exploded? The Chinese are making small cartridges containing a secret mix of what they call gunpowder. It explodes by the heat made by a pin indenting a cartridge.'

'How long will you require to make the tablet?'

'I fear it will take over a year.'

'Don't worry. I'm not intending to die for some time.'

Al-Nasir had been Caliph for forty-five years when he died in 1225, but he saw Al-Jaziri's masterpiece completed. The ten-digit code mechanism – a rotating crank that had to be aligned correctly by positioning the levers beneath the nacre squares – had proved to be difficult to get right. Only the ten squares opposite the hinges would work. Once the mechanism was perfected, the sequence of depression had to be chosen.

The Caliph wanted numbers relating to events in Mohammed's life within the code.

Al-Jaziri persuaded him that this would effectively reduce the number of possibilities by intelligent guesswork. 'It would be too obvious,' he said. 'Let us draw the numbers by lot.'

The Caliph agreed.

Experiments were conducted to explode the tablet if the hinges were forced. This, too, became a stumbling block.

'Over the years, perhaps centuries, the explosive mixture may deteriorate and will not work or, worse still, ignite of its own accord. If the idea is to destroy the portrait so that no infidel will ever see the Prophet's face, then I suggest we use several strategically placed small phials of concentrated acid. Internal pins will break the thin glass as soon as someone tries to force the box.'

Although not happy at the idea, al-Nasir agreed. 'Now that you are nearing the completion of the internal workings, I have been thinking of the decoration around the edges and on the upper face,' added the Caliph. 'I think the pieces of nacre and coloured glass on the top should be arranged to read: *Mohammed is the messenger of Allah.*'

'The best calligrapher in Baghdad is Ibn Muhaqi who has recently developed a beautiful, flowing, sophisticated script. Shall I ask him to show you some samples of his work?'

'No. The fewer who know of the tablet, the better. You get several proposals and do not tell him your reason. I will then choose the final design.'

The technique of polishing shaped coloured glass had been perfected on the Abbasid island of Cyprus. It was used to decorate the top face of the tablet that would protect Mohammed's portrait for the next 700 years.

★

Around 1206 AD, the Mongols, led by Genghis Khan, began expanding their empire. Beginning with northern China, one territory after another fell to his ruthless tactics. His warriors swept across Asia destroying everything in their path. The fierce tribal chieftain had begun to take over the world. Although Genghis died in 1227, he left his son, Ogodei, a territory that extended from north-east China to the Caspian Sea. In total, the area measured eleven million square miles. Genghis Khan had conquered more than twice as much territory as any man in history – before or since.

Ogodei Khan continued the Mongols' advance westward, pushing into Russia. By 1240, Kiev had been sacked and his hordes were rapidly ravaging the cities of Europe with the help of Chinese gunpowder. In March 1241, the vast Mongol Army arrived at Budapest and Ogodei's armies slaughtered one million Hungarians. It was one of the bloodiest defeats of all time. However, in December 1241, Ogodei Khan died unexpectedly. A power struggle began among Genghis' other sons and grandsons that fractured their empire so badly that it never completely recovered.

In 1258, one of Genghis' grandsons, Hulagu Khan, invaded Mesopotamia. He had been commanded by his elder brother, the Great Khan, Mongke, to conquer all the Muslim states of the Abbasid Caliphate. After subjugating the Persians, his huge army marched on Baghdad.

The Caliph, al-Mustansim, immediately saw the impossibility of defending Baghdad. He entrusted his equerry, al-Mustansir, with the Seal and its secret. With the Mongol army of over 250,000 men encamped on the east bank of the River Tigris, the Caliph arranged for his lieutenant to escape. In the middle of the night, al-Mustansir slipped away in a small boat with the Seal and sailed down the River Tigris to safety.

Hulagu's Army ransacked Baghdad. The Grand Library, containing countless precious historical documents and books on subjects ranging from medicine to astronomy, were destroyed. The waters of the Tigris ran black with the ink from the books flung into the river. Citizens attempting to flee were intercepted by the Mongol soldiers and killed; neither women nor children were spared. Resistance lasted less than two weeks. It ended when the Caliph was slaughtered by being wrapped in a carpet and trampled to death by Mongol horses. However, the Caliph's badge of office survived.

Over the following months, the Mongols looted throughout Mesopotamia, destroying mosques, palaces and hospitals. It has been estimated that the death was greater than a million. Grand buildings that had been the work of generations were burned to the ground. From being the most influential city in the world, Baghdad became a depopulated, ruined city for several centuries and never recovered its former glory.

Hulagu's plan was to complete the destruction of Syria before advancing on the Levant and Egypt. To get to Egypt, he had to travel around the Fertile Crescent as crossing the Arabian Desert would be impossible with such a large army. He conquered Damascus in March 1260, two years after Baghdad.

Meanwhile, al-Mustansir had sailed south to the Persian Gulf. Coastal trading ships had taken him to Oman and Yemen, before entering the Red Sea. From there, the safety of Egypt was in his grasp as Egypt was ruled by the Mamluk family – still very much a part of the Sunni Abbasid Caliphate.

As Hulagu's Army was preparing to advance through Palestine, prior to invading Egypt, his brother died and Hulagu had to return to Mongolia to claim the succession. Believing it sufficient, he left behind an army of only 20,000 men to control Syria. The Head of the Egyptian Mamluks, Sultan Qutuz, saw his chance. Quickly raising an army and declaring al-Mustansir as the new Caliph before departing Cairo, he defeated the Mongols in a battle near the Sea of Galilee on 3rd September 1260. It was the first major loss suffered by the Mongols, who never again ventured south-west towards Palestine and Egypt.

However, Al-Mustansir's adventures had taken their toll on his health. On his death bed in late November, he handed the Seal of Office to al-Hakim who became Caliph for the next forty years.

Over the years, the ferocity of the Mongols had driven tens of thousands of Muslims west into Anatolia, modern day eastern

Turkey, where the fiefdoms of various beys, or chieftains, offered sanctuary. The small beyliks had proliferated as the Eastern Roman Empire, the Byzantines, had declined.

By 1300, there were twenty small Turkish principalities. As a result of treaties and battles, the beyliks began uniting and Sultan Osman emerged as the most powerful bey. When he died in 1326, Osman controlled most of Anatolia – the beginning of the Ottoman Empire. His son and grandsons eventually ruled all of Turkey and much of the Balkans. The fall of Constantinople in 1453 ended the rule of the Byzantines and it became the capital of the Ottomans until they were defeated in World War One, by which time the city was universally known as Istanbul.

As the Ottoman Empire expanded, the Sultan began accumulating titles from the empire's subjected peoples. In 1362, although Ottoman Sultan Murad I claimed the title of Caliph, it wasn't until the Ottomans conquered Egypt in 1516 that the last of the Abbasid caliphs, al-Muttawakkil, surrendered the caliphate to Sultan Selim I. With Fatima's portrait secure, the Seal that had resided in Cairo for over 250 years moved to Constantinople where the Caliphs resided until after World War One.

The Ottoman Empire, with a professional army of over a quarter of a million men, grew rapidly in the sixteenth century. Within a few short years, it controlled all of North Africa, the Balkans as far north as Hungary, the coastal countries around the Black Sea and all of the Middle East. By 1914, the Sultan was revered universally as the Sunni Caliph by over 300 million Muslims. Ironically, the British in the nineteenth century had encouraged the Muslims in the Indian sub-continent to accept the Ottoman Sultan as the true Caliph. In exchange, the Ottomans urged the Indians to accept British rule.

★

By the beginning of World War One, the Ottoman Empire had shrunk from its former days of glory. Known as the "Sick Man of Europe", the Ottomans had lost the Balkans when Serbia gained independence, the Black Sea states when the Russians freed Romania and Bulgaria, as well as the control of Egypt to the British.

The Ottomans were initially neutral when World War One began, but joined the German alliance when two battleships being built in Sunderland for the Turkish Navy were sequestrated for the Royal Navy. There were several important Ottoman victories in the early years of the war, such as at Gallipoli and Kut. However, the Arab Revolt that began in 1916, led by Faisal, with TE Lawrence as his liaison officer, turned the tide against the Ottomans. They accepted defeat on 30th October 1918 when the British forces led by General Allenby joined up with Faisal in Damascus. The subsequent armistice signed at Versailles in 1919 allowed the Turkish Sultan to retain his title despite vast areas of the Ottoman Empire being ceded to France as a result of the implementation of the 1916 Sykes–Picot agreement. The consequent French occupation of large areas of southern Turkey led to the Turkish War of Independence. Under the leadership of Mustafa Kemal Atatürk, who had defeated the Allies at Gallipoli, victory against the French came in November 1922 when the modern state of Turkey was created. The secular Atatürk immediately abolished the sultanate. The last sultan and Caliph, Mehmed VI, left the country on 17th November 1922 and with him the Caliphate finished.

Married five times, Mehmed, along with the Seal of Office, went into exile with his four remaining wives and three children: two surviving daughters from his first wife and a son, Ertrugel, from his third wife. The entire family settled in San Remo on the Italian Riviera, near the French border.

As far as history was concerned, the Caliph's Great Seal of Office, that few knew existed, seemingly disappeared forever when Mehmed died in 1926.